ROMERO

ROMERO

(The Moreno Brothers series #4)

Elizabeth Reyes

ROMERO

Elizabeth Reyes
Copyright © 2011
All Rights Reserved.

This book is dedicated to my loyal readers. Particularly the ones who emailed me more than once to request that I write Romero and Isabel's story. This story was never going to be and if it hadn't been for you guys it may never have blossomed the way it did and now I'm so glad it's part of the Moreno Brother series. Just beware. Romero is ... well Romero. =)

I hope you enjoy!

Chapter 1
High School Graduation

Romero

Manny was on his third disposable camera. His girl-friend Aida stood next to him, wearing a dress that looked like he just picked her up on a street corner.

"Can you wind up your plastic camera a little faster so we can get out of here?" Max said. "It's hotter than shit out here."

"Shut up and get in there, will you? I'm sending every damn one of these to Cousin Lou in Texas. That asshole didn't think we could raise this kid." He smiled at Romero, and if Romero didn't know any better, he'd think Manny was getting choked up again. *Jesus.* "C'mon smile, will you?"

Romero's uncles had always insisted he use their first names.

"You know, if you break down and buy a digital camera like everyone else, you can send them to him tonight in an email," Max said.

Manny took a few more pictures. Romero got tired of telling him about his finger on the lens. Let him be pissed about it when he got all the pictures back. All he could think of was getting the hell out of there to go party with his friends.

"I can do the same with these as soon as I get them back. They give you a disc over at the drug store, smartass. Besides why would I buy a digital camera when I got a load of these?"

Romero frowned. His uncles had plenty of friends with "connections." They constantly hooked him up with things that *fell off* of delivery trucks, in exchange for favors. Because of the business his uncles ran they had plenty of favors to barter with that those types of guys would really enjoy. The latest hook-up had been a few dozen boxes of disposable cameras. "Are we done?" Romero asked.

"Yeah, with this one." Manny dumped the camera in a tote and pulled out another brand new disposable camera. "Go get your friends. I want a few with them in it."

Romero began to protest, but it was pointless. If he didn't obey, his uncle was bound to start yelling for his friends to get their asses over here anyway. Rather than endure another one of their usual public scenes, he complied. "All right, I'll go get them but make it fast because I got somewhere to be."

"Yeah, yeah, you'll go when I say you go. We're going to dinner, remember? I didn't get all dolled up for nothing."

Aida fixed his uncle's bright red tie. Both his uncles had worn suits for the occasion. As usual, their choice in clothes didn't disappoint. Manny, a heavyset man, was in a white suit with a black shirt and bright red tie. Max looked like something out of a zoot suit movie. But it was all good. Romero was used to this. This was nothing compared to the matching powder blue suits they'd worn to his middle school graduation, and the scuffle they started in the crowd during the ceremony. "That fat bitch got right in front of me just as I was taking the picture!" was Manny's argument.

That fat bitch's husband didn't take too kindly to

his uncle's foul mouth and it was on.

As he walked through the crowd of bodies, many still in their graduation robes, he spotted Claire—sweet, quiet, bookworm, Claire. Ever since the tenth grade when he'd caught her trying not to laugh at one of his lewd remarks, she'd been on his get-to-know list. Up until then he'd only had a to-do list when it came to girls. In fact, there were only two girls on his get-to-know list ever. Ironically, the other one, Libby, was a lot like Claire. Only unlike Claire, he'd never gotten the feeling Libby might actually be attracted to him, except for the few times he caught her staring and he thought she might've blushed. Unfortunately, they'd been in class and she'd spun her head around so fast he wasn't able to tell. Another unfortunate thing about her is she'd moved away a year ago.

He'd been surprised to see Claire in the Forensic science class he'd taken this past semester on the weekends as part of their school's regional occupational program. He hadn't told anyone about the class. Not even his uncles knew. He'd told them he enrolled in a weekend program but said it was a weight training thing.

Like in school, he hadn't expected to have much interaction with Claire, until they were partnered up on a project. There was no denying the attraction she tried so desperately to hide. He saw right through her. Even now, it made him smile at the times he'd broken through that sweet innocent wall of hers, and gotten her to admit a thing or two. Like when he teased her about being so holier-than-thou, she'd probably never even had a naughty dream. Not only did she admit to having had some, but they hadn't all been about her boyfriend.

Her boyfriend—that wiped the smile right off his face. He'd waited too damn long to get to know her and by the time he started talking to her in the ROP class she was taken. If she had wanted to, it wouldn't have been the first time that Romero had borrowed a little time with someone else's girl. Only thing was, with Claire he hadn't been too sure if he could handle sharing her. He never got a chance to find out though.

As strong as he felt her attraction had been, she wasn't the cheating type and apparently things between her and her boyfriend were pretty serious. Of course, that only made Romero want her more. What had really thrown him was when he smugly asked her if any of those dreams had been of him. He completely expected her to blush and deny it vehemently. Instead sweet innocent Claire smiled the wickedest smile that nearly made *him* blush and she pled the fifth.

But even that didn't top what he remembered most fondly about her. With all the suggestive teasing he'd done, he expected more demure responses. But after they finished up their project, instead of demure she'd teased him right back, calling him closet-smart. Something that for some reason always shut him right up.

Romero slowed down watching her pose for a picture with a woman he could only imagine was her mom. She noticed him after the picture had been taken and smiled, making Romero breathe in deeply. He smiled back and began walking toward her. She'd only taken a few steps, when her boyfriend stepped in front of her with a bouquet of flowers. The moment was over and he decided to walk away.

He rounded up his two best friends: Eric Diego and Angel Moreno. "Don't ask me why, but Manny wants pictures with you guys in 'em. Let's get this over with.

The sooner we're done, the faster I can get dinner with them out of the way and we can meet up."

"No fights this time uh?" Angel smirked.

"Shit, we're not out of here yet." Romero laughed.

They posed for a few hundred more shots, and the whole time Manny came up with more reasons why he had to take another.

"Do you have to make that face in every picture? This isn't a mug shot. Max, will it kill you to fucking smile in just one of these? Stop with the tough guy poses, Moe, no one's buying that shit."

Eric and Angel stifled in laughs. Romero had always gone by his last name to everyone else but his uncles. His first name was Ramon, though he'd never gone by it. Manny and Max both called him Monie when he was a kid. Over the years it morphed into Moe. His uncles loved introducing themselves as Manny, Max, and Moe any chance they got. They thought it was cool but Romero knew people's first thought, especially considering his two uncle's appearances were the Three Stooges.

They finally got out of there and went to the Lucky Dragon for dinner. Besides his friend Angel's family's upscale Mexican restaurant, this was the only other fancy restaurant his uncles liked going to. They'd gone there for so many years the owners knew them well. The owner's name was Pak Mi and even after all these years it never got old. "Pak Mi? No Pak *you*!" Then his uncles would go into a fit of laughter as if it were the first time they used that one.

After plowing through his food, Romero checked his phone again and replied to a text from Eric.

"Put that shit away, will you?" Manny pointed his chopsticks at Romero's cell. "How many times do I have to tell you, not during dinner?"

"But I'm done." Romero continued to text.

"Take that thing from him," Manny said to Max.

Romero scooted out of the booth before Max could reach for his phone. He leaned in and hugged Manny and then Max, then smiled and nodded at Aida. "Eric is outside—party time." He grinned. "Thanks for dinner. Don't wait up."

"Hey, Moe," Manny called out as he began to walk away. "You got condoms. Use them."

Romero turned to the women in the next booth who looked up at him after hearing his uncle's loud statement. He smiled and winked. "Don't worry. I always do."

Angel's family went all out as usual. They owned a restaurant and closed it up for the evening, just for the occasion. They'd party there for a while because they could sneak the free liquor from the bar and then move on to after-parties.

His two best friends couldn't be more different than him, but they'd been his best friends since they were kids and they'd always gotten along great. Romero knew if he hadn't lived up the street from them, they would've never been as tight they were now. That's how different they were.

Angel came from a big family—two brothers and a sister, and his parents owned one of the most renowned restaurants in La Jolla. His two older brothers were in college on full scholarships. Angel was on the same path. He'd been the star football player most of the four years in high school. The only time he hadn't been in the spotlight was when his brothers were in it.

Eric was an only child so he could relate to Romero in that sense, but that's where any similarity in their family lifestyle ended. Eric's dad was a businessman and the epitome of class. He jetted all over the world, was well-read and educated. Both Eric and Angel's futures were carefully planned. They'd be attending college in the fall and knew exactly where they were going.

Romero, on the other hand, hadn't even looked into college. His uncles were under the impression that he'd join the family business. But Romero had other plans. Plans he hadn't shared with anyone.

His uncles, while a little rough around the edges, were good guys—now. They'd come a long way from their days of being thugs. His grandmother told him stories when he was younger. They ran with the worst of them and got his dad, their youngest brother, involved. Then his dad was arrested for drug trafficking—something to which his brothers introduced him. Romero was just a baby. His grandmother said his uncles, full of regret, decided to turn over a new leaf. Lead a life on the straight and narrow.

They gave up trafficking for gambling on the ponies in Del Mar. Manny was surprisingly lucky. He planned on saving up his winnings and opening up his own business. Then a few years later, his uncles decided they needed to step up and be the role models they never were to their younger brother. So they gave up the life of gambling for a more respectable way of life— they opened up a titty bar.

Romero's dad was supposed to do fifteen years in the can, but he was out on parole earlier that year. Just a few months later, he was back in for possession. The judge wasn't messing around either, since he was still on parole—slapped another ten-year sentence on him. Romero didn't care. He'd never known his old man anyway. As far as he was concerned, his uncles and grandmother were the only parents he ever had.

Romero would've never believed his graduation night would turn into this. Because Angel had met and fallen completely head over balls for the new chick in school senior year. She'd be coming along with them to party, like she had for months. Even worse? Now that Angel's highly guarded younger sister, Sofia, had turned seventeen, she was allowed to date. Eric had staked his claim immediately. Not that they hadn't been sneaking around for months, but now they'd be at the party out in the open for everyone to see they were a bona fide couple.

Romero couldn't understand how anyone would want to get tied down so young. He lived to get wasted and bag a new piece of ass every chance he got. That was the whole reason why he joined the football team to begin with. Ever since he'd made the starting line up and started bulking up, he never left a party without knowing he was getting laid, or at least blown by some of the girls who still tried to act like doing that was somehow more respectable than going all the way. Either way, it was a happy ending and he'd take it.

They were at a backyard party for over an hour and Romero had already thrown a few back. Eric and Angel were too busy honey-mooning to even get a buzz. Romero kicked it with some of the other football players. Ozzie, a third stringer but a good buddy of Romero's, brought a bottle of Jack Daniels. "Your dad actually bought you this shit?"

Ozzie smiled, taking a swig then looking like he might throw up in his mouth. Romero laughed. Ozzie was no drinker. This was going to get ugly. "Give me that."

Ozzie handed him the bottle. Romero took a drink and grimaced as the warm liquid slid down, burning his throat in the process. "Smooth," he said, in a voice so hoarse the guys laughed.

Running into Claire and her boyfriend again at the party was an unpleasant surprise. He'd only seen her at these types of parties a handful of times — each time with her boyfriend — a basketball player who had frat boy written all over him. They were made for each other. What surprised him even more was her walking away from her boyfriend to come over and say hello to him.

"I was gonna say hello to you today when I saw you after graduation, but you walked away."

Romero glanced at her boyfriend who looked in their direction but avoided eye contact. Smart guy, because the liquor only intensified his regret of waiting too long to get to know Claire. It wouldn't take much now for Romero to snap. "Yeah, well, you looked busy."

She shrugged. "Anyway I just wanted to say congrats." She leaned in and whispered, "Mr. Closet Smart. I'm sure you have big plans."

Of course, Claire would be the only one who'd think that. "I have a few," he smiled. "What about you?"

One of the girls in the group with her boyfriend called out for her. Figures her coward ass boyfriend wouldn't even look their way, pretending he wasn't the one who'd put the girl up to calling for Claire. Claire turned and nodded.

"Looks like you're missed already."

She rolled her eyes. "Best of luck to you, Romero. I know you'll be successful at whatever you end up doing."

"Thanks," he smiled. "And I know you will, too."

He watched her walk back to her group and her boyfriend wrapped his arms around her as soon as she reached him.

A couple of hours later Romero was behind the garage with his hand down a cheerleader's pants. His fingers found their way to a spot that made her gasp and she moaned spreading her legs a little further. He kissed her even deeper.

"Romero," she spoke in his mouth.

He tried but couldn't remember her name. "Hmm."

"I've only done it once."

"Nice," he said, sucking her neck. "We'll get a few more in tonight."

"Right here?"

Romero stopped for a moment and looked at her. He hadn't really planned on doing it there. Usually, this was just the starter. They could head to the beach or a backseat later, but something about her anxious eyes told him she might change her mind.

He took the few steps over to reach for the back door of the garage. One turn, and it opened. Romero smiled. There had to be a car in there. He pulled her by the hand and she followed willingly. A peek inside, and he realized this was better than he thought — an SUV, and the windows were open. He turned back to her with a smirk. "Happy Graduation, sexy girl." He would've added her name instead of the endearment if he'd remembered it.

Isabel

Isabel summed up her valedictory address with a

smile. She glanced at her father who was behind the video camera that sat on a tripod just below the stage. He stood tall and proud, clapping. Her mother and siblings stood with everyone else, to applaud the speech she'd worked on for weeks. The immense relief of getting it over with was more than reward enough.

The last month and a half, she'd been a wreck. The only one of her siblings who hadn't made Valedictorian was her brother Art, but then he'd gone to a highly regarded military school, and had graduated with honors, so that seemed acceptable enough. Isabel had struggled the last few months with her AP classes becoming increasingly difficult. She was so worried that her scores on her finals wouldn't be enough. As relieved as she was that this was finally over, she knew this was only the beginning.

Both her oldest sister Pat, and her brother Art were following her father's example and going into law. Her father was a criminal judge. Her other sister, Gina, had just transferred to Cornell, and knew before she even graduated from high school that she'd be majoring in civil engineering.

Isabel was still undecided about her major. Her mother had been a schoolteacher for years before being diagnosed with breast cancer a few years ago. Thankfully, she'd beat it. Even after the chemo taking so much from her mother and her father insisting she not go back to work, her mother insisted she had to.

Growing up, Isabel heard all the stories her mother told her about her students. She seemed to revel in it and even though her dad often made cracks about how unappreciated teachers were for all the hard work they did. Isabel noted how he never came home speaking fondly of his day at work, like her mother did so often.

As much as her sister was pushing for her to go into law — maybe someday between them they could start their own firm, Isabel's heart was leaning towards her mother's first love — teaching.

After the ceremony, they went out for a swanky dinner in Laguna, at one of her dad's favorite restaurants. A few of her friends had mentioned getting together later that evening to celebrate, but Isabel had plans early the next morning. Even though she was attending the University of San Diego, just over an hour away from her home in Laguna Beach, she would be staying in a dorm. Even more than her parents, her sister Pat that had always pushed her to excel. She did it all through grade school and high school. Unlike her brother, who was going to Loyola, Pat was studying close by and living at home. Isabel needed to get away. Already, because of their insistence, and because none of them had taken the summer off after high school, she was enrolled in summer school. Both her father and sister Pat had been hammering at her for months now, "Knock it out, no sense in wasting time."

So tomorrow was orientation and her summer classes started in a week.

"I'm really proud of you, Isabel." Her father squeezed her hand during dinner. It was rare for her father to say anything heartfelt. It almost brought a tear to her eye.

"Yeah," Pat added, "and you were worried about not making Valedictorian." Her sister rolled her eyes. "I knew you had it in you, Bell, you just have to believe in yourself more."

Isabel smiled. "I'm just glad it's over."

"Now the real fun begins," Gina said. "College life and college *men*." Her eyebrows bounced up and down.

Her mom chuckled. "Just don't get too caught up in that stuff and let your grades slip."

"I won't." Isabel couldn't even imagine getting *caught up* in that. She had one boyfriend all through high school. The rest of the time, she spent most of her weekends studying and reading. Just like tonight, while everyone else was out celebrating graduation, she'd be hitting the hay early.

"Art, I thought you were bringing Sabrina to dinner tonight." Her mom said, taking a sip of her wine.

Art shrugged. "Changed my mind."

"Why?" Her mom asked.

"Is she still working at the Quick-Mart?" Pat asked, with a smirk.

"She's putting herself through school, Patricia."

Isabel chewed slowly, taking in the glare her brother gave Pat.

"It was just a question."

"Yeah, well those kinds of sarcastic questions are the reason I didn't want to bring her."

Pat's eyes opened wide as if his comment surprised her. "It's nothing personal, Art. You should know by now, no one will ever be good enough for my little brother, least of all some trailer trash working at the Quick-Mart."

"Pat," her mother warned.

"I'm just—"

"Oh, but that arrogant asshole you're dating—"

"Hey!" Her mom reached over and swatted Art on the back of the head. "I will not have that kind of language at the dinner table."

"Your mother is right," her father added, "lower your voice and apologize to your sister."

Art apologized through his teeth, though it was anything but sincere. That pretty much ended any mood for small talk between her siblings. Her father asked Gina about her flight itinerary. Everyone agreed to keep their schedules open to be there to see her off since she'd be gone for months. Isabel never understood why Gina had chosen to go so far to school. As much as her family could drive her nutty sometimes, they meant the world to her and she'd miss them terribly if she was ever away from them for that long.

Even now that she'd be staying at a dorm, she was still close enough that she could drive back on a whim if she ever needed to.

Chapter 2
The Real World

Romero

Now that he was eighteen, Romero could be a door-man at his uncles' bar. He knew they expected him to be there for good, eventually graduating into working inside when he turned twenty-one, but that wasn't in his plans. He'd let them down easy when the time came, but for now, he'd enjoy the dancers and wait-resses so easily accessible to him.

After high school, he continued to work out, main-taining the physique needed to man the door for un-ruly drunks who wanted in or needed to be thrown out. He'd been working there all summer.

Romero enjoyed the job. It gave him the experience he needed for what he was planning. While his friends would all be in college, he was doing his own prerequi-site work. For years, he'd thought about possibly be-coming a cop, then making detective like the ones he saw in movies and on television. But he decided not to go that route. He hated being on a schedule. That was the same reason he decided college wasn't for him. Unlike Angel and Eric, he barely managed to stay eli-gible to play football during high school. It wasn't that the classes were too hard for him. He just never really cared enough to pull top grades.

He'd already knocked out the joke of a test he needed to be licensed as a security guard. Not that his uncles required it, it was just step one of the goals he'd set for himself. Just like the sparring and grappling he'd taken up practicing for over a year now with some of the guys at the gym who did mixed martial arts.

Romero walked into the front room. He could hear Manny in the kitchen with Aida. "I put four meats in Max's sandwich, sugar." Aida said. "How many do you want in yours?"

"How 'bout I put my meat in you." Manny said, making loud kissing noises and Romero knew his uncle was attacking his girlfriend in the kitchen. *Again.*

Aida screeched then laughed loudly. Romero frowned. He was seriously going to have to get his own place. "Hey! I could hear you in here!"

"Well cover your ears 'cause it's about to get louder."

He heard Aida laugh, then snort. Romero laughed. *Sick bastard.* He sat down on the sofa and grabbed the remote. "You want me to fix you a sandwich, Moe?" Aida asked.

"Nah, I'm good. Thanks."

Max walked out of the hallway with a newspaper under his arm. "I have the squirts."

Romero didn't even look at him, just shook his head, staring at the television. "I need my own place *now*," he muttered.

"What was that?"

"Nothing."

His uncle walked toward the kitchen. "Don't we have medicine for the shits?"

Romero tried concentrating on the reality show on criminal investigations. But his uncles, as usual, were too loud.

"It's in the bathroom," Manny said.

"No it's not, I didn't see it."

"It's right there in the cabinet. I had the shits the other night, too. I took some."

"I'm telling you it's not there."

Romero turned off the television and headed back to his room, trying to ignore his uncles, who were still arguing about the shit medicine on their way to the restroom. Manny walked in first. "Holy mother of fuck!"

"I told you, I'm sick! What did you expect, roses?"

"Well, can you open a ga-damn window for the love of Christ!"

Romero rushed by the open door, holding his nose. "And you left your splatteration all over the toilet, you sick fuck!"

"I couldn't find the brush to clean it!"

The whole neighborhood could probably hear them, especially since his uncle had made such a racket opening the bathroom window. His uncles told him months ago that it was okay if he wanted to bring girls home to spend the night—he was a man now. Yeah, he really wanted to bring a girl home to this shit.

Romero grabbed his phone off the dresser. He had a text from Angel's older brother Alex.

Working out in 20 min at the gym.

He'd sent it ten minutes earlier. Romero grabbed his gym bag and swung it over his shoulder. He squeezed his nose as he walked by the open bathroom door. Max was in there scrubbing the toilet.

"I'm outta here, Max. See you tonight."

He walked through the kitchen to get to the back door. Manny and Aida were eating at the table. "Where you going?"

"Gym." Romero took an apple from the fruit bowl

on the counter and bit into it.

"I wanted to talk to you."

Romero stopped at the door and turned around. "So talk."

"Did you bang that new girl, Cici, already?"

Romero smirked, "Not yet."

"She's got a crazy-as-shit boyfriend."

"And?"

"Stay away from her. I don't want any trouble."

Romero laughed and opened the back door. "All right, Manny. Whatever you say."

What a joke—this guy's girl was working at a titty bar. What did her boyfriend expect? She wasn't even all that, but now things were interesting. Manny should know better than to tell him to stay away from someone. What little interest he had in the girl, which was close to zilch, had suddenly spiked.

*

With summer officially over, the nights were beginning to take on a chill. Romero stood in front of the bar, wishing he'd worn a long sleeve shirt instead of a tank. He hadn't worked the last two nights, but his uncles had filled him in on Cici's boyfriend showing up and sitting at the bar while she worked, then trying to attack a guy who got friendly with her. He'd been thrown out and he wasn't allowed to come back when she was on duty. His money was still good when she wasn't there.

Cici had smiled at him tonight when she got there. Just like the first few times he'd seen her, he got the distinct feeling her eyes were saying more than her mouth was when she said hello. He was used to it. All these chicks were suffering from daddy-didn't-love-me syndrome. They were looking for love in the worst of places. He almost felt sorry for them.

He took some solace in knowing that while he'd never promised any of these girls more than a few moments of pure unadulterated fun, he always made sure they were as satisfied as he was. Not that it was important to him really, but nothing turned him on more than to hear a chick moaning in pleasure. Not the fake kind either. He knew the difference. There was no faking the trembling and the out-of-control heartbeat. Hearing and feeling their euphoria was the fucking best.

Cici walked out the door and gave him that smile again. Her perfume was overpowering, as usual. "Break time?"

"Yeah." She worked the lashes.

No question about it—this was going to happen. "What are you gonna do?"

"Sit... in my car."

Romero glanced around the parking lot. "Which one's your car?"

Cici pointed to the furthest end of the dark parking lot. *Perfect.*

"Mind if I join you? It's about time for my break, too."

"Sure." Her smile stretched out even more.

Romero radioed in that he was taking a break. In less than two minutes, another security guy came out to cover for him. Never one to beat around the bush, Romero touched Cici's dark hair as they walked to her car. With the roots showing, he could see it was obviously dyed. "You don't like the blonde?"

"I change it all the time. I get bored."

They reached her car. Cici stood against the driver's door and stared at him. Aware of the time constraint, and not the least bit unsure of what she wanted, he leaned in and kissed her. His uncle's words rang in his head. *Stay away from her.* All the motivation he needed. He smiled against her mouth.

As expected, she didn't protest, instead she opened her lips, welcoming his tongue. He took her face in his hands and kissed her deeper, pushing his body against her. Her hands pulled his shirt out of his pants with an urgency even he wasn't feeling yet. This was even easier than he'd thought. She started to undo his belt. Instinct made him look up. A guy stalked toward them, his furious eyes bouncing from Cici to Romero.

"Cici, is that you? You fucking bitch!"

Cici froze. "Oh shit."

Romero didn't pull his body away from her. "Is that your boyfriend?"

"Oh my God," she whispered, "yes!"

Romero smirked, taking a step back. "It's cool, you'll be fine. What's his name?"

"Freddy."

"Get the fuck away from my girl," the guy yelled as he got closer.

He wore a dirty mechanic's uniform. Romero had been around enough drunks to know the guy had been drinking. He lifted his hands in the air and smiled. "You're not supposed to be here, Fred."

"Fuck you!" He pointed at Romero. "Cici, get your ass over here."

Cici began to walk around Romero, but he put his hand on her shoulder, before she could get by. "She's on duty."

Fred charged at Romero. "I told you to get the fuck

away from her."

Romero grabbed his hand and spun him around, throwing him against the car. He held his arm behind his back. "You need to calm down, Fred."

Fred squirmed but Romero held him tight. Romero frowned when he heard the voices and footsteps behind him. He was hoping this wouldn't get back to his uncles. Fred stopped squirming. "You gonna be calm?"

The other security guys reached him. "You got things under control?"

"Yeah, we're good. Right, Fred?"

Fred nodded, staring at Cici. Romero let go of him, and smiled at Cici, whose eyes still looked very frightened. In the next moment, he understood why. Fred backhanded her so hard she flew back more than three feet, hitting the fence behind her and fell to the ground, her purse spilling all its contents everywhere.

"You fucking cu —"

Before he could finish, Romero slammed his fist into Fred's mouth, blood splattering all over. He got in a few more fists to Fred's face, before being held back by the other security guards. More people spilled out of the bar and hurried toward them. Romero managed to free his arm and slammed another fist into Fred's stomach. Someone caught his arm before he could hit him again. "That's enough, Moe!"

Romero turned to face his uncle, feeling that familiar uncontrollable rage that had only gotten worse lately. "He hit her!"

His uncle turned to Cici, who was picking up her things from the ground. Fred looked up from where he'd doubled over after Romero landed one in his gut. Manny backhanded Fred one time. "You fucking asshole!"

Cici walked around the car. "Get inside, sweetheart." Manny grabbed Romero by the arm and began walking away. "Get him the fuck out of here guys. He comes back, have him arrested."

"No, call the cops on his ass now!" Romero yelled.

Manny shook him. "Are you outta your mind? I call the cops now, they'll take you both in."

Romero yanked his arm away from his uncle, feeling an immense urge to go back and pound on Fred some more. Manny must've seen the look on his face. "Keep walking, boy. Keep that temper of yours under control, son, before it buries you. Don't you even think about going back there."

Cici's sister picked her up at the end of her shift. She said she was going back to her sister's and not the apartment she shared with Fred. Jesus, she lived with the guy. She looked too young to be in such a serious relationship. Although it was so serious, why the hell had she been moments from pulling Romero out of his pants? That whole night Romero tossed and turned.

She was a no-show the following two shifts. She called a week later to say she wasn't coming back. Romero already knew it. Though she didn't tell her uncle, he knew she'd gone back to Fred and he'd made her quit.

Weeks later, Romero still struggled with the fact that if he hadn't made it his mission that night to bag her, she wouldn't have gotten slapped. In hindsight, that slap probably wasn't the first she'd gotten from Fred and definitely wouldn't be the last. Those kinds of women couldn't be helped. At least that's what his grandmother said about his own mom. "Les gusta la mala vida." *They loved the bad life.* Yep, Cici had to know the risk she was taking that night, and she'd taken it so eagerly.

After that night, Romero never touched another of his uncle's employees again. Any time one of them flirted with him now, it brought back the memory of Cici being slapped. It was a memory he'd probably never forget. He couldn't stand it.

Isabel

All summer, Isabel had had her dorm to herself. It was heaven. She'd always been a neat freak, so she dreaded having to share a room with anyone. She'd been warned that fall would be different. With twice the amount of kids enrolling in the fall, there was no chance she was going to keep her room to herself. She could only hope she got someone she got along with.

She was still holding out hope when she got back from her second class and no one was in her room. Then there was a knock at her door. The door opened and in walked a petite blonde girl, with her hair in a ponytail. She read the paper in her hand. "Are you I. Montenegro?"

Isabel nodded as disappointment sunk in. "Isabel."

"Oh good, then I'm in the right place. I'm Valerie." She dropped the two bags she carried, then peeked out the door. "This is it, Alex."

Valerie held the door open. Isabel had seen some muscular guys in her time, but this guy took the cake. Not only did his head nearly hit the doorway, he barely fit through the frame. He carried her luggage in and dropped it just inside the door. He glanced at Isabel who immediately felt inadequately dressed. She'd taken her bra off when she started reading. She hugged herself. "Meet my new roommate, Isabel."

"Hey, Isabel." He smiled at her politely, showing off a very nice pair of dimples before turning back to Valerie. "I'll go get the rest." He kissed Valerie before walking away.

The rest? With the bags Valerie dropped and the ones her boyfriend dropped, they were up to five. Valerie looked around for a few minutes.

"I take it this is mine, right?" Valerie plopped down on the empty, sheetless bed.

Isabel nodded, still hugging herself. "That whole side is yours."

Valerie took everything in and was about to say something when Alex walked in with two more bags. "This is it," he said, dropping them on the already crowded floor.

Valerie stood up and climbed around all the luggage to get to him. She tiptoed to reach him and gave him a peck. "Thank you."

Her boyfriend wrapped his arms around her, picking her up effortlessly, making her screech. Isabel turned back to her laptop and tried not to think of how invisible she felt. They stood at the door smooching for what seemed like an eternity. Valerie kept giggling because he wouldn't let her go. "I have to unpack, Alex."

They went silent for a while. Isabel dare not look up, since they were obviously making out right there in front of her. She could literally hear the exchange of bodily fluids.

"Stop," she finally heard Valerie whisper. "Alex, we're not alone."

Thank you!

Isabel pushed her glasses up a bit and pretended to be engrossed in the screen of her laptop. After an unbelievable few more kisses, Alex finally left.

Valerie closed the door. Now Isabel could look up.

"Sorry about that," Valerie said, still standing by the door. "He gets a little carried away sometimes."

Isabel nodded, not sure how else to respond to that. She only prayed this is not what she would have to put up with for the rest of the semester.

"I'll just unpack and let you do whatever it is that you're doing."

Two hours later, Valerie had unpacked most of her stuff, but as far as Isabel could see, she hadn't really put much of it away. For the past half hour, Valerie had been on the phone with Alex again.

"Yeah, I'm done unpacking."

Isabel jerked her head up from her book. Most of her things were still all over the floor and she'd stacked a lot of stuff along the walls. They had drawers, bookshelves and a closet. Was she not planning to use any of them?

"No, I'm not coming home this weekend but you can come here."

Isabel squeezed her eyes shut and took a deep breath.

*

Two months later, Valerie's things were pretty much in the same place where she'd *unpacked* them, and there was never a dull moment. Valerie and her boyfriend had a turbulent relationship. Things were wonderful for a few weeks then Valerie would get into a noticeably bad mood, grumbling that she hated him and slamming things around for days.

Isabel never asked her anything about it. They hadn't exactly warmed up to each other. Things got tense between them after the few times Isabel had to remind Valerie about not leaving her clothes on the bathroom floor after she showered.

Isabel had a ritual when it came to studying. She needed absolute silence. She'd explained this to Valerie, who said she understood and would try to keep it down, then proceeded to blow-dry her hair.

"I didn't know you were studying," she'd responded to Isabel's complaint. "Who studies on a Friday night anyway?"

After a few more blow-ups, they officially hated each other.

Isabel sat on her bed. It was Friday night and she'd decided not to head home until the next morning. One of her friends told her about a party tonight just off campus, but as usual, she passed. She'd just finished talking to her sister, Gina, who couldn't believe Isabel was sitting in her dorm room on a Friday night. Isabel had always envied her sister who was not only smart, but always fit right in with the popular, party crowd.

To her surprise, the door opened and in walked Valerie. Ever since the beginning of the semester, Valerie had gone out every weekend and sometimes during the week. She glanced at Isabel, her eyes and nose bright red.

"You okay?"

Valerie shook her head and walked into the restroom. Isabel had witnessed many of Valerie and Alex's over-the-phone arguments. She'd been mad at him plenty of times, but this was the first time she saw her cry over him, if her tears now in fact were because of him.

Valerie came out of the restroom and pulled a t-shirt out of a bag from the floor. She took the blouse she wore off, and pulled the t-shirt over her head. Isabel had already decided she'd let her be and not pry, until Valerie sat down on her bed and buried her face in her hands, sobbing.

Out of pure reaction, because it was what she'd do if it was one of her sisters, Isabel jumped from her bed and sat next to Valerie, putting an arm around her. Valerie leaned against her, welcoming the comfort of Isabel's gesture.

"I don't even know why I care anymore," she said, finally looking up. "It's not like he's ever promised me anything."

Isabel stared at Valerie's wet face. She grabbed the box of tissue from the desk and handed it to Valerie.

"He does this all the time." She stopped to blow her nose. "And I pretend like it doesn't bother me, then I find out the truth and..." she put the tissue to her eyes and took a deep breath. "It hurts like hell."

Isabel had only been in one relationship in her life. It was long, but boring by most standards. She didn't have much to offer in the way of advice. "What did he lie about?"

Valerie told her how long she'd been going out with Alex, and that she'd been drooling over him since grade school. Theirs was an open relationship, which Isabel didn't get. Supposedly, they were both okay with seeing other people. From what little Isabel knew about Alex and the body language she saw when he was with her, he didn't strike her as someone who would be okay with that kind of understanding. But she listened without interrupting.

"The longer I keep this up, the more it hurts to know I won't be spending time with him because he's with someone else. I used to shake it off, but sometimes it really hurts, especially coming off a week like this one."

"So why don't you tell him?"

Valerie shook her head. "I can't."

"Why?"

"It's always been like this between us. Either I accept our relationship for what it is — take what he will give me — or walk away and lose him completely." She took one final deep breath, and wiped her eyes. "I'm done crying. This isn't the first time and I'm sure it won't be the last." She gave Isabel a pathetic little smile. "I'm starving. You wanna split a pizza?"

They ordered a large pizza. As tiny as Valerie was, she devoured more than half within minutes. They sat on the floor exchanging stories about high school and their families back home. "You live in La Jolla and you're paying for a dorm? Isn't that like twenty minutes away?"

Valerie nodded. "Alex." Valerie must've read the look of confusion on Isabel's face because she clarified, "I was hoping the time away from home would help me eventually get over him."

Valerie told her more about her relationship. Isabel told her about her high school sweetheart, Jacob. They talked until almost three in the morning.

"Two and a half years, *really*?"

"Yeah," Isabel smiled. "We started going out my sophomore year."

"So why'd you break up?"

"It wasn't so much a break up, as it was a to-be-continued type of deal. He enlisted in the Navy. He wanted us to stay together, but I just didn't think it would work. Plus," Isabel shrugged. "I was kind of over it already anyway. When he told me about enlisting, I was actually relieved. I'd already started to practice my break-up speech."

"You weren't in love with him?"

"I thought I was. But looking back now, I think I was just in love with the idea of *being* in love, you know? He was my first everything, and even though that was exciting, it was never spectacular. I've read so much about that warm fuzzy feeling and how you can hardly wait to see him again—when you're with them the world seems to stand still."

Valerie pouted. "I know that feeling."

Isabel pouted too. "Well at least you've felt it. I never did. I think we were just too comfortable with each other from the very beginning. Everything was perfect all the time. I don't even remember ever arguing with him. We agreed on everything."

"What about the sex?" Valerie grinned.

"It was okay." Valerie's expression made her laugh. "I mean at first, of course it was. We were both each other's firsts, so *that* was exciting. But neither of us knew what we were doing, it was always over so fast— never mind-blowing like I've read so much and seen in the movies."

She left the part out about how after two years with him she'd never even had an orgasm. On her own, certainly, but never with him. A big part of the reason was since they were so young, most of the time they were sneaking around so they had to make it quick. That was probably the most exciting thing about it. That she was doing something bad, and though she never admitted it to Jacob she liked being bad sometimes. It was so unlike her she doubted Jacob ever knew how thrilling it had been for her to take such risks.

Isabel didn't even have to ask, but she did anyway.

"How 'bout you and Alex?"

Valerie smiled so big, and although it made Isabel green with envy, she laughed anyway. She was really enjoying her time with Valerie. If she could get past her roommate's messy side of the room and her habit of leaving things everywhere, she might actually get used to this.

Chapter 3
Moving On

Romero

Manny and Max weren't happy when they found out that not only was Romero not going into the family business, he wouldn't even be doing the doorman gig anymore. Of course, he'd help out if they were ever in a bind and needed him, but he had a goal and he was sticking to his plan.

After a year of doing the doorman thing exclusively, he started landing jobs at other bars and clubs. He needed the experience of dealing with more than just throwing a bunch of drunks out on their asses.

He landed a job at a sports arena working security during concerts and events. The bigger celebrities had their own security, but the small-time celebs needed to be escorted in and out. As different as the venue was, compared to his uncles' bar, the sexual encounters were surprisingly similar. His choices in this case, were of a more sophisticated caliber but the outcome was still the same. The women may have been classier on the outside, but to Romero they were just as hollow on the inside and the act itself, just as meaningless.

The biggest difference was while the women at his uncles' bar looked up to him as if he were on a higher level because his uncles owned the joint, these women had the fucking nerve to look down on him because he was the security guard to their gig. They'd spread their legs just as easily as the girls from the bar and moaned just as loud. It was laughable. Though most of the time he didn't feel much like laughing.

One night he walked the back stage, keeping an eye out for any eager fans that might sneak back to get a closer look at the musicians performing that night. The music blared so loud you could actually feel it vibrate through the halls.

Thoughts of his next step to get to his goal consumed him. He'd already enrolled in an online course required by the state to get his business license. Talking to Angel and Eric helped him stay on course. They were always talking about the next semester and having to pass this or that prerequisite. Even though he never talked about his own goal, he had a lot to take care of before he got to where needed to be.

The main thing slowing the process for him now was money. His uncles had it, but he wasn't about to hit them up. He was doing this on his own. That was part of the reason he sought out another job—more money. His uncles had offered him more money to stay but he knew it was a hand out. Most of the time he sat out there for hours. Some nights he saw no action at all. How the hell could he justify a raise for doing nothing more than sitting and keeping an eye out?

Loud voices jolted him from his thoughts. He turned to see a man and a woman arguing just outside the ladies' room at the other end of the hall. He hurried toward them. From what he could see, they both seemed to have the proper backstage passes around their necks. Their argument was escalating. The music was loud, but so were they, and Romero could make out what they were arguing about.

"You don't talk that way to a man in his position!"

The man barked right in her face, but she didn't back down.

"The hell I don't. He insulted me!"

The man grabbed her arm and she pulled it away. "Get your paws off me!"

The second Romero saw his other hand go for her throat, he broke into a sprint. He felt something ignite in him and the memories of that night with Cici in the parking lot assaulted him. "Get your fucking hands off her!"

They both turned, startled by his voice. The man backed away from the woman just seconds before Romero reached them. Romero slammed him against the wall. "You think you're a tough guy, hitting women? Hit me, mother fucker!" He held his hands open to his sides dying for this guy to take a swing.

People from inside one of the backstage rooms walked out after hearing the commotion.

"I didn't hit her," the guy said, holding his hands in front of him warding off any punches Romero might take.

Romero grabbed him by the neck and squeezed. "You like how this feels, asshole?"

"All right that's enough," someone from behind Romero yelled. Romero kept squeezing and the man's face began turning red. The rage he felt got worse by the second. The coward didn't even try fighting him off. Romero reached for the passes that hung around the man's neck with his other hand and ripped them off. He had every right to throw anyone out who started trouble. This guy had started more than that.

He pulled his hand off the guy's neck and grabbed him roughly by the collar of his shirt instead. Romero hauled him off toward the exit. "Where are you taking him?" A bald man surrounded by a few bodyguards asked.

Romero didn't even turn to look at him, trying desperately to calm himself before he did more than he should and responded. "He's out of here."

"Do you know who that is?"

"I don't give a shit."

As it turned out, he should've given a shit. The man he'd thrown out was the brother of one of the boys in the wannabe boy band performing that night. Even though the band was still up-and-coming, their clout was big enough to get Romero fired.

It was a pisser, but a well-worth-it pisser. All this time he thought he was over what had happened to Cici that night. Seeing that man put his hands on that woman brought back the ugly memory. He played the scene repeatedly in his head every night. The look in her frightened eyes just before he slapped her, then seeing her body fly backwards. Images of her swollen bloody lip made him squeeze his eyes shut. There was no doubt in his mind that if he had to do it over, he would pound Fred's face into the ground until he was unconscious.

After what happened at the concert, he was wondering about Cici again. Was Fred still beating her? Was she even alive still?

His uncles had been arguing, going back and forth all day. This time it was about Aida. "I'm not busting your nuts, Man. I'm just saying you've only been seeing her a few months and already you're talking about moving her in? How do you know she's the one so fast?"

"I just do. She's not like them other skanks I've dated. She's different, okay."

Manny stopped at his open door when he saw Romero still lying in bed. "What's with you?"

"Nothing,"

"What do you mean nothing? You've been lying around a lot lately. You feeling okay?

Max stuck his head in the door. "You sick?"

"Nah, I'm fine." Romero sat up. "Did you guys ever hear anything about Cici after she quit?"

"Who?" Manny asked.

"Cici, the waitress with the crazy boyfriend last year. She only worked at the bar for a couple of weeks?"

Max still looked lost but Manny frowned. "Oh, her. No, why?"

"Just wondering whatever happened to her."

"Probably working at another bar. She was trouble. It was better that she quit." Manny walked away from the door.

Max still appeared to be trying to figure out who they were talking about. "You don't remember her, Max?" Romero didn't understand his own sudden interest. It bothered him to no end to think she wouldn't have had to live through that, if it hadn't been for him.

"I think I do now." His confused expression went hard. "If it's the one I'm thinking, Manny's right. Trouble—so stop wondering about her and get your ass outta bed. We're going bowling and you're coming with."

Isabel

If it hadn't been for Isabel's insistence, Valerie might've taken her real estate license exam and dropped out of school. Valerie didn't share Isabel's enthusiasm for school. But in an act of friendship, and the selfish need to keep her new best friend around longer, she convinced her to stay and at least get her AA. Once Valerie had earned her degree, she was gone. Not wanting to get used to a brand new roommate, and knowing without Valerie there, things just wouldn't be the same, Isabel decided to finish school while commuting from home.

Pat had transferred to a school out of state, making Isabel's last two years of school easier. No one loved her decision to become a schoolteacher, least of all Pat, but her parents supported her decision. She knew her mom was secretly thrilled that Isabel had decided to follow in her footsteps.

"I just hope you're not going to stop just because you get your credentials, Bell. If teaching is what you want to do," Pat had said, with the roll of her eyes. "No offense to Mom, but you can at least take it a step further and teach at a university level."

Unsure why she'd never been able to stand up to her oldest sister, Isabel actually agreed to consider it. Her sister had cheerfully made the announcement to everyone in the family. Ever since she'd started teaching full time, not only her sister but her father began asking her when she was going back to school. She was just getting used to her new role in life and they wanted her to squeeze in more school time?

Valerie moved out of her dad's place months ago and had kept trying to convince Isabel to move in with her ever since. She was on the phone with her again on the way home from work. "Isabel, you promised when we were in school that we'd get our own place once we graduated. You can organize this place however you want. I'll follow the rules, scout's honor!"

The school district she worked for was actually closer to Valerie's place than her parents' house, and if she did go back to school, she *would* be much closer to the university also. The only reason she hadn't agreed to it yet was because she was the last one home now. Pat married a highly decorated Navy Lieutenant Commander and moved out over a year ago. Her other siblings never bothered moving back into the nest after they left for school. Gina now lived in New York, while Art stayed in Los Angeles. Their dad was supposed to retire a few years ago but he kept putting it off. Isabel hated leaving her mom alone. But she *had* promised, and deep inside she really did feel it was time to get her own place.

"Okay?"

Valerie squealed, then laughed. "Is that a question or an answer?"

"It's an answer," Isabel smiled, beginning to feel the excitement of it. "I'll tell my parents tonight."

"Oh my God, this is going to be great!" Valerie gushed. "And Alex has his own place now too, so he won't be over that much. He prefers we hang out at his place anyway."

Isabel didn't comment. Valerie and Alex still had their off and on roller coaster relationship. At the moment, it was on. But she knew it was just a matter of time before things went south again. Isabel didn't understand why Valerie couldn't just let go once and for all.

*

A few weeks later, she'd moved in and everything was put away exactly as she required things to be put away.

Of course, Pat came by to put in her two cents about her new place. "Personally, I would've stayed with Mom and Dad until I saved up to buy my own place. But since you're going back to school, maybe this is best for now."

As usual, Isabel took the criticism with a nod and a smile.

The months passed, and Valerie kept her promise about not having Alex over too often, though Isabel didn't mind having him around. He was pleasant enough, but he was clearly more comfortable having Valerie stay over at his place. Valerie spent so much time over there, Isabel began to wonder if maybe she'd move in with him. Then one night after he'd disappeared for almost a week, Valerie went to his place and confronted him.

Isabel had seen Valerie upset about Alex many times since meeting her, but this was by far the worst. After years of speculating and assuming she knew what he was doing when she wasn't around, she caught him with another girl at his place. Valerie knew all along he kept the company of other women when she wasn't around but seeing it for herself was devastating.

Even after Valerie cried for hours and probably the entire night — Isabel finally left her alone in her room — Isabel still assumed that within days or perhaps weeks this time, Valerie would get back with him. But it didn't happen. She finally decided she'd had enough.

As hard as Isabel knew this must be for Valerie, they both agreed it was for the best.

Valerie hadn't dated anyone in months, so Isabel felt a little guilty when Lawrence, a guy from a few doors down, asked her out. He was a little older and a professor at UCSD. It seemed ideal. Valerie was excited for her.

Pat, of course, found reasons not to like him. "Why is he still living in an apartment at his age? He can obviously afford a house."

"He says he's comfortable here and he says being a real estate owner does not define you as a person."

"That," her sister said with a sneer, "is lack of ambition. I hope he doesn't put those kinds of thoughts in your head."

Isabel couldn't muster up the energy to argue. Maybe if she actually *liked* Lawrence, she would. She'd dealt with his kind before plenty of times: know-it-all, brainy guys. What she couldn't get past was how boring he was. She was so sick of boring. From her first boyfriend to Lawrence and every guy she dated in between—boring. But then how did she expect to attract anything different? It's not like she was Ms. Excitement. Just about anything she'd ever done in her life that was remotely exciting had been thanks to Valerie. She sighed. She was doomed to be with a boring guy. Just like her sister's husband and she hated to say it, as much as she loved him, just like her dad.

Chapter 4
First impressions

"You're kidding me with this shit, right?" Romero glared at Angel.

Angel didn't even look at him. "Nope, it's not happening." He shot the basketball into the hoop.

Eric caught the rebound and bounced the ball. "Why what happened?"

"Nothing happened." Angel held his hands up for Eric to throw him the ball. "I just don't want a bachelor party. What's the big deal?" He shot the ball again.

"The big deal is," Romero grabbed the ball as it bounced off the rim. "we had this whole Vegas thing set up—an entire weekend, Angel. You can't just rank out on us like that."

Angel shrugged. "Well, I appreciate it, but cancel it. It's not happening."

"You're fucking serious?"

Angel laughed. "Yeah, I'm serious. You guys can still go if you want. Celebrate for me."

Romero knew it had something to do with his fiancée, Sarah. Angel was so damn whipped it was a joke. She either told him not to have one or worse, threatened to have one of her own. Romero had been looking forward to this, too. He'd finally reached his goal of starting his own security firm. All the goals he'd set for himself in the last few years had finally come together. It was a little rocky at first but things had started taking off in the last couple of months. He'd just received his

P.I. license, had two employees now, was already looking to hire more, and the money was finally rolling in.
What better way to celebrate than partying his ass off
in Vegas? Now Angel had pulled the rug out from under him. "We gotta do something for you, man. Even if
we don't go out of town we can do something around
here."

"Nah, I don't want shit. We got all kinds of showers
and other crap my parents are planning. I don't need
anything else." Angel stopped to take a swig from his
water bottle.

Romero shook his head as he watched Eric take another shot. "Damn shame. I'll think of something."

"Drop it, Romero. I don't want anything. So let it
go."

Sarah, his fiancée had definitely pulled a fast one on
him. There was no way he'd be this adamant about it.
This was bullshit. He'd never understand how a girl
could have such a hold on a guy. Romero stood there
baffled about Angel's refusal to give in.

*

"Let's go over this again," Isabel said, as Valerie
glossed her lips, looking into the visor on the passenger
side. "Remember, indifference is key. You've been over
Alex now for a year. That's proof enough you can live
without him."

Valerie nodded. They were on their way to Valerie's
cousin's wedding shower. She was marrying Alex's
younger brother and Valerie was the maid of honor.
This was a disaster. Valerie exceeded Isabel's expectations this past year. She actually managed to stay away
from him for that long. But now she had to be there for

all the wedding events. And so would he.

"I got this, Isabel. I'm *so* over him. You're being silly right now."

Isabel took a deep breath. "Okay, I hope so, but if anything comes up, remember I'll be right there for you."

Valerie laughed. "I'll be fine."

They walked into the elaborate set up in Alex's family's backyard. Valerie had told her that their family was big on gatherings and parties, but this was outrageous. The entire backyard was transformed into this outdoor wedding heaven.

After saying hello to her cousin Sarah and her fiancé Angel, they made their way to the outdoor bar. Alex and few other guys were huddled there already. Valerie squeezed Isabel's arm when Alex came into view. The jerk looked hotter than ever and Isabel had a bad feeling Valerie would be a goner.

"Be strong," she whispered as they reached the bar area.

The guy pouring the shots behind the bar lifted a brow when he saw Valerie approach. "I'll take one," Valerie said.

God that was the worse thing she could do—get drunk. "Valerie no," she warned, hoping Valerie would listen to reason.

"Who brought the narc?"

Isabel immediately turned to the idiot behind the bar, pouring the shots. "Pardon me?"

He did the stupidest show of bowing down with his hand over his head and then added in the most antagonistic voice. "Pardon *me!*"

Isabel's face warmed in reaction, as the people around her chuckled. He poured a few more shots.

"You in, Narc?" he asked, looking at her with a smar-tassy smirk.

"Easy Ramon," Alex said.

"Yes, pour her one please," Valerie, said.

Isabel's jaw dropped, then remembered how hard it must be for Valerie to be here standing so close to the man she used to be hopelessly in love with.

Ramon pulled out another shot glass. "Coming right up." He was your typical muscle head. Isabel expected no less from Alex's friends. Though he wasn't as big as Alex, she could see even under his dress shirt, he had enough muscle to call attention from most girls.

She ignored the shot in front of her for as long as she could, until he finally called her on it. "So... did I pour that for nothing?"

Valerie turned to her, then to Ramon. "Romero, this is my roommate, Isabel. Isabel, this is Romero."

"I thought it was Ramon."

His expression hardened. "It's Romero." He pushed the shot closer to her.

Isabel turned to Valerie, exasperated—the things she did for her. Grudgingly, she took the shot. Romero smiled as she grimaced, feeling the alcohol warm her throat.

"Want another one?"

"No." Her voice was hoarse and he laughed.

"Is that your first shot ever, Narc?"

"My name is Isabel."

He smirked. "Too long. But all right, is that your first shot, *Izzy*?"

It was better than Narc, and it wasn't the first time she'd been called that, so she didn't protest, staring at him as she sucked on a lime. "No, it's not."

His golden brown eyes seemed to sparkle in

amusement as he poured more shots. The crowd that was there when they arrived had dispersed. Just Isabel and Valerie—who stood right behind her, talking to Alex—were the only ones still there, leaving Romero to scrutinize only her. She pushed her glasses up, trying not to stare at his impressive forearms as he poured the shots. "Take another one."

Isabel stared at the shots in front of him—one for him—one for her. "I'm driving." She lifted her chin.

"It's early. You'll be fine." He took his shot and smiled at her.

She turned, hoping Valerie could get her out of this but both she and Alex were gone. Really? Already? After all they'd gone over on there way there? She hadn't even noticed them walk away. Her shoulders slumped and she took the shot, immediately sucking on a lime. Romero grinned from ear to ear. "You see? And you were fighting it."

"That's my last one." Her voice was a rasp. "I mean it." She'd never understand why people enjoyed doing shots.

Romero set the bottle aside and leaned his elbows onto the bar. "So how come I've never met you? You and Valerie been friends long?"

Unlike most guys who tried being discreet, he did nothing to hide the fact he was taking her in, *completely*. She felt utterly invaded, the way his eyes went from her hair to her cleavage. They even spent some time on her hands. She tried hiding her unease with his bald-faced demeanor. "Years, we met in college."

"College girl, uh? What are you doing now?"

Isabel still felt the burn in her throat from the two shots. "I'm a teacher. And you?"

She was used to limited eye contact when first

meeting someone. Not Romero. He seemed to seek her eyes out, and then smile confidently. "I should've known."

"What does that mean?" She'd heard this before. Even with her mom being a teacher, she knew most people's image of a teacher — straight-laced, unattractive, mousy women, usually with a ridiculous bun in their hair.

"I'm just sayin'."

"You're saying what?" She lifted her eyebrow.

It was annoying the way every one of her statements or questions seemed to amuse him. "You *look* like a teacher."

She felt herself warm inside. "And what exactly does a teacher look like?"

The corner of his mouth lifted as he blatantly looked her over again. "Sweet...and sexy, apparently."

She felt the heat rush to her face and Romero smiled even bigger. "Did I embarrass you?"

"No," she said too quickly. "You didn't answer my question. What do *you* do?"

"I just started my own business this year." He poured another shot and lifted it to her.

She shook her head. *Not even one more.* "What kind of business?"

He didn't even bother with a lime after downing the shot he poured. "I'm in the security business."

Of course. "Like a bodyguard?"

"Somethin' like that." Isabel studied his stubborn jaw and the way he'd smirk at everyone he glanced at, like he had some kind of inside joke going with each one. She wondered if *she* was the joke. Here was this tough looking bodyguard, or whatever he was having some fun with the nervous schoolteacher at the bar.

She was glad now that Valerie had convinced her to wear her hair down. Well, half down. The front was still up in a barrette, but she let the back hang loose.

Angel came by looking for something behind the bar.

"What do you need?" Romero asked.

"Water." He bent down still searching. "Didn't you bring bottled waters out here?"

Romero shook his head. "I'm in charge of the booze, son. Fuck the water."

Angel frowned, shaking his head. "Useless."

"Take a shot, Angel. You need to relax."

Angel barely glanced at him and stalked away.

"So you're in charge of getting everyone drunk?" Isabel noticed ever since her last shot, Romero's eyes kept making their way back to one place, especially when she spoke—her lips. It unnerved her. Had he no tact at all?

"Yep, you ready for another?" He reached for the bottle.

"No. I'm not having anymore."

"Sure you will."

He was so damn sure of himself. "No, I *won't*."

"You will," he said, looking up behind her with a smile. "Ready for another one, big guy?"

Angel and Alex walked up to the bar. Angel had a box of bottled waters and Alex held a box of some other kind of bottled beverage. Isabel glanced around but didn't see Valerie. "Where did Valerie go?"

Then she saw it. Alex looked visibly shaken. He wasn't the same Alex as when they'd walked in. *Great.* Something happened already. "I'm out." He said, his jaw tight.

"What?" both Angel and Romero said almost at the

same time.

"I gotta go to the restaurant. I'll be back." He walked away without even glancing at Isabel.

"That guy works too much," Romero said.

Isabel searched around the backyard. She hadn't even noticed how many more people had arrived. Every table in the big backyard was just about full and there were many people still standing. Then she spotted Valerie. She stood at the opening of the canopy that covered the entire backyard. Something was definitely wrong. She slipped off the bar stool, grabbing her purse.

"Where you going?" Romero asked.

"To see about Valerie."

"Bring her over here."

Isabel pressed her lips together as she hurried to Valerie. Yeah, that's exactly what Valerie needs — to get drunk and stupid, just in time for when Alex got back.

*

"Will you move?" Romero made way for Angel to finish dumping the bottled waters into the ice chest next to the bar. He hadn't taken his eyes off Isabel. His first impression of her when he saw her walk up to the bar, he knew she'd be uptight. He was right — definitively not his type, if he even *had* a type. But he knew for sure uptight schoolteachers weren't it — or at least he knew *he* wasn't *their* type.

He just hadn't expected her to be fun. He'd never met someone whose facial expressions did so much telling. From the moment he called her *narc*, he noticed it. Everything he said or did, her face had so much to say about it. From the way her eyebrows pinched in, to

the way her eyes opened wide at some of his comments. And her lips were something else. The way she
pressed them together suddenly, then fell open in the
next instant. He'd also never seen anyone blush so in-
stantaneously. Her face turned beet red in a blink of an
eye. It was highly entertaining.

"Don't even."

Romero turned to look at Angel, who glanced at
Isabel, then back at him. "What?"

"Sarah said she's a brain—not for you."

"What? You don't think I've banged a few brains in
my time?" He tried not to show how annoyed Angel's
comment made him.

"Easy," Eric said, as he walked up to the bar.

Romero glanced at Eric then glared back at Angel.
Angel laughed. "Trust me, she's not your type. She's
got some class. Don't go embarrassing her either. Sarah
said she's shy."

Romero shook off Angel's comments when he saw
Isabel was on her way back to the bar without Valerie,
and smirked. "Too late."

Both Angel and Eric followed Romero's wicked
smile. "Be cool," Angel warned.

"Always," Romero said, pouring himself a beer
from the keg.

Angel walked away holding several bottles of water
in his hands. Eric asked for a cup and Romero handed
it to him. Isabel seemed down when she reached the
bar. "Where's Valerie?"

Isabel took a seat at the bar. "She went to the ladies'
room."

"You mean restroom."

Her eyebrows pinched. "What's the difference?"

"We're at someone's house, not a public place. So

there is no ladies' or mens' room."

She pushed her glasses up, frowning. He stared at the design on her French tip nails that he noticed earlier. He reached for her hand, and found it was soft, just as he expected. She flinched at his touch but didn't take her hand back. He pulled her hand gently to him for a closer look. This close, he saw it was the letter M in calligraphy. He glanced up at her but didn't ask. It obviously didn't stand for Isabel. He let her hand go and she glanced around, not offering an explanation.

"You wanna beer?"

Her lips twitched slightly. "You have wine?"

There was another ice chest off to the side, with some wine bottles chilling. He'd never been into wine, or into chicks who drank wine. He glanced back at her as he pulled two bottles of wine out. White and pink— was the only distinction he saw. She asked for the blush, which he assumed to be the pink, and poured her a glass.

He noticed the keychain that hung out of her purse with the San Diego Padres emblem. "So you're a fan?" He gestured to the keychain after placing the cup of wine in front of her.

She frowned. "I was, but after the year they had last year... I dunno. The Diamond Backs are starting to look good."

"What?" Romero stared at her in disbelief, loving the way her startled eyes opened wide. "You don't just turn your back on your team when they have a bad year."

"*One*? They've had like three or four in a row." She sipped her wine.

Romero shook his head adamantly. "You from the San Diego area originally?"

"Laguna. I moved to La Jolla after college."

"Close enough. Number one rule for a true sports fan. You're born to your team. Choice was never an option. And even if you move away, that's your team forever. You carry the keychain around daily. You should know that."

Isabel laughed and he finally got to see what her face looked like lit up. All her cute expressions had slowly given away that she wasn't as uptight as he initially thought—now that sweet smile that brightened her entire face was another tell-tale sign. He gulped hard. She was something else.

"No, I didn't know that. Thanks for enlightening me." They talked for a while longer about The Padres. Then he asked a few random questions about where she got her nails done and they made small talk about the horrible parking at the mall, but after seeing her bring the tip of her thumb to her mouth for the second time, the M on her finger stared at him. He finally asked something that actually interested him. "So who's the M for?"

Her eyes did the asking.

"The M on your nail." Romero handed her a second glass of wine.

"Wow, this is a lot," she said, taking the cup. "Maybe I can pour half of it in another cup for Valerie."

He watched her take a sip and he waited, taking a swig of his beer. She glanced around, looking antsy.

"Izzy?"

She looked back at him. Again she didn't even have to speak, her eyes expressed her confusion.

He couldn't help smiling. "The M on your nail. Who's it for?"

She brought her hands up to look at her nails again. "Oh, my name."

"Your name's Isabel."

"My last name is Montenegro."

Romero took a big satisfying drink of his beer then said, "Ms. Montenegro. Is that what your students call you?"

She nodded. "Romero is your last name, right?"

"Yep."

"So how come you don't go by your first name?"

He shrugged. "Never have."

"Why?"

"Long story. I just don't." He turned away from her questioning eyes. "You sure Valerie didn't leave?"

"No, I'm driving. She didn't bring her car," she sighed. "But she is taking long. I hope she's okay."

"Why wouldn't she be?"

She seemed apprehensive but finally said, "I think she was upset about something she and Alex talked about."

"Ah," Romero nodded, remembering all the drama those two had gone through over the years. "The never-ending booty call."

"Is that what he calls it?"

"No." He smirked at her murderous glare. "It's what I call it. Those two have been going back and forth forever. They should just get it together or get it over with."

"Well it's been over with for a year now."

"Hmm," he chuckled, bringing his cup to his mouth.

"It *has* been," she insisted.

"So why is she still getting upset about something he says?"

Her lips pressed shut. Romero couldn't help feeling smug as she glanced away. Then her expression changed — softened. "That must be Sal."

Romero turned to see Angel's oldest brother being greeted by Angel and Sarah. "Yeah, that's him." He turned back to her. "Why?"

"I've heard a lot about Alex's brothers. He looks just like them."

Sal was still working on his master's in business management, something no doubt Valerie had mentioned to Isabel — exactly the kind of guy Isabel was probably into. Of course, even without the education, Angel and his brothers always got this kind of reaction from chicks. He watched her, feeling a little disgusted, as her eyes lingered in Sal's direction for too long, her dark eyes almost twinkled. For some reason he thought women like Isabel would be immune to this kind of shit, but her eyes even brightened, then there was an all-out smile.

Romero turned, fully expecting to see Sal giving her the same goo-goo eyes. Instead, he saw Valerie walking toward the bar, also smiling. Sal wasn't even within eyesight anymore. As Valerie got closer, he could see her eyes were a little red.

"Are you okay?" Isabel asked as soon as she was close enough.

"Just dandy," she said to Isabel then to Romero she said, "I need a shot. In fact line them up, I'm gonna need more than one."

"Valerie, don't," Isabel warned.

"You said you're driving right?" Romero poured the shot.

"Yeah, but — "

"So what's the problem? If she needs a few shots,

she needs a few shots."

Valerie didn't share anything about why she was feeling down. Isabel didn't push either. Romero sensed it wasn't something they wanted to talk about in front of him. He almost left them alone to talk, but then Valerie something that made him stop and pour himself another beer. "Did you meet Sal?"

Romero pretended to concentrate on pouring his beer with as little head as possible, as if he hadn't had it down to an art since high school.

"No, but I saw him."

"What did you think?"

It's not like he cared. He wouldn't even begin to pretend he and Isabel could possibly have anything in common. But the thought of a seeing those cute facial expressions, while she lay under him, *had* begun to cross his mind. He had to know now, if Sal was going to be doing some cock-blocking.

"He's exactly like you described — Alex, only not as huge."

"I'll introduce you if you want. He'll probably come by a little later. He just makes me a little nervous." Valerie put out her empty shot glass for a refill.

Romero took it. "Why's that?" He poured the tequila a little higher this time. "Why does Sal make you nervous?"

Valerie glanced around. "I don't know. He's a perfect gentleman and all, but he's so smart."

"That's stupid. He's just like Angel and Alex only he's gone to school longer than them."

He saw Valerie's eyebrow shoot up when he used the word stupid. But it was. So he stayed in school longer, that made him different? Romero grew up with all three. Only difference with Sal is he could hold out longer before blowing a fuse, but it's not like he never had. And unlike his brothers, he'd never gotten hung up on any one girl, but there certainly wasn't a shortage of them.

"I know," she said sounding a little defensive. "For some reason he just makes me nervous, okay?"

Romero rolled his eyes. "I'll introduce you, Izzy." He handed Valerie her shot, "That is, if you really want to meet him."

He glanced at her casually and saw she blushed again, but not quite as dark as she had when he called her sexy. "If I meet him, I meet him. Don't go out of your way."

She didn't have to tell him twice. He certainly wouldn't. As luck would have it, by the time Sal made it over to the bar, the girls had gone over and sat with Sarah and the other bridesmaids. Isabel spent the rest of the evening away from the bar and Romero found himself fighting the annoying urge to look her way every five minutes.

Chapter 5
Outranked

Even though it was heartbreaking all over again for Valerie, Isabel was proud of her. She'd confronted her demons. As sure as she was the day of the shower that she was completely over Alex, seeing him again had been so much harder than she had imagined. The devastating kiss he planted on her when he got her alone, almost did her in, but she managed to stand her ground. Isabel hadn't been mistaken about Alex being shaken at the wedding shower. Valerie had lied telling him she was seeing someone else now.

There were a few more events coming up before the wedding, but Isabel was determined to get Valerie through this. If that meant she had to be there for her at all the events, so be it. That made her think of something else—Romero. Since he was one of the best men in the wedding, he'd be at all the events as well. In the two weeks since the shower, she hadn't quite been able to stop thinking of his smug smirk, and that look in his eyes when he called her sexy.

The woman doing her nails smiled at her suddenly, and Isabel realized she'd been smiling silly. She felt her face warm. What a goofball she must look like, sitting there staring into space with a big, inane smile.

As she usually did when her nails were drying, she wore her earpiece and spoke with one of her sisters or her mom. Since she'd been so busy lately with all the papers she had to grade, she had to get creative about making time to keep in touch with her family. This time it was Pat.

"Hear me out, okay?"

Isabel laughed. "Nothing good ever comes after those four little words."

"But this is a good thing, Bell."

"So why the forewarning?"

Her sister sighed. "Because I already know how you are. No is always the first word out of your mouth at the mention of anything out of your little comfort zone."

"Not true." But it was. She could almost see her sister rolling her eyes.

Instead her sister took a deep breath. "Whatever you say, Bell. Anyway, Charles has a friend visiting in a few weeks. He's a highly ranked officer and—"

"Pat, you said you wouldn't do this again."

"Will you let me finish?"

Her sister would never stop trying to set her up with her husband's highly ranked friends. Just like with her education and her career, Pat was such a control freak. She just *had* to have a hand in her sister's love life as well. Isabel took a deep breath. "Go ahead."

"He's a very nice man, Bell."

"So why's he single?"

"Well... just like you. He hasn't found that right person yet."

Ouch! "Just give it to me up front. What's wrong with him?"

The last guy Pat set her up with was the creepiest guy she'd ever met. Pat hadn't met him until that night either. His eyes would bug out sometimes for no reason.

"There's nothing wrong with him. I've actually met

this guy a few times. Only I didn't realize he was single, or I would've had you two meet a long time ago. He's very good-looking, Bell. I promise, and he'll only be here for a couple days. He's stationed in Germany right now, but he'll be back in California for good in a few months. Charles and I were going to have dinner with him when he flies out, so I thought it would be nice if you would join us."

Who was Isabel kidding? Pat wasn't going to take no for an answer. "When?"

"Some time in the coming weeks." Isabel could almost hear her sister's smile. "I'll let you know when I know for sure what day."

She wrapped up her conversation with Pat and gathered her things. On her way down the escalator, she was lost in thought. Visiting Germany might be nice one day.

"Izzy!"

She glanced around, spotting him at the bottom of the escalator. Romero stood there in jeans and snug black t-shirt. Since the t-shirt was much tighter than the dress shirt he'd worn at the shower, she could now see his impressive build. She could definitely see why he was in the security business.

That playful smirk she'd been thinking about for the past two weeks was now an all out smile.

"Hey," she said as she reached the bottom.

"Fancy meeting you here." He reached his hand out to make sure she didn't trip on that last step.

She took his hand, taking notice of the firm grip. They stepped aside to let everyone else go by and stood off to the side of the escalators. "I was getting my nails done. What are you doing here?"

"Let me see?" He held her hand in his, examining

her nails. "Very nice—no M this time?"

She shook her head, taking her hand back and examining her nails again. "No, they always get me with something extra. This time it was my toes."

Romero looked down and smiled. "*Very* nice."

The way he said that made her face heat up and she prayed he wouldn't notice. "So what are *you* doing here?"

Just like at the party, even a simple question like that seemed to amuse him. "I just came down to uh, find a few tools I needed."

"Tools?"

"Yeah, at Sears."

"Oh." She nodded. "Did you find them?"

"Nah, they didn't have what I needed." Isabel got that same feeling when he looked at her, that there was some kind of inside joke, and she'd been left out again. Only this time there was no one around whom he might be conspiring with. "So what do you do after you get your nails done?"

"Go home." Maybe she should've said something more exciting.

His smile dissolved. "But it's Friday."

God, she felt pathetic. "I came here straight from work." That smile would be the end of her.

"So you don't have plans for tonight?"

"Um... well—"

"Good. Let's go grab something to eat."

"I'm... uh... now?" He caught her so off guard. She couldn't come up with an excuse fast enough. Why she was trying? She had no idea, but she'd always been that way. Her first reaction to an invitation from any guy was to think of an excuse to say no.

"Yeah, why not?" For the first time, he didn't seem

so sure of himself. But he'd asked the perfect question. *Why* not?

"Okay. I *am* getting kind of hungry."

The wicked smile was back. What could he possibly be thinking that was so damn amusing?

To her surprise, he suggested her favorite restaurant at the mall, calling it his favorite as well — Frisco's, the fifties style burger joint with servers on roller skates. The waitress brought over their menus, but Romero told her he already knew what he wanted. The double Frisco with onion rings, and a strawberry shake. He asked her to bring out the onion rings first, like an appetizer. Isabel ordered the same. She handed her menu back to waitress. "Only make mine a single."

Romero didn't even wait for the waitress to leave before asking, "So, really? Friday night and you didn't have plans?"

He made it sound so unheard of. "I don't always make plans until the last minute." As if all her plans weren't meticulously thought out days in advance, but she kept a straight face.

He cocked an eyebrow. "You might still be doing something tonight?"

"Well, that depends."

The eyebrow shot up even higher. "On what?"

She had to think fast. "Like who calls." Because God knew, her phone would be ringing off the hook. "Or if I'm even feeling up to it, by the time I get home."

"True," he said, with that evil, *evil* smile, "because I just might wear you out."

Isabel could've kissed the waitress for interrupting the moment. The waitress set their shakes down in front of them, and though Isabel pretended to be completely distracted by them, she couldn't help but notice him sit back and really take her in again. As if when he'd done so at the shower, it hadn't been enough.

"Wow." Again, he didn't bother to wait for the waitress to walk away. "I've never met someone who blushes so fast. It's..." He snapped his fingers and laughed. "Just like that."

Isabel noticed the waitress glance at her before walking away. Her face got even hotter. She took the straw in her mouth, closing her eyes for an instant. Her phone rang in her purse and she didn't care if it was telemarketer, she was answering. "I gotta get this," she said to a still smiling Romero. She pressed talk without even looking at who it was. "Hello?"

"Bell, I almost forgot. Daddy's birthday is next week. I'm making dinner for him at my place. Keep Saturday open, okay?"

"Sounds good."

Romero's eyes were on her the entire time. His lips wrapped around the straw of his milkshake, but his eyes never swayed from hers. "Are you near a computer? Can you look something up for me?"

"No. I'm not home yet. I'm out having dinner."

Her sister was silent for a second then came the inevitable, "Umm... okay... with who?"

Isabel glanced at Romero again who hung on her every word. "With Valerie."

Thankfully, the waitress dropped off the onion rings. "Oh... okay, tell her I said hello."

"I will."

Romero picked up an onion ring and took a bite. He glanced around very obviously. "I don't see Valerie."

Isabel picked up one of the onion rings, tearing it in half. "Trust me. If you knew my family, you'd understand why I said that. That was my older sister. If I had said I was having dinner with a guy, she would've had me on the phone forever, giving me a complete interrogation. She's very... inquisitive about that kind of stuff."

"Ah." He nodded. "One of those. So I take it you're *not* currently in a relationship, if she'd be that damn nosy about who you're having dinner with."

Isabel laughed. "I like the way you put it better."

He didn't laugh. "Are you?"

For a moment, she thought she'd evaded the question. "No, I'm not." She bit her onion ring. "But my sister's determined to find me the perfect guy, yet. So who knows?"

Finally, the man frowned. Even his frown was a very nice one. "Your sister? Why do you need her to find you a man?"

Isabel shook her head. "Not *a* man. I said the *perfect* man. You see, my sister is convinced only she can find someone good enough for me. Apparently every guy I've ever dated wasn't." She shrugged. "I just humor her. Not much else I can do. Aside from being too inquisitive, she's also very assertive." She stirred her shake.

"And you just go along with whatever she says?"

Isabel looked up from her cold drink. Now it was her turn to be amused. Romero seemed almost irritated. Funny how her sister could do that to people before they even met her. "I'm telling you, if you knew her, you'd understand. It's easier to just go along with it than to argue. Besides, I don't see the harm in going out on a few blind dates. She'd never steer me wrong. And as long as I'm single and ready to mingle why not?"

She couldn't believe she threw that last comment in.

Who even says that anymore? She felt her face warm again.

Romero jumped right on it with a grin. "You ready to mingle, Izzy?"

She sat up a bit, clearing her throat. "It's... just an expression." She bit into her onion ring, hoping he'd have mercy on her since she was obviously blushing *again*. But no such luck.

"You do that a lot."

Admitting it would be her best bet. She didn't want him to get the idea he had some magic power over her. Not that she could remember anyone else making her blush as consecutively as he had. "I know. It's a curse." She took a sip of her shake, unwilling to meet his eyes.

"I heard you're shy."

She looked up at him. "Not really. Just *some* things make me a little... uncomfortable."

He sat back again. "I'll have to start keeping tabs on what those things are."

"Why? So you can torture me?"

"Exactly."

Isabel rolled her eyes. "I think I can make it through the rest of this dinner without turning into a turnip again."

"You wanna bet?"

Their eyes met and she smiled, giving in. "No."

He laughed. "I didn't think so. But you know what you're good at?" Isabel waited. "Dodging the questions that make you uncomfortable. Why would admitting you're ready to mingle make you uncomfortable?"

"It was a silly way to put it. I just meant as long as I'm not involved in a relationship, what harm is there in my sister setting me up?"

Their food came and they were silent while they set

themselves up to eat. Romero took a bite of his cheese-burger while Isabel placed her napkin on her lap. It wasn't until she was halfway through spreading the mustard evenly on the bun that she noticed he was staring at her. "What?"

"What are you doing?"

She looked down at the bun in front of her. "What do you mean? I'm putting mustard on my bun."

"Yeah, but you do it like you're painting, not a smidge outside the lines," he laughed. "And the salt and pepper, it's like you were counting each grain. Do you always do that?"

She frowned. Valerie had always teased her about her eating habits, as well as all her other habits. "Too much salt isn't good for you."

He wiped his mouth shaking his head. "That's fuck-ing hilarious."

She didn't get it. "What is?"

"You!" He pointed at her plate. "The foods been here for five minutes and you haven't even taken a bite."

"I was about to."

"No, you weren't. You were still busy *painting* your bun."

Ignoring his comment, she pressed her bun on her burger and picked it up. He watched her with that never-ending grin as she took a bite.

"I wasn't rushing you, I was just sayin'."

They finished their meal and the waitress came by to offer them dessert. They both passed. If Valerie had been there, they would've shared something. The wait-ress put the bill down on the table and Romero took it. Isabel reached for her purse. "How much is it?"

"Get out of here. I got this."

She bit her lip, unsure how she felt about him footing the bill. "Are you sure?"

"Yep, plus I'm not done yet. When she comes by again, I'm gonna order a beer. You want one?" Then he rolled his eyes. "That's right, you drink wine. I don't know if they have any here." He reached for the drink menu. "I've never—"

"I drink beer."

"You do?" he asked, bringing his attention back to her.

"Yeah, just 'cause I didn't have any at the shower." She hated that he obviously had her pegged as a prudish teacher who only sipped wine. "But I've been known to throw a few back here and there."

Romero smiled, flagging the waitress down. After several rounds, Isabel said she had to drive, but she asked for water and they continued to talk. She'd never felt as witty as he made her feel, because he laughed so much at some of the things she said. Though the majority of the time she wasn't *trying* to be funny.

"So you said your sister sets you up a lot. Obviously, these guys she's picking are not the winners she thinks they are, if you're still single."

For a second Isabel entertained the preposterous idea that he might actually be interested in her single status. But she shook the thought away, remembering Valerie's comments about how Romero, the former bouncer, went through women like Isabel went through books. She lifted a shoulder, stirring the ice in her water with the straw. "They've all been *nice*. But there has to be more than just what *she* thinks is perfect. There has to be chemistry."

"And what *is* perfect to her?" He swallowed the last of his beer and set the bottle on the end of the table.

"Respectable, good career, good place in society, someone she thinks will take good care of her little sister."

His expression went serious for a moment. *"Good place in society.* What the hell does that mean?" The waitress came by and took the bottle. Romero held up a finger for another beer.

Isabel took a deep breath. Normally, she wouldn't get so personal but over the course of the evening she'd begun to feel more and more comfortable talking to him. She found him to be a breath of fresh air, especially compared to all the uptight guys she usually dated. Not that she considered this a date, but having someone like Romero even as just a friend could be a fun — different. "Everyone in my family, with the exception of my mother and me has at least a master's degree. My sister is married to a Lieutenant Commander in the U.S. Navy. Most of the men she sets me up with are up there in rank, either that or someone she met in graduate school." Isabel sipped her straw. When she looked up it was strange to see not even a trace of a smirk on Romero's face. "That's the way she's always been." She shrugged. "She just wants the best for me."

Halfway through her explanation she'd begun to rethink telling Romero all this, especially since she still wasn't sure exactly what he did for a living. He might take offense.

The waitress set the new beer in front of Romero and he took a swig. "Well, good luck finding Mr. Perfect based on a fucking rank or degree."

And there it was. She definitely wasn't asking him what he did for a living now. She didn't want him to think she was judging him. "So what about you? You have any brothers or sisters?"

He shook his head. "Nope, just me and my uncles. Which reminds me." He pulled out something from his back pocket and handed it to her. "I almost forgot why I came here."

Her attention went from the paper in her hand to his eyes. "I thought you said you were here looking for tools?"

The smirk was back and now it was *his* turn to look a little embarrassed. Isabel felt a flutter in her belly and her face warm. "I uh, was hoping to run into you, actually. I was here last Friday, too. I remembered you saying you got your nails done here on Fridays."

Isabel was floored, but at the same time filled with a strange excitement.

He ran his fingers through his hair. "My uncles get Padres tickets from some of their clients sometimes." With the smirk gone, their eyes locked and Isabel felt her heart speed up. He pointed at the tickets but kept his eyes on hers. "I thought you might wanna go. It's tomorrow night."

"I... uh." She gulped, still trying to get past the fact that he'd sought her out two weeks in a row. "I have a lot of papers to grade this weekend."

Why did she always do that? She saw the disappointment in his eyes. "You sure? Can't you do that on Sunday?"

Yes, she could. She finally pulled her eyes away from his and looked down at the tickets. She hadn't been to a game in a while.

"It's a good one," he said. "Against the Dodgers. They're both tied for second right now."

She could do this. Romero was one-hundred percent the opposite of any guy she ever dated, but there was nothing wrong with going to a ballgame with a *friend*. She looked back at him. "Okay, I think I can work something out with those papers." His face brightened immediately. That smile was beginning to do things to her.

Chapter 6
Stealing first

Romero pulled into the parking lot of Isabel's apartment building and parked. He hadn't stopped thinking about her since the shower and after last night it got even worse. There was something about her. He thought he'd seen all of her expressions at the shower, but she'd put on a show for him last night. Her face was so damn animated, and he especially liked when he embarrassed her. Those eyes of hers, it was hilarious the way she fidgeted with her glasses when she got nervous, and those lips — okay, this was getting stupid.

The whole damn time between the shower and yesterday he told himself it was curiosity, not interest. Not since high school had he met a girl he enjoyed just talking to, but most importantly, it had been that long since he met one as sweet as Isabel who seemed to enjoy talking to him, too. It might be cool to hang out with her and she was Valerie's friend. That was another point for her. He'd always thought Valerie was cool.

He got out of the car and headed for her apartment, almost laughing at the anxiety beginning to build in his stomach. Just like yesterday at the mall when he saw her on the escalator, the anxiousness he'd felt was completely unexpected. Then dinner had been near perfect. He couldn't even remember having such a good time with a chick — a good time despite not having even touched her. Everything about it had been great, except for when she told him about her sister's expectations about the guys she dates. Fuck her sister. He knocked on the door.

Valerie opened the door with a big grin. "Hello, Romero."

"Hey, Val," he said, matching her grin.

Isabel came out of the hallway, wiping the grin right off his face. Her long dark hair was down and curled. The glasses were gone. He already thought her eyes were sexy but how the hell could a little makeup make such a difference? They looked amazing. The outfit she wore, a light sweater that came off her shoulder with jeans and high heels was sexier than hell. He didn't even try to hide what he was feeling. She smiled, her cheeks already beginning to flush.

Romero gulped, feeling completely struck. "You ready?"

She nodded, pulling her purse strap over her shoulder. They walked to his car. He had to restrain himself from going for her hand, an urge he'd never felt before.

Opening the car door for her and waiting for her to take her seat before closing it, he smiled. It had just occurred to him, this was all so new to him.

Halfway to the stadium he had to ask, "All right, what are you wearing?"

"What do you mean?" He couldn't get enough of her expressions.

"What's that scent? It's driving me fucking nuts."

"You don't like it?" she asked, smelling her sweater.

"That's not what I meant by driving me nuts," he laughed, changing gears. "I can barely concentrate. You smell so damn good."

"Oh." She cleared her throat. "It's old school. I've worn this forever. It's called Envy."

"Envy, uh? I love it." He laughed.

When they got to the stadium, she walked around his car and they met in front of it. Deciding not to hold back any longer, he reached his hand out for hers and they walked hand in hand toward the entrance. Holding a girl's hand while they were both still sober and fully dressed was definitely a novelty for him, but it wasn't so bad — not bad at all.

Romero immediately noticed how men turned to look at Isabel. Some blatantly checked her out even as he stood next to her holding her hand. It was fucking irritating. One guy flat out smiled at her and she smiled back, looking away quickly. "You know him?" The question flew out without thought.

"No, do you?"

"Nope." It was a strange irritation and he tried to shake it.

Before they got their seats they stood in line to buy beer. The place was so crowded they stood inches away from each other. At one point, his body was up against hers and her hair brushed against his chin. He pulled a few strands of it away from her face and she looked up at him. One look at her lips and he was done. Fuck this. He leaned in and kissed her, softly at first, not sure what to expect, but she parted her lips and he went for it, kissing her deep. Trying not to get too carried away in this crowded place, he pulled away, taking a much needed breath but brought his arm around her small waist. She seemed a bit startled but didn't pull away.

They stood in line for a few more minutes. It amazed him what just rubbing her back and playing with her hair did to him. She shivered when he ran a finger down her spine. "You cold?" he smiled.

"No," she smiled back and to his surprise, she didn't blush.

He tipped her chin and kissed her again. He had no idea what was happening here, but he was going with it, keeping it short because they were next in line. They got their beers and walked to their seats.

"Why'd we get four?" she asked as they sat down double fisted with beers.

"You wanna stand in that line again?"

She surprised him again with a grin. "It was fun."

Damn. As soon as their beers were in the cup holders and they both had a free hand, he took hers in his. The entire time, all he could think about was kissing her again.

They were on their way to the restrooms for the second time, when he pulled her to him and kissed her again, this time longer than he had all night. It surprised him she was so willing. All that talk about her sister and the high-ranking bullshit, he thought maybe she'd be apprehensive. She still hadn't even asked him about his job, though he got the distinct feeling she was avoiding the subject.

When he finally pulled his lips away from her, he stared into her eyes. They seemed to plead. "What?"

"I really have to go."

Romero laughed. "Oh yeah." They walked the rest of the way and split up. Like the first few times they'd gone in, he was out before she was. He stood outside the restrooms, watching the game. The Padres were down by two but had two men on and their big hitter at bat. He ripped one out of the park and the place went wild. Even Romero put his fingers to his mouth and whistled. He was still clapping when he turned around to see if Isabel had come out yet. She had, and she was walking toward him. Damn she looked good. She smiled, asking, "What did I miss?"

"Home run," he said, pulling her to him. "Padres scored three, so we're up now."

Isabel pouted. "I can't believe I missed it."

He kissed her again. He'd never felt such an urge to kiss a girl. Sexual urges were one thing. That, he understood, but this was just kissing and he couldn't get enough. Through the years he'd had his share of good kissers. Hell, he'd been praised about it plenty of times, but with Isabel it wasn't even about that. She was a good enough kisser but it was more about her taste, her mouth. *Her.* With every kiss, gentle as it may be his body wanted more.

Everyone applauded, drunks and rowdy fans hollered and whistled as the inning ended. Romero and Isabel made their way back to their seats. Just as they sat, her phone rang and she answered. Romero slipped his hand in her free one. "Hey, Art."

Romero turned to see her smiling face.

"I'm at a Padres game right now. Yeah, of course they're winning." She glanced at Romero with an even bigger smile.

He didn't smile back—he couldn't. He stared at her so hard, she glanced away.

"Tomorrow? Yeah, I'd love that. I know I miss you so much, too."

Romero dropped her hand and she glanced at him again. A heat, different from any he'd ever felt, flooded his insides. She brought her hand to her ear as the crowd started cheering again. "I can't hear you, Art. I'll call you when I get home." She hung up.

"Who's Art?"

"My brother." Romero literally felt the heat drain away. "He lives in Los Angeles and I haven't seen him in a while, but he's coming down tomorrow. We're gonna do brunch."

He'd hardly listened to anything after the first two words, instead he slipped his hand back in hers and leaned in to kiss her. "That's fucking great." He smiled, against her lips.

*

Before the evening even started, Isabel had prepared herself mentally that this was going to be different. Romero was different. But in no way was she prepared for his kisses. She'd never been kissed like that. Not in all the time she'd been with Jacob in high school, not *any* of the guys she dated in college.

From the moment she'd met him at the wedding shower, she got that he didn't hold anything back. He said whatever was on his mind, no holds barred. He'd certainly reconfirmed that last night and tonight. That's what made her wonder if he was like this with every girl he went out with. Was this just a date or was this the beginning of something? Did she even *want* it to be something? How could it possibly work between them? They were completely different.

"Something wrong?"

She didn't even realize she'd been spaced out on the ride home. She turned away from the window and faced Romero. "No."

"You got real quiet all of sudden."

"I just have a busy day tomorrow."

The light turned green and Romero continued driving. "What else are you doing besides seeing your brother?"

"I have all those papers to grade. Then I was going to go to the show in the evening but I don't think that's gonna happen now." Even though she'd stopped seeing Lawrence a while back, they remained friends and still got together to see a movie every now and then. He shared her love for reading, and they often swapped books.

"The show, huh? With Valerie?"

She nodded—no need to get into details. "But like I said, I highly doubt that's gonna happen now. It's okay though, I can go another time. I haven't seen Art in too long. I'm really looking forward to seeing him."

"Is he anything like your sister?"

Isabel noticed the way his features hardened when he asked that. She was really beginning to regret ever mentioning her sister's attitude about the guys she dated, especially after the way things had gone tonight. "No, not at all. He rarely even asks about my personal life."

When they got to her apartment building, he got out and came around the car to meet her, kissing her as soon as he was close enough. Not once the entire night had he asked her how she felt about him kissing her. He just did it, and not once had she protested. It was so unlike her to let things move this fast but she was powerless to stop it. She didn't *want* to stop it.

He paused for a moment, leaning his forehead against hers, his breathing labored, but said nothing. Isabel brought her hand up to his hard chest, as if to bring the moment to an end, but when her eyes met his, she moved her hand further up around his neck and he kissed her again, pushing her gently against the car. His tongue was like magic and feeling his big hard body against her worked her into a frenzy. *Insanity.* How could a kiss make her so crazy? She finally pulled her lips away from him, catching her breath.

"Wow," she said, breathlessly. "We gotta stop."

"Why?" His expression went very serious.

"Because I don't want you to get the wrong idea."

His eyebrows pinched. "And what idea would that be?"

"That I do this." She moved a little, hoping he'd pull his body away but he didn't. "This isn't like me. This was just supposed to be a night out at a ballgame. Not a..."

He finally pulled his body away from her. "Not a what?"

"Not a date. Even on a date I don't—"

"I was on a date."

She lifted an eyebrow. "And you do this on all your dates?"

He thought about it for a moment then smiled. "Can't say I've been on many dates." She rolled her eyes. "What? It's the truth. Ask Valerie. I've never been the dating type."

That she believed. "And suddenly you are?" She crossed her arms in front of her, eyeing him.

"Well, if it's anything like tonight. Sure, I'm down if you are."

Isabel pushed herself away from the car and started toward her apartment. He slipped his hand in hers and walked with her, stepping in front of her just as they reached her door. "When do we get to hang out again?"

Hang out? She eyed his lips, knowing that in moments they'd be on hers again and she could hardly wait. "Next week?"

"Next week?" His voice went up an octave and his eyes widened at her apparently offensive suggestion.

She laughed. "Well, tomorrow's out of the question. I'll be busy all day."

"What about *during* the week?"

"I work."

"Not all day. You're a teacher. You're out by what, two or three?"

"Three thirty."

He smiled. "Perfect. I'll pick you up at four on Monday."

Before she could protest, his lips were on hers and she gave in to his kiss completely.

*

Isabel *hung out* with Romero almost every night for the next three weeks with the exception of a few times when she had dinner with her mom and sister Pat. They'd finally talked about his security firm. She was actually very impressed. He hadn't gone to college, but he'd mentioned at least half a dozen certifications he had mostly from online courses or state exams he had to pass, and he had an intricate knowledge of every piece of equipment used in his business. Some of it looked very complicated, not to mention his expertise in countless security softwares, including some he said he wasn't supposed to know so well.

She saw the excitement in his eyes when he spoke of his business. He'd hired a few more employees in the last two weeks alone and was actively searching for more. It kept him busy, too. Some of the nights they'd hung out for only about an hour before he had to leave.

The kisses were getting heavier but Isabel was hesitant to take it any further. She still didn't know what his intentions were. As up front as he was, he still hadn't mentioned how he characterized their relationship. The comments he made were about having fun with her, and enjoying their time together. None of that said *exclusive relationship* to her. She could do the friendship thing if they stuck to just kissing. She'd never once had what some of her friends in college referred to as friends with benefits. And after seeing how painful it was for Valerie to carry on her non-exclusive relationship with Alex, it made her nervous to think about getting involved in something similar. Though she had to admit, just from his kisses, she knew sleeping with Romero would be an exciting first for her. That alone was making it harder and harder for her to resist trying the friends with benefits thing for once.

At the same time, thinking about an exclusive relationship with him made her even more nervous. How could he possibly fit into her world?

They'd gone to the show once before, but this time they hardly saw any of the movie. She felt like a teenager in the back row of the theatre, getting felt up. Every time she hesitated, feeling like they were going too far, he backed off, but each time she went back for more and they continued where they'd left off.

His hand made its way between her legs but over her jeans. Still, even through the thick material, he knew exactly where and how to rub to make her tremble. "Let's get out of here," he whispered against her mouth.

"And go where?"

"My place."

Her instincts said no, but before she could respond, his tongue was in her mouth again. If his kisses alone could drive her insane, she wondered what else he could make her feel. "Okay," she whispered and he stopped and stared at her.

"Yeah?"

She smiled and nodded.

"Let's go." He stood up and took her by the hand.

She followed him out. As soon as they were out of the theatre in the cool parking lot, he stopped in front of her and cradled her face. "Will you stay the night?" She stared at him surprised by his request. "Please?"

But her own response surprised her even more. "I have to pick up some things at my place first."

He smiled and kissed her unlike he'd kissed her all night. They were soft gentle kisses and the way he stopped and stared at her in between made her melt.

They stopped by her apartment and she threw a change of clothes and some toiletries into a bag. Valerie was busy trying to get something on her keychain as she walked by, hoping her roommate wouldn't notice the bag in her hand.

They were just outside her apartment when she got a text from Valerie.

Was that an overnight bag you were carrying?

Isabel smiled and texted back. She still couldn't believe she was doing this.

Maybe.

The next text came when she was in the car.

Isabel you whore!

Isabel laughed then covered her mouth when she realized Romero was staring at her.

"What's so funny?"

"Nothing," she said, as she texted back with a big smile.

Friends with benefits =)

Romero was still staring at her. He hadn't even started the car.

"Just a silly text," she said, not about to tell him what it said.

He lifted an eyebrow and started the car.

Chapter 7
Just Friends

The studio apartment Romero rented was small but it was good enough for him. It beat living with his uncles. Sure, he missed the noise sometimes, and he still spent more time over there than he did at his own place, but he loved having his own space, especially at times like this. Even though his uncles had told him long ago he could bring girls home, some of the freaky things he did with them would've been too much, even behind his closed bedroom door.

He'd had plenty of girls over since he'd moved out years ago, but only a handful of them had ever spent the night. Those had only been because he'd been too wasted to drive them home. The awkward, sober morning after was always the pits, so he avoided it at all costs. When it did happen, he couldn't get them out of there fast enough the next morning.

They walked in and he watched as her eyes pored over everything. Everything included a bed, his one nightstand, a sofa, the plasma T.V. on the wall and a few boxes on the floor. "Did you just move in?"

Romero laughed. "No, I've been here two years." As usual, her eyes said it all. "I don't need much. Besides, I'm hardly ever home."

He walked to the kitchen, still holding her hand. He frowned when he opened the fridge. There wasn't a whole lot to choose from. "I can order a pizza if you're hungry."

"I'm not." She still held her bag in her hand.

"Did you bring enough stuff for the whole weekend?" He took the bag out of her hand and placed it on the floor.

"No." Her face flushed. Damn, that would never get old. "Just something to change into in the morning."

He leaned in, kissing her softly as he caressed her face with his hands. "You're so beautiful," he whispered.

He'd told girls they were hot plenty of times, but he couldn't remember ever using the word beautiful. There was no other word to describe Isabel, except maybe adorable with all her different expressions. Right now, right here, so close to making her his, she was blushing in his hands, utterly beautiful.

She brought her hand around his neck and kissed him back with the same eagerness as she always had. He'd been blown away by her willingness from the very beginning. He was so sure she'd be more hesitant. Instead, here she was practically swallowing his tongue. He moaned, picking her up and setting her on his kitchen counter. She never once unwrapped her arms from around his neck and continued kissing him even as he nudged her legs open and pulled her to the edge of the counter.

With her neck at eye level now, he dove in, kissing the soft skin just under her earlobe. He sucked the small gold stud on her ear, feeling her tremble just like she had at the theatre, just like she had every time in the past three weeks when he kissed her neck and wanted so fucking bad to do more. He could hardly contain himself now, and he didn't even have to.

"Izzy," he whispered in her ear.

"Umm?"

"I want you, baby."

"I want you too," she said immediately.

That was all he needed to hear. He lifted her off the counter and walked the few steps to his bed in his front room. He set her down then lifted her knit blouse over her head. Her black lacy bra barely held in her soft, pale breasts. She scooted back and unzipped her jeans. There'd been many women in his bed and he'd watched them do the very thing she was doing now, yet he didn't remember ever feeling like this. His heart hammered away. Sex had never been emotional to him. The only feelings he ever had during sex, was insatiable hunger — if that even counted as a feeling.

All he did now was watch, and he could barely catch his breath. He worked the buttons on his own jeans and slipped them off. As he watched her slide her pants down his body went through the usual emotion he felt just before he was getting ready to satisfy his hunger, but something new accompanied it. Normally, he didn't think past the act itself.

Like the anger that seared through his veins when he flew into a rage and he was helpless to stop it, he now felt something new. An emotion almost like a slow growing alarm, overtaking him by the second. Something in his heart was trying to warn him this was an experience he may not be ready for. A place from which he might never return. But deep inside he knew the truth. He was already too far gone. Still the alarm grew as he slowly crawled on his knees, his heart racing. From day one, he'd thought of having her beneath him like this.. Owning her, even it was only for a few hours. Now, he wanted more.

Kissing her belly as he passed it on his way up her

body, he took the intoxicating scent, and taste of her warm skin. She'd removed her bra, and she lay there naked except for her black lace panties. She quivered as he traced gentle kisses up her torso then took her breast in his mouth, slowly sucking her nipple, feeling her shudder and her breathing hitch.

Even with her practically naked body beneath him, he yearned for her mouth. He'd come to love kissing her, something he couldn't stand going a day without. From the moment he first kissed her at the ball game, he realized kissing Isabel was different. It was what he felt when he was that close to her that made it different. He *needed* that feeling.

Romero thrust his tongue in her mouth, mimicking what he'd soon be doing to her body. She squirmed beneath him, pulling her mouth away to catch her breath and he stared at her. That feeling again overwhelmed him. It scared the hell out of him, but in a strange way, he welcomed it.

He reached over to his nightstand and pulled out a condom. Isabel stroked his shoulders and arms. That alone did things to him he'd never felt before. This was crazy. "It's been a while for me, Romero. Just so you know."

He squeezed his eyes shut, chasing away any thoughts of his Izzy with someone else. "I'll be gentle. I promise."

He kissed her again, and continued to until the intensity of his kisses had her moaning. He could be doing anything to her at that moment but he couldn't pull his lips away from hers. Each kiss was deeper and each kiss made that unfamiliar emotion grow stronger and even more beyond his control.

Finally, he let his hands travel lower, caressing her

over her panties, loving the way she continued to moan into his mouth. Then he pushed the thin fabric aside and slipped a finger in. *She* was so ready.

"You ready, baby?"

"Yes," she said willingly.

Romero had never felt the need to be so excessively gentle. Hell, he'd never cared enough to ask anyone if they were ready, and he'd had his share of virgins.

As she pulled down her panties he put on the condom, still incredulous of his nervousness. The only time he vaguely remembered being nervous before sex was way back when he'd done it for the first time, but the anxiety he felt now was unreal.

Nudging her legs apart gently he stared into her eyes as he positioned himself to enter her. She was tighter than he expected. He promised he'd be gentle but he suddenly wanted nothing more than to be in her completely — claim her.

She lifted her hips up against him, wrapping her legs around him, making him groan in delight.

He squeezed his eyes shut, driving himself in all the way and she cried out. He continued to do so again and again, slowing down when he felt she was getting close. Sex was usually simple. He knew exactly when to slow and when to move faster. As wild as things could get, he always managed to stay in control. But today, with Isabel, he couldn't steady his responses.

He started up again slowly trying with all his might to hold back for her, but then she began to twitch and squeeze around him moaning even louder and then he felt her trembling explosion. He was done restraining himself. Burying himself deep inside her, the emotion he'd felt earlier now nearly suffocated him. He collapsed onto her, kissing her forehead, her cheeks and all around her mouth, barely able to catch his breath.

It was a struggle but he eased himself off of her and lay there, breathing hard. His heart felt like it could shoot out of chest any at second. He'd never even heard of anyone feeling all this. "That was..." He couldn't think of the word to describe what he was feeling.

She turned to him. "Incredible."

"More than that. It was the best." For him it was and he could only hope it was as good for her. He couldn't remember ever feeling so satisfied. Nothing had ever felt so perfect. She was perfect.

They lay there for a good while in a absolutely comfortable silence. Romero was content just listening to her breathe and feeling her heartbeat so close to his own. Even with everything he was feeling now, one thing gnawed at him. He didn't want to ruin the moment or the night. but he'd never been one to hold back saying or asking about something the instant he wanted to, and he'd held this off this long.

He lifted himself onto his elbow and leaned into her. "Who made you laugh earlier, Izzy?" He kissed her eyebrow when it questioned him. "The text you got in the car?"

The look she'd given him when he asked her in the car was a strange one. Up until that moment in the car, he hadn't put much thought into the possibility that Isabel might have other guys in her life—a thought that now had him grinding his teeth.

"Oh." She lay there naked next to him, and the thought of that text made her blush? He tried not to frown. "Valerie was teasing me about my overnight bag. She can be so silly."

The smile matched the one in the car and the irrepressible jealousy he'd begun to feel the moment he thought another guy was responsible for his Izzy's silly mood, subsided. He exhaled, then kissed her. "You hungry?"

"Yeah, I think I worked up an appetite."

Romero got out of bed, disposing of the condom, pulling on his briefs. "Growing up, I never learned to cook much of anything, but if there's one thing Max taught me, it's how to make a kick-ass grilled cheese sandwich."

"Mmm, that sounds so good right now."

"Coming right up," he said, pulling his pants on. "You do any cooking?"

He watched as she pulled her blouse over her head without a bra. He had to fight the urge to jump back into bed and attack her.

"Yeah, a lot actually. My mom was big on cooking and I do all the cooking now at home for Valerie and me."

Romero laughed. "One thing I remember about that girl is how much she can eat."

"Tell me about it. The good thing is I never have to do the math to cut down the recipes since most serve four. With Valerie it all goes."

"Any specialties?" he asked pulling the cheese out of the fridge.

"Many, but I'm told my albondigas are to die for."

Her phone rang, and she hurried to her purse to get it. "I gotta take this."

Romero nodded, spreading butter on the bread.

"Hi, dad."

He frowned. Just about every time he'd been with her, one of her siblings or parents called. Obviously, she was real close to all of them. He'd thought about what it would be like when he finally met them. Something told him it wasn't going to be pretty. He hadn't even met her sister and already he couldn't stand her.

*

Isabel began to worry about how sleeping with Romero would change their relationship. If things got more serious, she'd inevitably have to tell her family about him. If things stayed between them remained casual—well, she wasn't sure how she felt about that either. She'd seen the box of condoms in his restroom. She hadn't meant to snoop, but she'd forgotten her razor and was hoping to find a new one under his sink. The box was big and it was almost empty. Then there was the nightstand by his bed where he apparently kept *more*.

The idea of him having other women in his life was not a new one. She reasoned that there hadn't been any promises. She slept with him knowing full well what she was getting herself into. Just a few days later, when she thought she'd heard a girl's voice in the background during one of her conversations with him, she discovered with surprise that maybe it would bother her more than she'd anticipated.

For the most part, his interest hadn't paled. He called her all the time and they'd slept together every chance they got. With a growing fear of getting in too deep, she decided to slow it down—at least until she knew for sure what she wanted. Until she knew if he even wanted anything more than to just *hang out*.

Valerie insisted that he seemed very serious, and even suggested Isabel just ask him straight out. Afraid of what his answer might be, she did the cowardly thing instead. She decided to tell him she was busy a few of the nights he normally would stop by to hang out. He'd asked her what she was busy doing, but she kept it vague.

For the first time since they started hanging out, she'd gone several days without seeing him. It scared her how much she missed him and how erratically her heart beat when her phone rang and she saw it was him. "Please tell me you're not busy tonight."

"I'm not," she smiled.

"What are you doing now?"

"Nothing."

"I'm on my way."

He picked her up in less than twenty minutes, and greeted her with a breathtaking kiss. Then said exactly what she was feeling. "God, I missed you."

"I missed you, too." Her heart pounded. This was bad—or good. She couldn't decide.

They went back to his place and barely made it through his door before they were all over each other. It was almost frantic, the way he kissed her and made love to her again, and again. It was frenzied but at the same time thrilling. They lay there afterwards trying to catch their breath. "You thirsty?" he asked.

She nodded, kissing his hard chest. After one more long kiss, Romero got up and pulled his pants on. She admired his chiseled chest and big arms. Then she heard her phone ring. She almost didn't answer, but she remembered she was supposed to call Pat tonight and it had already rung several times during their time in bed. After Romero called, she'd forgotten all about Pat. She sat up grabbing her phone from the side of the bed. "Hey, Pat."

"You were supposed to call me."

"I know. I was about to. I just got out of the shower."

She looked up and took the bottled water Romero held out for her. He walked back to the kitchen. "Oh good, so you're home. I wanted to stop by."

Shoot. "Well, I'm home now, but I was on my way out."

"Uggh, never mind then. I just wanted to show you the gift I got Gina for her birthday. It's a dress, but you know her taste better than I do so, I wanted to get your take on it."

"Send me a picture."

Pat huffed. "Okay, I will when I get home."

Isabel hung up, opened the bottle of water, and took a big drink. "Oh, that's good."

Romero leaned against the sofa directly in front of the bed, staring at her. "How come you told your sister you were home?"

She took another slow drink to give herself a moment to think. "I dunno. I told you how she is. I figured it was the fastest way to get her off the phone."

"What does she think about you and me?"

She felt her eyes open wider and she pressed her lips together.

He chuckled, but she could see it was forced. "You haven't told her. What's the matter, Izzy? Afraid big sis won't approve?"

"No."

"Have you told *anyone* in your family?"

She took another drink of her water.

"I get it," he said, walking into the kitchen. He downed the rest of his water and slammed the bottle into the trashcan.

"It's not what you're thinking."

"Then enlighten me, Isabel. Because you're on that fucking phone with them all the time. Telling them about your new boyfriend seems like something you might wanna share."

"I wasn't sure that's what you were. I thought maybe we were just friends. We never — "

"Just friends?" He stalked toward the bed. "We've been seeing each other non-stop for weeks. What did you think this was?"

She swung her legs off the bed. "I wasn't sure. We never talked about it. Everything just happened so fast."

His expression went from angry to hurt. "You're not sure?"

"I meant about what our relationship was. I couldn't just assume we're exclusive."

That triggered something. She literally saw the color of his eyes darken. "Is that what you were *busy* doing these last few days?"

"No!"

"According to you ten seconds ago we aren't exclusive." His voice went up a notch and his nostrils flared. "Who were you with these last few days?"

"No one. I was home."

His eyebrows pinched. "You said you were busy."

She pulled her shirt on over her head. "I was slowing things down."

"What...Why?"

She stood up. She couldn't do this sitting in the bed. "I don't know."

He walked up to her and stood looking down into her eyes. "Look at me." There was something desperate in his eyes now. "Do you wanna be with me?"

"Yes."

"But you were slowing things down?" He searched her eyes. "I've been going fucking crazy wondering what you were so busy with? Can you just tell me why?"

"I wasn't sure if this is what you wanted. I got scared."

"Well, now you're scaring me. I know what *I* want. I want *this*. To be with you and *only* you. What do you want?"

"I want this, too."

"Are you sure?"

"Yes," she said, putting her hands on his face. She'd never been so sure about anything in her life. She felt terrible now that she'd ever questioned it.

He put his hands over hers then kissed her. "You're sure?"

"Absolutely," she smiled. "I should've just asked, but I was afraid of coming off as one of *those* girls."

"You are *nothing* like *any* girl I've ever met."

This close, she could feel how hard his heart pounded. "I'm sorry."

He leaned against her forehead and took a deep breath. "You owe me."

"I know."

He pulled away from her, the panic in his eyes now replaced with a trace of that humor she loved to see so much in them. "No, you really owe me. I want Albondigas."

Isabel laughed. "You got it. I'll make some tomorrow."

Romero kissed her deeply before pulling her back into bed.

*

She felt like such a spineless coward. "Okay, I'll be there."

Isabel had forgotten all about the date her sister had set up with her husband's friend.

Thankfully, Romero was booked that evening working. This wasn't worth the interrogation she'd have to deal with from her sister if she refused. Her brother-in-law's friend would only be in town for a few days. She could knock this out and get her sister off her back without having to get into it about Romero just yet.

She told Romero she was having dinner with her sister, leaving out who else would be there. He was so caught up in his business for the evening, he didn't ask much else.

As expected, Michael, the *perfect* guy her sister set her up with, wasn't that perfect. For starters, he had no sense of humor. Isabel never considered herself to be a funny girl, but for some reason Romero thought she was *fucking* hilarious. Michael's humor paled in comparison to Romero's. He didn't think half the things she knew she and Romero would be laughing at were at all funny. Including the guy showing off on the dance floor, who twisted his ankle. Romero *so* would have laughed with her instead of giving her the appalled look Michael did when she sniggered.

He did seem interested in her, but she noticed the more he drank, the cockier and more flirtatious he became. She did her best to fend off any advances, and he'd made plenty. She was just glad it was over now.

When Michael asked for her number, she gave him the number to the landline in her apartment which was used mainly for Valerie's faxes. She didn't want her brother-in-law to be offended that she'd snubbed his friend, even though that's what she wanted to do.

She texted Romero as soon as she got home.

You still working?

He responded immediately.

If I wasn't I'd be there with you.

She was so tempted to tell him she loved him, but she knew that was the wine talking. Though she'd thought of him the entire night…

Goodnight baby.

Goodnight Izzy…dream of us.

She smiled, her heart completely taken.

Always.

Chapter 8
Fucking Fantastic

The next day Isabel met her mom and Pat for lunch. She'd already told them she couldn't hang out and chat for too long like she normally did. Valerie was having a meltdown because they were going to a bonfire gathering as part of her cousin's pre-wedding celebration. Alex had been working Valerie. He'd left her a heartfelt message that had her nearly in tears, then last night he met up with her and just about sealed the deal. He wanted her back bad. Today would be the test. Valerie either got past this or she'd be back on that rollercoaster ride with him. Isabel was meeting her after her lunch and they were driving there together.

"So?" Pat smiled as the waitress walked away.

Her mother waited, eyeing Isabel as well, making her uncomfortable. "What?"

"You know what." Pat said, still smiling. "What did you think? Because Charles said, Michael really liked you. I mean *really* liked you."

Isabel shrugged. "He was nice."

Her mother started in on her salad. Pat stared at her. "Isabel, he was more than nice and Charles said when he moves back—"

"I'm seeing someone now, Pat."

Both her mom and Pat stared at her blankly. "You are? Since when?" Pat seemed disappointed. This was just like her.

"It's been a few weeks. I didn't want to say anything until I knew how serious it was. But now I know it is."

"Why didn't you tell me? Charles and I went through a lot—"

"I didn't ask you to. Besides when I agreed to this, it was before I started seeing Romero. And I didn't even know until just recently that—"

"Romero? That's his name?"

Isabel pressed her lips together. She wouldn't tolerate her sister putting him down in any way. "He goes by his last name. His name is Ramon." She took a deep breath and chewed a spoonful of salad before speaking again. "So I can't get involved with Michael... or anyone else. Not anymore."

"I'm glad for you, honey." Her mother touched her hand. "When do we get to meet Romero?"

Her sister obviously didn't share the same enthusiasm. She'd all but stopped eating. Isabel pretended not to notice her glare. "Soon. I'll have to plan something and I'll let you know."

To her surprise, her sister didn't give her the inquisition she was expecting. Isabel figured it was the shock of it. As soon as she got over it, it was coming. There was no way Pat wouldn't demand to know *everything* about Romero. Isabel was ready for it. Her feelings for Romero surpassed her fear of any disapproval from her family now. They'd just have to accept him for who he was.

*

They set their chairs around the unlit bonfire. Isabel got a text from Romero as she left her apartment saying he was running late but he'd be there. Once settled, Valerie poured her a wine cooler in a cup and handed it to her. They sat down facing the fire pit.

"So how did the date go last night?"

Angel and his sister's boyfriend, and not to mention Romero's other best friend, Eric, were just a few feet away, throwing wood in the pit. "Not here, I'll tell you later."

"Oh, right." Valerie nodded, her eyes on the guys.

"Not much to tell anyway."

"Not much to tell about what?" Romero's voice behind her startled her.

She and Valerie exchanged glances while Romero waited. His expression gave nothing away, so she had no way of knowing if he'd heard everything.

"Girl talk, Romero. Go help out," Valerie said, gesturing toward Eric. "I've heard legendary stories of your fires."

"All lies." He turned to Isabel, leaning in for a kiss.

The kiss was so sweet Isabel knew he couldn't have heard. She remembered the look on his face when he questioned her about who'd she been with the days she tried slowing things down. No way would he just let this go if he'd heard. He walked over to where the guys were and started helping with the wood.

"Oh. My. God," Isabel said, taking a big swig of her wine.

Valerie giggled, but Isabel could see the look of remorse for having brought it up here. Isabel assured her if Romero had heard, he most definitely would have said something.

Alex arrived, and as the time passed, Isabel could see Valerie was giving in. After a walk to the ladies' room, Valerie let her know she was going to come clean with Alex about not having a boyfriend. When they got back from the restroom, Romero sat on the ice chest next to her chair and kissed her again. "I missed you last night."

Feeling a slight pang of guilt, she smiled. "I missed you, too."

"So where'd you and your sister go?"

Isabel glanced away from him to take a sip of her cooler, but mostly so she wouldn't have to look him in the eye. "Blemberg's, on the Marina."

She glanced at him and his face soured. "I know, but it's one of her favorites."

"Figures." She eyed him, lifting an eyebrow and he kissed her again, shrugging. "I'm just not into that fancy shit."

She'd been right about Valerie. After disappearing with Alex for a long while, they came back holding hands. She sat down and leaned over to Isabel. "I'm going home with Alex." She bit her bottom lip. "I'm doing the right thing, Isabel. I promise and I'll explain why later. But we're taking my car, so he can leave his with Sal. You'll be okay going home with Romero?"

Isabel could see, not only in Valerie's eyes but also in Alex's earlier, something had changed. Valerie was smart. If she thought she was doing the right thing, then Isabel wouldn't try talking her out of it. She squeezed her hand. "Yes, I'll be fine. I'm happy for you."

Since Valerie wouldn't be home tonight, Isabel invited Romero back to her place. Not that Valerie would have a problem with him staying over. Isabel just felt a little weird about it still, especially since she'd been right. Romero was like no other man she'd ever been with and Valerie's room was just across the hall.

Romero looked around her room. "Damn, Izzy, I

knew you were neat but this is… "

"What?" She'd never tire of his sexy smirks.

He sat down on her bed. His eyes went from her dresser to her nightstand and back to her. The moment she was close enough he pulled her to him and sat her on his lap. "Is there anything about you that's not perfect?" he said, kissing the corner of her lips.

"Like I'd really tell you." She wrapped her arm around his neck.

"I don't think there is." He turned her over gently then pinned her to the bed.

Isabel stared at him, her breath caught when she felt his hand in between her legs. He'd already made reference to her easy-access sundress at the beach. He kissed her as he pulled the sliver of panty aside and slipped a finger in. She kissed him deeper, instantly aroused. "You're so ready," he said against her lips.

"I am." She ran her fingers through his hair, as the second finger entered her. She moaned, squeezing his shoulder. Then he slid the third in.

He pulled his mouth away from hers and sucked her neck, all the while his fingers playing with her, his thumb tormenting. She squirmed, feeling the sensations run through her body like an electrical current. It was building, the more his thumb rubbed the more she felt herself losing control. "Romero!"

"Hold on, baby."

He pushed her up slightly and pulled himself down to the edge of the bed. She wasn't sure what to expect, but the jolt like lightning that torpedoed through her body when she felt his tongue on her, was not it. She cried out in pleasure. She'd already been so close. Her entire body trembled as he continued to work her with his tongue—his lips. Her hands fisted the blankets around her as she felt the incredible explosion of pleasure. She moaned, arching her back, willing him to stop. She couldn't take anymore.

She felt him kiss her one last time before having mercy on her. The waves of pleasure still pulsated through her as she lay there, breathing heavily.

Romero lay down next to her, staring at her as she tried to catch her breath. "Izzy?" he whispered.

"Hmm?"

"You're perfect."

*

Waking up next to Isabel was a mixed feeling for Romero. On the one hand, he loved seeing her first thing when he woke up. On the other, he was afraid if he got too used to it he'd never want to wake without her again. He wasn't sure if she was ready for that. His feelings for her had taken him by storm. He was afraid of freaking her out.

Hearing something in the front room, he sat up. He frowned when he realized he woke Isabel, but then smiled at her perfectly naked body. "That's probably Valerie. What time is it?"

"Nine."

"Really?" She sat up. "Already? I never sleep that late."

Romero smiled, remembering why. "We had a long night."

Isabel got out of bed and searched her closet. "What are you looking for?"

"My robe. It's in here somewhere."

She found it, flung it on and hurried out of the room. Romero sat up and pulled his jeans on. He walked out into the bathroom. When he walked out of the bathroom, he saw Isabel hurry back into the room. The phone in the kitchen rang.

"I got it!" Valerie yelled from the front room.

It kept ringing, so Romero walked out into the kitchen. He froze when he came face to face with Valerie. She seemed surprised to see him, especially since he was still shirtless and barefoot. Her expression amused him. "You gonna get that?"

"No," she said, her eyes obviously trying to avoid his bare chest. "The answering machine can pick it up."

The machine went off just as Isabel came out of the room, now dressed in shorts and a blouse. Romero turned back to Isabel when the machine beeped.

"Isabel this is Michael. I just wanted to tell you I had a fantastic time with you Friday night..."

Isabel took a step toward the machine, but stopped when Romero stepped in front of her. The heat inside him was already on the rise. The kind of heat that made him do things he never wanted Isabel to be witness to. He swallowed hard, trying to understand what he was hearing. She'd said she was with her sister Friday night. He listened as the message went on.

"... I'll be here a little longer than I thought, so I was hoping I could see you again before I leave..."

He couldn't take his eyes off Isabel, feeling his heart beat pick up with every word the fucker on the machine said.

"... I hope we can make this happen." He left his number for her, then hung up.

"Funny story," Isabel said, attempting to make light of it, but Romero felt on the verge of exploding.

He tried to stay calm, hoping she did have a reasonable explanation. "Yeah, Isabel? Tell me about it."

"My sister set this up before we even started going out."

Romero saw red. "You were on a date with this guy Friday?"

"No, we just had dinner—"

"That's a date! What else did you *just* do with him?" He had a vision of her with another guy and the guy's words slammed into him. "You know what? I don't wanna know." The urgency to get out before he snapped had reached a disastrous stage. He rushed to the bedroom. "Whatever you did, it was *fucking fantastic!*"

Romero pushed the door to her room open, slamming it against the wall. There were only a handful of times he's felt this way in his life and each time he'd exploded beyond his control. He didn't want that to happen now. That side of him was off limits to most people he knew, but especially Izzy. He grabbed his shoes and slipped one on as she walked into the room, closing the door behind her. He couldn't even look at her.

"I'm sorry, Romero. She'd set this up a long time ago."

With his heart already pounding away, he attempted to speak. "Why would she still expect you to go if you're with me now?"

She didn't say anything. He stopped what he was doing and stared, feeling the hurt pummel through him. She still hadn't told her sister.

"I just didn't think it was a big deal to get—"

"Not a big deal? You lied to me!" She flinched when he yelled and he immediately regretted it. That was it, if he didn't get out of there now, he might do or say something worse that he'd regret.

Feeling his temper reach a level there was no turning back from, he slipped on his other shoe and grabbed his shirt, rushing past her.

"I'm sorry, Romero," she said, as he walked past a very stunned looking Valerie.

"I'm sorry, too. Go call him back, Isabel. *Make it happen.*" He grabbed his keys and wallet and rushed out.

He fought the incredible urge to go back and demand to know what the *fuck* was so fantastic about Friday night. No guy would call a date fantastic if nothing had happened. That's the reason why he stopped her before she answered. If she so much as kissed the guy, he would've gone off the deep end for sure.

What confused him most, was he was used to the rage. That he'd been dealing with it all his life. And like today, he'd gotten pretty good at keeping it down to a roar. But the pain he felt now was new. At first because she lied to him, but then when he realized she was obviously too ashamed to tell her family about him. *Still.* Even after the bullshit about her not being sure about their status. That was harder to take than her having gone on that fucking date.

Not that he wasn't *beyond* pissed about that. But it almost felt like the times when he'd been physically hurt as a kid. The lie had been the blow that knocked his teeth out, making him see stars. The realization that she was ashamed of him, was the swift knee to the groin that followed immediately after. That pain overpowered everything else.

He drove past his apartment, knowing Isabel would most likely come by since she knew he'd taken the day off. The entire day—to spend with her. He didn't want her to see him like this. If she already didn't think enough of him to tell her family, what would she think if she saw him lose it? The way he felt now, he was one flick away from losing it completely.

He drove to his uncles' house instead, and went straight to their liquor cabinet.

"What's with you?" Manny asked, as Romero downed a huge swig of tequila.

Romero didn't respond.

"You drinking tequila in the morning now? What are you, stupid?"

Manny was a strange one. He had drug dealing in his past, gambling and even ran a titty bar but he didn't drink — never had.

"Leave me alone." Romero said, feeling the burn in his throat… and his heart.

Max walked into the room. "What's wrong with you, Moe?"

"Nothing. Just leave me alone." He took another swig.

"What do you mean—"

"I don't wanna fucking talk about it! Can we just drop it?"

Manny stalked over to him and grabbed the bottle out of his hands. "No! I won't drop it!" He put the bottle back in the cabinet and slammed the door shut, pushing Romero into the chair behind him.

Romero put his elbows on his knees, and ran his hands through his hair, letting them both rest behind his head. Despite the pain and anger he felt, he wanted nothing more than to be with Isabel again.

"What's your problem, boy?" Manny nudged him with his knee. "Business not so good?"

"Business is fine." He knew his uncles well enough

to know they wouldn't let this go.

As annoyed as he was that he chose to come here, he knew why he did it. He needed to be near them. Needed to be the only place where he knew he was accepted even with all his flaws.

Max walked over and crouched down next to him, putting his hand on his shoulder. "Is it a girl?"

Romero nodded, still not looking up.

"What?" Manny said. "All this for a skank?"

Romero jumped up, out of his chair and stood right in Manny's face. "She's not a skank. Don't you *ever* call her that."

Manny stared at him for a second, before smiling. "Well, well, well. Looks like you got it bad." He laughed. "Who is she? How come we haven't met her?"

Romero was still breathing hard from what Manny had said. Max stared at him, looking more concerned, and not quite as amused as Manny. He thought of Manny's question, and felt like a complete hypocrite. He'd always prided himself in that these were his uncles and he loved them no matter how unrefined they could be. If anybody didn't like it, they could go fuck themselves — until Isabel. At least she'd told him about *her* family, warts and all. He'd hardly mentioned Manny and Max to her at all. He'd never actually admitted it to himself, but he had to now. He hadn't really mentioned them to her because he was afraid of what she'd think.

"You'll meet her soon," he said. "We just had a fight, that's all. I'll get over it."

He grabbed his keys off the table.

"You sure, boy?" Manny asked. "You looked real upset there for a minute."

Romero smiled and hugged him. Then turned around and hugged Max. "I'm good."

He wasn't really, but he was better. Only now on top of everything, he felt like an asshole. He took a deep breath. "You guys wanna go get some breakfast? I'll tell you all about her."

Manny and Max exchanged glances then Manny shrugged. "Sure, I already ate." He glanced at his watch. "But that was about an hour ago. I can eat again."

Chapter 9
The one

All day Isabel tried in vain to get a hold of Romero. She'd left messages, texted him and gone by his place twice. His car hadn't been there. Valerie left to spend the night at Alex's place again a few hours earlier and Isabel had finally allowed herself to cry like she'd really wanted to.

Banging her fist into her pillow, she cried like she'd never cried in her life. She'd finally met *that* guy. The one she couldn't stop thinking of day or night. Even at work, she found herself constantly thinking of him. He was the first guy that made her feel sexy, but it wasn't just about the sex. It was the way he looked at her. There was something so incredibly intense. He told her he thought she was perfect and almost made her believe it.

She didn't feel like she had to impress him with her intelligence or her family, the only things she ever felt she *could* impress anyone with. This was the first time she didn't even like to talk about her education because she didn't want him to think she was rubbing it in and he'd been completely impressed with her anyway. She still didn't understand why, only that she loved the feeling. She didn't even realize how hard she'd fallen, until the possibility of losing him hit her.

For so long, she'd yearned to feel that magical feeling of true love. That feeling of needing to be around someone always, and as scary as that feeling was, it was also intoxicating. Then just like that, because of her stupid inability to stand up to her sister sooner, she'd blown it.

After one long sob into her pillow, she heard the knock at the door. She sat up, and tried to catch her breath, contemplating whether or not to answer it. Lawrence often came over unexpectedly to drop off or borrow a book. Sometimes just to chat. She was in no mood to talk to him or anyone.

"Izzy, you there?"

She jumped off her bed, not caring what a mess she must look like, and rushed to the front door. She opened the door with her hand over her mouth, feeling like sobbing again when she saw him.

Romero hesitated, then took the one step up and wrapped his arms around her.

"I'm so sorry." she said, against his shoulder.

He squeezed her tight, kissing her temple and head, then pulled away to look at her. He wiped the tears with his thumb. "We need to talk."

Romero closed the door behind him and took her to the sofa in the front room. They sat down, facing each other. Isabel was overwhelmed with relief, but more than anything, filled with a happiness beyond any she'd ever felt. Even with her stupidity, he'd come back to her. But she cautioned herself, she still didn't know why or what exactly he wanted to talk to her about.

He moved a few strands of hair away from her face and wiped the corners of her eyes. He stared at her for a moment, too serious, and she wished to God, she could see that smug smirk of his again so she'd know everything was okay. His expression went suddenly even more rigid. "I need the truth." His jaw clenched. "Did you do anything with him?"

"No." She shook her head adamantly.

"Then what was so fucking fantastic about it?"

"I don't know. My sister and Charles were with us the whole time. But I promise you nothing. I would never..." Isabel moved over and straddled him, feeling how tense he was.

He brought his arms around her. "You gotta know how crazy that would make me if you ever did. Izzy. I don't know what I'd do."

"It'll never happen." He kissed her neck. She loved how she lost all her inhibitions around him. He made her feel like an entirely different person. Being with him made her not care about anything else. None of the petty things that bothered her so much before mattered anymore. She'd actually begun to escape the need for everything to be perfect. Something bigger was much more satisfying now.

His expression softened but very little before he spoke again. "I need to know that your sister is not—"

"She's not! That was the last time. I promise."

"I know to your family, I'm not much—"

"No!" She reached for his hand. "Don't say that."

"It's the truth, Isabel."

She squeezed her eyes shut. "Please don't call me that. I've never hated the sound of my own name so much as I did this morning when you called me that."

His jaw tightened. "I was pissed."

"I know, and it felt so *wrong*. I don't like you being pissed at me."

He squeezed her hand. "Izzy, I don't blame you for not telling your family about me."

"But I did. I told them yesterday. Well, my mom and Pat, and they want to meet you. I told them they would—soon." She took a deep breath, still feeling drained from her cry earlier. "I'd been so caught up with you these last few weeks, I completely forgot about the date. So when she called the other day to tell me about it, it was too late, she'd already planned it. I didn't want to get into some long drawn out explanation. I wasn't ready yet. So since you were working, I figured I might as well get it out of the way." She stared into those beautiful hazel eyes that could flare up so quickly. "It was so boring. All I thought of was you the whole time. I kept waiting and expecting him to make me laugh like you do."

She saw his expression harden again and his eyes darken. "Why would you?"

"I just told you?"

"I meant I *know* nobody will ever make me feel the way you do. So I'd never even expect it. Why would *you*?"

She shook her head. "My point was, all I could think of the entire night was you. The first thing I did when I got home was text you." She leaned her forehead against his. "You forgive me?"

"I wouldn't be here if I didn't," he said, tightening her hold around her. "Truth is, I was being a hypocrite today."

That confused her and she stared at him. He laughed. "I was mad at you for not telling your family about me, and I did the same thing to my uncles. I didn't tell you about them because I was afraid of what you might think."

"Why?"

"They're… different, but they're good guys. You'll see when you meet them."

She smiled. "Okay. But first you're meeting my mom and sister." She tried to act as if it were no big deal, but she was more nervous about it than she'd ever admit to him. "Tomorrow we're having dinner with them."

The first thing she did after Romero stormed out today and he didn't pick up any of her calls, was call her sister and mom and made sure they kept their evening open for her. She had no idea Romero would be coming back tonight, but she was hoping by tomorrow she would've at least heard from him.

He stared at her silently for a moment, that intensity in his eyes that made her that perfect kind of nervous. "I think I love you," she whispered.

His eyes widened. She held her breath. It was too soon. She shouldn't have told him.

"You *think*?"

She was suddenly choked up. This day was too much. "Is it too soon?"

He sat up, putting his hands around her face. "You love me?" His expression looked almost frantic. Had she scared him that much? She stared at him, afraid to answer.

"I fucking love you, Izzy. I've been so scared to freak you out, but I do."

She fell into his chest. "I love you! I do! And you're *happy*?" This was insane.

"Yes, I'm happy!" His big hands swallowed up her face. "Are you crazy? I can't stop thinking about you!"

His expression suddenly went from ecstatic to troubled. "What?" She searched his eyes.

"I don't know about you, and I don't think I wanna know, but I've never done this relationship thing. I probably won't be very good at it. And I sure as hell never met any girl's family, and your family..." His eyes were genuinely horrified. "I'm gonna screw this up, Izzy."

"No you're not," she said, with a nervous laugh.

But the magnitude of this jolted her. She'd never dealt with anybody like Romero in her life. She was a peaceful spring day to Romero's level-five tornado. She'd suspected it before, but he confirmed it today when he blew up. Oh, she saw him try to conceal it, but there was no hiding the inferno in his eyes. In the past, like any sane girl with even an ounce of sense, she would've run the other way from a man like Romero, but strangely, it was part of the attraction.

My family is going to love you. She almost said it, but she didn't think she could pull it off with a straight face. "We can do this," she said instead, kissing him.

"You really love me?" he asked, against her lips.

"I really do," she smiled.

He stared in her eyes, as if he was still trying to find the doubt in them. He'd never find it because as much as it scared her, she'd never felt like this for anyone. It was everything she ever dreamed of and so much more. He kissed her, pulling her down on the sofa and pressing his body against hers.

She pushed away thoughts of asking him to wait for her to get a towel, so they wouldn't mess the sofa. Okay, maybe she wasn't entirely cured of her obsessive need for neatness and perfection. But she could work on it.

*

Yesterday had been one of the most emotional days of Romero's life. One he wouldn't be sharing with anyone else. Not even his uncles had gotten much out of him, except for an explanation of how he met Isabel and what she was like. Each time he'd started describing her he had to remind himself his uncles were watching him closely, because he got so into it. By the time he realized he was laughing about things there was no way his uncles could understand until they met her, they were staring at him as if they didn't even know the guy in front of them.

Maybe they didn't anymore. Maybe he *was* a new person. He sure as hell felt like one. Hearing Isabel say she loved him last night, had to be *the* best moment of his life. If he hadn't heard her himself, he would've never believed it. Not only had he been certain what he was feeling for her was completely nuts, he'd known from the very beginning they were from different worlds. It was easy to understand how even then, he'd fall so hard for her. Even as he spoke about her to his uncles he couldn't believe the crazy emotions he felt just talking about her. But he never expected someone like her to fall for *him*.

The anxiety he'd been so unfamiliar with, until he started seeing Isabel, was the only thing annoying about the whole situation. He felt it even now, as he drove into her apartment parking lot. Meeting her sister tonight was going to be a challenge. He'd never been one to fake what he was feeling and he already knew he wasn't going to like her, but he didn't want to screw things up, so for once in his life he actually planned on biting his tongue if he had to.

Alex's truck was in the parking lot. Romero wasn't surprised. Valerie had obviously spent the night with him the night of the bonfire, and last night he'd called Romero to ask how things were with him and Isabel. Romero started to bust his balls, because Alex almost never called him, especially not to talk about relationships, but then Alex admitted Valerie had put him up to it. Apparently, they'd been together all weekend and here he was again. Romero always knew Alex had it bad for Valerie.

The door was open, so he knocked once before letting himself in. He expected to see Alex who stood waiting in the front room. "Hey, Alex."

Alex greeted him but Romero barely paid him much attention. What he didn't expect was to see some dude in Isabel's kitchen talking to her as she sliced up food.

"Izzy? You cooking? I thought we were going out for dinner?" He barely managed a smile, feeling that same agitation he'd only ever felt since he met Isabel.

He checked the guy out as he walked past him, toward Isabel. He saw it immediately. Even though the guy looked a little older than all them, he was bothered by Romero. Was this another one of her snobby family members or...

"No, I'm just making snacks," Isabel said.

As soon as he was close enough he kissed her, and it was no peck, but she pulled away too quickly. Romero gulped, trying not to get worked up. Her not wanting to make out in front of other people was understandable, but the look on the dude's face was almost as bothered as Romero was beginning to feel. So he brought his hand down from Isabel's back and rubbed her ass, hoping the fucker would say something. Isabel stiffened at the touch of his hand on her behind, and he felt bad about making her uncomfortable, but not bad enough to move it away.

The guy cleared his throat loudly, clearly afflicted by Romero's actions. He waved the book in his hand at Isabel. "Let me know, Isabel, when you're ready for some more Tolstoy. I have them all."

"Tolstoy?" Romero asked.

The asshole shook his head and gave Romero that look he'd seen all too many times growing up, usually directed at one of his uncles who were either talking too loud or cussing in a public place. That repulsed, *your kind are all the same*, look. "Nothing you'd be familiar with, I'm sure."

That almost set Romero off, but before he could react, Isabel moved away from him suddenly, catching him off guard and walked around the counter. "I'll walk you out, Lawrence."

Romero watched as Isabel walked out with this guy who, apparently, she didn't think was important enough to introduce to him to, or was this someone else she didn't want knowing about him?

"Who is that guy?" he asked Alex.

Alex lifted an eyebrow and shrugged. "Their neighbor."

Their neighbor?

Valerie walked out of her room and said something to Alex while Romero was still preoccupied with thoughts of *Lawrence* the neighbor. "Oh hey, Romero. Where'd Isabel go?"

"Outside, with that dude. Does he come over here a lot?"

She glanced at Alex then back at him. "Lawrence? No. Not really. He was just here to pick up some books Isabel borrowed."

Alex and Valerie walked to the door. Romero followed them. Isabel was taking too long. Even though Alex stood in front of him, blocking his view, he still heard Lawrence. "…I mean really, Isabel. I can see Valerie with someone like that, all brawn and undignified.

But you? I gotta say, not only am I stunned, but a bit disappointed."

Instantly on fire, Romero jumped in front of Alex, down the two steps of her apartment and right into Lawrence's stunned face. "What the fuck does that mean?"

Lawrence backed away a step but stood his ground. "I was just making an observation. There's no law against that."

Romero knew he was close to losing it but as usual, there was little he could do about it. "You don't know shit about me, asshole!"

When he saw Lawrence start to point a finger at him, that was it. Romero pushed him hard in the chest with both hands. The guy stumbled back flipping over the bushes in front of the apartment. "Oh my God!" Valerie gasped.

Alex jumped in front of him before he could charge at him. "Easy."

One glance at Isabel and he saw she was completely stunned and he gulped hard, glad he'd decided to push Lawrence instead of clocking him like he'd really wanted to. This probably never happened in her world.

"You see!" His attention was averted back to a red-faced Lawrence, who barked at Isabel, then pushed her hands away as she tried to help him up. "This is exactly what I was talking about."

Romero lost it. "Did you just push her?" He nearly broke free from Alex's hold, who bear hugged him in reaction.

"Get him out of here, babe." Alex warned Valerie, then to Romero he said, "Relax, dude. If he'd pushed her, I'd let you at him."

Lawrence didn't have to be asked twice. He left

quickly and they all went into the apartment. Romero didn't even care that Alex and Valerie were still there. He was livid. "Why does that asshole even care who you're with?"

He hated to see that apprehensive look in Isabel's eyes. The last thing he wanted to do was frighten her. So when she turned to Valerie and Alex who announced they were out of there, he tried to get a grip, but he couldn't bring himself to even look away from her.

As soon as they walked out, she turned back to him. "Okay, so he's an idiot," she said, stating the obvious.

"Why does he care?"

"We used to go out."

Romero stared at her. Her words felt like a slap, even though she'd said them in the calmest of tones. Last night he said he didn't want to know if she'd ever done the relationship thing. Now he wondered how many she'd been in. Would she be comparing him to this uptight asshole? Who else would she be comparing him to? He took a deep breath. "How long?

"Not very long at all." She slipped her hand into his. "I stopped seeing him because he was so arrogant, but we stayed friends because we're neighbors and I didn't want things to be awkward."

This could be a problem. If Romero ever ran into the prick again, things could escalate real quick. "Look, Izzy," he said, trying to sound calm. "This is your place. I can't tell you who you can and can't have over. But you can't expect me to be cool if you have another guy here, especially an ex."

To his surprise she laughed. "I seriously doubt Lawrence is ever setting foot near my place again. The only other guy you'll probably run into around here now, is Alex."

Just seeing her smile made some of the tension he felt dissipate, but not completely, there was still the matter of dinner with her sister. She wrapped her arms around his waist. He breathed in deeply, hugging her and kissing her forehead. He'd put the thought of Lawrence aside for now. There was something he'd wanted to ask her even last night, but he'd never had make-up sex and there was no fucking way he was ruining a night of that. "So what did your sister have to say about me?"

"Surprisingly, not a whole lot. I think she was in shock. She had no idea I was seeing anyone but she'll be grilling me soon, I'm sure."

Romero looked down into her eyes. "What are you gonna tell her?"

The corner of her lips went up. "What do you think I should tell her?"

"What I told my uncles."

"And what was that?"

Every time he thought he'd seen all her expressions she surprised him with a new one and he smiled even more certain about what he told his uncles. "That you're the one."

Her eyebrows pinched just as her eyes filled with tears. "Really?"

"Yeah, really." He kissed her softly.

"I love you," she whispered.

He stared at her wishing his brain could get past the *I think* part when she'd said it the first time. As unreal and amazing as it felt to hear her say it, her facial expressions were beginning to give too much away and he'd been staring at her then, too. The uncertainty was as plain as the tears in her eyes now. He, on the other hand, was one hundred percent sure of what he was feeling. "I love you, too, Izzy."

Chapter 10
Pat

Knowing Romero wasn't into *fancy shit*, and knowing if she left it up to Pat, that's exactly the kind of place they'd be having dinner, Isabel chose a trendy Italian chain restaurant at the mall. She almost suggested Frisco's, but with the possibility of this not going too well, she hated to tarnish that memory of their first dinner there, especially if they ever wanted to go back.

They reached a stop light and Romero squeezed her hand. "What are you smiling about?"

She was glad she'd begun to stop blushing about every little thing or her face would be warm right about now. "I was just thinking about when we just so *happened* to run into each other at the mall."

He smiled. "Aren't you glad we did?"

"Yes, very glad." She squeezed his hand back.

Before the whole Lawrence incident, Isabel thought she might give Romero a heads up about her mom and sister, but even though he'd calmed down since, he still seemed a little tense. She didn't want him thinking she needed to tell him how to behave, or that she didn't want him to be himself. Still, for his own sake, she decided to let him in on one thing.

They pulled into the parking lot of the restaurant and got out of the car. "Just so you know," she said, as she came around to meet him. He reached out for her hand. "My mom does not have a problem with cussing. Not too much anyway but..." Romero peered at her.

"She has this thing about cussing at the dinner table. Don't ask me why, she's always made a big deal about it. I'm not telling you that you shouldn't. Just consider yourself warned."

He flashed that smirk she was now in love with and he patted his chest with his fist. "I got this."

Isabel smiled taking a deep breath, hoping he didn't see the nerves behind the smile. No matter what her family's opinion of Romero was, there was nothing they could do or say to change the way she felt about him now. She just wasn't looking forward to any kind of unpleasantness… from either side.

Pat and her mom were already there, looking through their menus. Her sister was completely engaged in it as Romero and Isabel approached.

"Do you see anything that sounds even remotely appetizing?" Pat asked her mother without looking up. "I don't know why Isabel likes this place so much."

"Try the swordfish," Romero said.

Both her mom and Pat looked up at the same time. Her mom smiled at the sight of Isabel. "Hi, honey." Isabel leaned in, hugging and kissing her. Then she turned to Romero. "Romero this is my mother. Mom, this is my friend, Romero."

"Her boyfriend." Romero said, reaching out and shaking her mother's hand.

Her mom smiled. "Yes, I heard. Nice to meet you, Romero. I haven't heard too much else about you, but I look forward to getting to know you better."

Just what she needed, a reminder to Romero that she hadn't told her family much about him.

"I look forward to it, too."

Isabel glanced at him but couldn't get a feel for what he might be thinking, only that his usually easy going smile appeared a bit forced. She turned to her sister and they walked around to her side of the table. "And this is my sister Pat."

Suddenly, the smirk reappeared and for some reason that made Isabel more nervous. "I've heard about *you*, Pat." He reached out to shake her hand.

Pat glanced at Isabel then back at Romero and shook his hand. "I hope that's a good thing."

Romero smiled and nodded but didn't say anything else. They walked around and took their seats at the table. Isabel sat next to Pat, Romero directly across from her, next to her mom.

"So you said the swordfish is good here?" Her sister glanced over the menu at Romero.

"Yeah, it's what I always have." He didn't even bother to open his menu, instead reached across the table for Isabel's hand. "It's the best."

Her mom put her menu down. "Well, I think I'll try it then."

Romero smiled. "You won't be sorry."

"I don't really care for seafood," Pat said, looking back at her menu.

After finally deciding and the waiter taking their orders, her sister got right to business. "So Isabel said something about you being in the security business, are you a security guard?"

When Isabel called her to ask Pat to leave the evening open for dinner with her and Romero, she'd specifically told Pat that he owned his own security firm. She glanced at Romero, who smiled as he took a drink from his beer bottle. The waitress brought a glass for him to pour it in, but apparently he wasn't going to use it. "I was for years," he said. "Until I opened up my own firm. I'm branching out now — also doing a little private investigating."

"Oh, really?" Her mother's eyebrows lifted. "Do tell. You mean like tracking down criminals?"

"Not exactly." Isabel squeezed his hand. She was very proud of him. "More like background checks for employers, maybe investigating someone they suspect is doing something shady. I've had a few instances of spouses wanting their better half followed around because they suspected infidelity. That kind of stuff."

"Sounds really interesting," her mom said.

"What kind of degree did you obtain for this line of work, Romero?" Pat chimed in.

Isabel stiffened. Pat already knew this. It was the first thing she asked Isabel when she called to tell her about tonight.

"A diploma from the school of real life," Romero smiled. "High school diploma. After that I got all the necessary credentials required by the state to run this kind of business."

Isabel smiled at him, taking a sip of her wine. He smiled back.

"So you didn't attend college at all?"

"No he didn't," Isabel said sharply. "Did you forget already? I told you yesterday when you asked me then."

Pat cleared her throat, obviously surprised at Isabel's reaction.

"Who cares about that?" Her mother interceded. "I wanna know about this private investigating. You know," she turned to Pat, "maybe this is something Charles's sister-in-law could use."

"Mother!" Pat loved digging in other peoples business but she hated when her and Charles' personal stuff was brought out.

"What?" Her mother arched her brow at Pat. "He talked about it openly at the barbeque a few weeks ago." Her mother waved her sister's protests away and Isabel couldn't have been happier that she'd turned the tables on Pat. She always had a way of about keeping the conversation under control. "You see," her mom turned back to Romero, "Charles' sister-in-law owns a small gift shop over on the pier and he says she's been having issues with the register coming up short a few times and a few others things have gone missing. She suspects one of her employees but without any proof there's really nothing she can do."

"Does she have a security camera?" Romero asked.

Isabel noticed her sister pretending to be completely engrossed in the menu and not at all interested in the conversation.

"She does," her mother said, stirring her martini and turned to Pat. "He said it's come up clean every time right?" Pat nodded but continued reading her menu.

The waitress stopped by to drop off breadsticks and ask if anyone needed another drink. Romero held his bottle up, making her sister lift an eyebrow but then her mother asked for another martini. "Another one, mother?"

"Yes, Patricia. Maybe you should have a shot."

Isabel's eyes met Romero's. She almost giggled. God, did she love her mom at that moment. Romero's eyes were as amused as hers. She was so glad he wasn't upset about her sister's obvious attempts to rattle him.

"Try the Patrón," Romero added.

Isabel nudged his knee under the table. Pat ignored him. Instead, she turned to Isabel. "Have you talked to

Daddy lately?"

"I did last week." Isabel had a feeling where Pat was going with this.

"Did he tell you he's thinking about running for Mayor next year?"

"Yeah, he did." Isabel glanced at Romero whose smile was now gone.

"Mayor uh?" Isabel could see Romero was trying to sound nonchalant, but there was a definite change in his overall demeanor. She should've mentioned it to him. This wasn't an insignificant little tidbit you forget to tell someone. "Of La Jolla?"

Pat smirked. "Oh, no. He'd never consider anything smaller than San Diego." She turned back to Grace, done acknowledging Romero. "I think he has a very good chance. I told him I'd help him campaign. Gina said she'd take a few months off and come home to help out, too."

The waitress dropped off the salad. Isabel was happy for the interruption. She was also glad she'd put her foot down when she did, otherwise Pat might've continued with her interrogation of Romero and things could've gone south real fast. By the time dinner was over, although the tension between Romero and her sister was still there, it was such a relief to have gotten their first meeting out of the way.

Pat wasn't done. Not by a long shot. Isabel knew this, but at least Pat knew now, that Isabel wouldn't be just sitting there, letting her do and say what she pleased.

When they were back at Isabel's apartment, Romero sat on her sofa and opened his arms out for her. She sat down at his side and leaned into him. "Your sister isn't *that* bad."

"Yeah, she is," Isabel smirked.

Romero stared at her for a moment before smirking himself. "Yeah, she *is*."

Isabel laughed. "Don't worry. I think she gets it now that she's not going to have freedom she thought she would to interrogate you like it's any of her business."

"I don't mind an interrogation as long as she can take it as well as she can dish it."

Isabel kissed him. "Well, that's what I don't want — you two starting a war. My brother and her hardly speak ever since he told her off. She's never approved of his fiancée. I don't want that happening between me and her but if it has to be that way, then so be it."

Romero smiled. "I think I'd like to meet your brother." His hand crept up her back under her blouse.

"You will." She smiled, kissing him. "Next time he's in town. So when do I get to meet your uncles?"

"Soon. I'll set something up. Neither will be making mayor of anything anytime soon. In fact, I'm not even sure they're registered to vote." He laughed. "But I think you'll like them."

"I'm sure I will." She felt him unclasp her bra. It sort of bothered her how good he was at doing that.

"Why does your sister care so much about who you and your brother date?"

Isabel frowned. "She's always been that way. Image is everything to her. So even though she won't admit it, it's about *her*. She loves nothing more than to brag to all her other snobby friends about her family, so who we're dating, or in my brother's case who he'll soon be marrying is just another thing she can brag about."

"What's wrong with your brother's fiancée?" Romero rubbed her back. It felt good.

It was so petty she was almost embarrassed to tell him but she did. "She lives in a trailer park. Her family is not the classiest I guess. She's also putting herself through school so it's taking her a lot longer than it did all of us who had the luxury of going full time."

She felt him stiffen and his expression changed. "So it's not just about her education; it's about how classy you are or aren't? Wow. Your sister is a piece of work."

"Don't worry about it." She straightened out, so that she faced him better now and kissed him again. "I'll deal with her."

He brought his hands around the front and cupped her breasts, smiling. "And I'll deal with you."

She lay back on the sofa and he moved over her, kissing her. Thoughts of them messing the sofa didn't even cross her mind this time.

*

The next morning, Isabel got the call she was expecting and she was ready for it.

"I just don't think he's right for you, Bell. Don't get all defensive about it."

Isabel was on her way to work and didn't need Pat to ruin her day before it started, but she wasn't backing down for the sake of not arguing like she had so many times in the past. "I'm not getting defensive. You're entitled to your opinion, but I like him and he's gonna be around a lot now so get used to it."

Her sister exhaled. "Daddy's not gonna like him either."

Isabel gripped the wheel. She dreaded her father meeting Romero. Though he wasn't as judgmental as her sister, appearance and image were a pretty big thing for him, especially now that he was considering running for Mayor. She hated to have to ask Romero to change anything about himself, but her father—who dealt with low class criminals all day—always said, *Only the less intelligent resort to foul language to color their conversation.* Romero had quite a mouth on him. "Well, he'll just have to deal with him, too. It's my life—*my* choice."

"Okay, okay. Change of subject."

This was a first. Had Isabel actually won an argument with Pat?

"Guess who I ran into a few days ago?"

"Who?"

"Jacob."

"What Jacob?"

"Your ex, silly. Your first love—high school sweetheart."

Isabel thought about it for a moment. She hadn't been sure before but now she was certain. She'd never been in love with Jacob. What she felt for Romero was a first. No one, not even Jacob, came close to making her feel like Romero did. "Oh, really?" She sounded as unenthused at the news as she felt. "Where?"

"Charles and I had dinner with a few of his friends and their wives on the base and he was there having dinner with a few buddies. Did you know he's on his way to make Lieutenant Commander?"

Isabel rolled her eyes. "I haven't talked to him in years, Pat. So, no, I didn't know."

"He's still single you know."

"Well, I'm sure now that he's making Lieutenant Commander, he won't be for long." Isabel pulled into the teacher parking lot at the school.

"He asked about you."

Isabel didn't say anything as she gathered up her things.

"I told him we should all get together and catch up. Wouldn't that be nice?"

Isabel almost laughed. Her sister was too much. "Oh, yeah. I'll bring Romero. I'm sure it'll be just lovely." She heard her sister huff. "Don't even think about it, Pat. I gotta go. I'm at work now. I'll talk to you later."

Isabel hung up before Pat could protest much. She should've known her sister wouldn't give up that easily.

Chapter 11
Manny and Max

"What's wrong with my tie?" Manny looked down at it.

Romero stared at him through the rear view mirror. "Nothing, but we're going to Moreno's. It's not that fancy. You don't need a tie."

"I think purple suits you." Aida just *had* to put in her two cents.

Ever since they'd gotten hitched, where Manny went—Aida went. He wasn't having it any other way. So Isabel would be meeting the whole lot of them tonight. Max was meeting them there, since he was working a little late.

"Yeah, I think so, too." Manny agreed with Aida. "And it matches my belt."

Romero sighed. Manny and Max wanted to go the Lucky Dragon but he managed to convince them to go to Moreno's. His uncles knew this was Romero's friend's family restaurant so they at least attempted to tone down the language when they ate there. They still slipped but if they started getting carried away and Romero had to remind them to knock it off, they'd think it was because of the restaurant and not Isabel.

When they got to Isabel's apartment he opened the door. "You guys don't have to get out. I'll be right back."

"Just remember, I'm a fat man and it's fucking hot back here, so hurry up."

Romero slipped the keys back in the ignition and started up the car again, blasting the air. The last thing he needed was to come back to the car to his sweating uncle cussing his ear off. "There—air's on. I'll be back."

Isabel was at the door when he got there. He loved seeing her in a dress. Not that she didn't look sexy as hell in jeans but there was something so feminine about her in a dress. The one she wore tonight was simple white cotton dress that hugged her just below her breasts, then flowed down to her knees. Seeing her in white made Romero wonder just for an instant what she would look like in a wedding dress.

He kissed her. "You're beautiful."

"Thank you." She turned around and locked her door.

It had been a week since he'd met her mom and sister and he still wasn't quite over Pat's comments. But Isabel hadn't brought up her sister since then so maybe everything would work out as long as he didn't have to be around her too often. "My uncles are a lot different than your family." He'd already told her this but for some reason he felt the need to remind her.

She squeezed his hand. "I don't *want* them to be like my family."

"And they call me Moe. Just so you know."

"Moe?"

"Monie was short for Ramon. Over the years it got even shorter. Now it's just Moe."

"You never did tell me why you don't go by your first name."

"I'll tell you another time." The more he knew about Isabel the more he wondered if she should know everything about him. Some things didn't need to be said.

Just as they reached the car, the back window went down and Aida's gum flew out, missing them by inches. "Oops, did I gitcha?"

"No, you didn't," Isabel said with a smile.

Romero muttered under his breath. "Aida, this is Isabel. Isabel this is my Uncle Manny's wife." He leaned over a bit. "And that's Manny back there."

Isabel reached over to shake Aida's hand and she waved at Manny who was too far. "Nice to meet you both."

"Likewise," Aida said.

"Yeah, nice to meet you, too. Moe's got it bad for you," Manny said, then added, "I can see why."

Nice. Let her know you were checking her out. Isabel got in the car and Romero walked around to the driver's side, wondering if this was such a good idea after all.

"So Moe says you're a teacher?" Manny asked.

"Yes, middle school—seventh grade."

"Ooh, that's the worst age," Aida said.

"Yeah, them little fuckers think they know everything." Manny patted the seat behind Romero. "I remember when Moe was that age. Son of a bitch if he wasn't a smartass. Luckily, Ma—God rest her soul—knew how to crack a whip. Otherwise he might've ended up like his dad."

"No, I wouldn't have! She was around when *he* was a kid and he still ended up like he did." Isabel squeezed his hand but said nothing. This was a fucking mistake. They hadn't even gotten to the restaurant and already his uncle had brought up the *last* thing he wanted to talk about.

"Maybe," his uncle said, not even noticing he'd pissed off Romero. "But this guy was a knucklehead,"

Manny laughed. "Did he ever tell you about the time he was trying to figure out how the fire extinguisher worked and he sprayed himself in the face?"

Aida cackled Manny wheezed. *Great. Fucking Great.* Was he going to break out with the naked baby pictures, too?

By the time they'd reached the restaurant Isabel had heard all the stupid shit Romero had done in middle school. Manny was getting ready to start with high school. Luckily, Manny and Romero got out of the same side of the car. Romero grabbed his arm and spoke low. "Will you can it with all the dumb shit I did? I'm trying to impress this girl, not make her think her boyfriend's an idiot."

"What? That was a long time ago. I'm just making conversation."

"Yeah, well talk about the time you shit your pants in Mexico. I'm sure Aida will be impressed by that."

Instead of balking, Manny laughed so hard he wheezed again. "I already told her, but if you want me to tell Isabel—"

"Just stop with all the vulgar talk." Romero took a deep breath. "Be cool. Okay?"

"I can be cool." Romero heard Manny say as he walked away.

He held out his hand for Isabel who took it then patted it with her other hand. "I like him. He's funny."

"Yeah, he's a real comedian. Just wait 'til you meet the other one." God this was going to be a long night. And to think he never gave a *shit* what anyone thought of his uncles. With Isabel, it was different. He'd hate for her to realize just how different her life was from his— maybe *too* different.

They were seated at one of the bigger tables. Manny

was doing his usual drumming of his fingers on the table as he looked through the menu. Romero nudged him casually. "What?"

Isabel looked up from her menu and Romero smiled at her then leaned into Manny. "Will you stop with the fingers? It's irritating."

Manny frowned but stopped. Alex walked over with Max. "Hey, the whole family is here." After all the hellos and introducing Max to Isabel, he took his seat, and Alex asked, "So are you guys ready to order? I can send someone over, or you need more time, Max?"

"Nope," Max said, sitting back in his seat. "I already know what I want—the usual—chimichanga plate."

After confirming everyone was ready, Alex said he'd put Max's order in and send over the waiter to take the rest of the orders.

Max dipped a tortilla chip into the salsa. "There was a *thing* at the bar today. Cops had to be called. I don't know if you wanna talk about it now or not but that's why I'm a little late."

"Talking about it later is better." Romero gave him a look. He'd told Isabel about his uncles bar but left out the part about the topless waitresses.

"Thing? What kind of thing?" Manny put his menu down.

Fuck.

"Some dick thought just 'cause he'd tipped one of the girls a fifty he could feel her up, so she slapped him. When he tried getting his money back she told him to go fuck himself. He was drunk and got all stupid and shit. The guys try throwing him out and he starts makin' a scene and demanded the cops be called 'cause our waitress stole his fucking fifty."

"You should've had the fucker arrested for feeling her up. They're there to look, not touch."

Romero was beginning to cringe every time his uncles cussed. Without even looking up from his menu he warned, "Will you guys watch the language? Remember where we're at."

Apparently, Max took that to mean he should just lower his voice, because he began to whisper. "The fucking asshole—"

Romero kicked him under the table—hard.

"Ow!" He turned to Romero with a pained and angry glare. "Whatcha do that for?"

Romero spoke through his teeth. "I told you to watch the language."

Max winced, leaning down to touch his leg. Manny looked at him and for a moment it gave Romero hoped that he got it and maybe they'd cool it finally. "Yeah, Max. Maybe we should wait 'til we get home to talk about this."

The waiter arrived with their drinks. "I'm told you're ready to order."

They all started putting in their orders. The waiter wasn't even done taking their orders when Max said, "Well it'll have to wait until tomorrow then, because I'm going out tonight. I need to get me some."

Romero downed half his beer. "Can I get another one of these?" he said to the waiter then added, "And a shot."

Isabel stroked his leg under the table and smiled at him. He could tell she meant to reassure him, but he was beginning to wonder if he'd survive this night.

Once their dinner was served, it helped to lessen the talking, so things seemed to settle down, though it wasn't without its moments. Like when Max spoke with a mouthful of food not bothering to even cover it with his hand or a napkin. Then there was Aida's snorting at most of Manny the Comedian's jokes. Romero had begun to count them—five so far. Isabel seemed to be having a good time, but it amazed Romero how he'd never realized just *how* crude his uncles were. Growing up he thought they were hilarious, just like all his friends did. He couldn't even imagine having this bunch in the same room with Isabel's family. Pat would have a field day.

Things got worse when they finished dinner. The belching started. After the third one Romero had had it. "Can you stop that already?"

"Hey, it's gotta come out one way or another," Manny said, pounding the side of his fist on his chest. "You pick your poison."

Jesus.

By the time the night was over and he drove Isabel home, he felt beat up. With all the cringing he'd done; he'd actually got a work out. They got to her apartment and he took her in his arms just outside her door. "Tell me I don't cuss as much as my uncles do."

"You do. But," she added quickly when she saw his jaw drop. "I've noticed you haven't been doing it so much lately." Then she laughed. "And I totally get now where you got it from." She cupped his face with her hands. "It doesn't bother me, but if it bothers you, I can start pointing out when I feel like you're going into one of your cuss modes. Sometimes I think you really don't even realize it. Like your uncles, it's just their natural way of talking."

"I never noticed how bad it was. When I was younger, it used to piss me off when they got dirty looks from people in public places."

They walked into her apartment. As usual, Valerie wasn't home—probably with Alex again. They went straight to her bedroom. He wasn't spending the night, just saying goodnight. And showing her how much he appreciated that she hadn't run away after meeting his family.

*

Isabel waited several days to bring up what she was hoping Romero would bring up on his own. They sat on the sofa in his apartment getting ready to watch a movie they'd rented. "Are you *ever* gonna tell me about your dad?"

Romero looked up from the back of the DVD case he'd been reading and shrugged. "He's been in jail most of my life. I don't know much about him, so there's not much to tell."

"What's he in jail for?" She hated talking to him about things that wiped the eternal humor off his face. But this was something she knew had to be important to him even though he didn't want to admit it. She'd heard it in his voice, seen it in his face the day he snapped at his uncle when he brought up his dad. She wanted him to be able to share not just the good, but the bad with her as well.

"Drugs—first trafficking, then his stupid ass finally gets out and he gets thrown back in just a few months later for possession."

She took his hand and kissed his knuckles one by one in an attempt to soothe him. He was suddenly so tense. "How long is he in for?"

He sat back. "Let's see." He counted on his fingers. "Wow, he's already done five years. So I don't know, maybe another three or four years if he doesn't keep fucking up. They almost tacked on another five 'cause he beat the shit outta someone in there. The guy nearly died. My uncles say it's what got him in so much trouble growing up. His fucking temper—"

"You're doing it again." She rubbed his hand and tilted her head. "Cuss mode."

"Well then let's not talk about him anymore." He stood up and walked to the DVD player. "Because I don't think I *can* without cussing."

"Okay, what about your grandma, tell me about her."

He turned to look at her. The smile was back. Isabel was so relieved. "Oh, she was the bomb. I never knew my mom. From what I'm told she was one of the druggies my dad sold to. So when she had me the state immediately gave custody to my grandmother since my dad was in jail, and she raised me. Well, her and my uncles, but I always felt like my uncles were my much older brothers, especially because they'd get scolded as often as I did." He laughed. "Believe it or not, she hated it when we cussed. So you *know* we heard it a lot. But she said my grandpa was worse than all of us. That's where my uncles got it from."

After putting the DVD in the machine he walked back, remote in hand and sat down next to Isabel. He filled her in on his childhood with his grandma, laughing all the while. She was glad to hear that her passing wasn't too excruciating for him. Alzheimer's took her life when he was in the eleventh grade, while hard, he said it had been more of a relief since she'd been sick for years.

"Manny took it bad. He talks all tough, but the guy's not afraid to cry." Romero shook his head. "He was a mess at the funeral."

To Isabel's surprise, a smile spread across Romero's face. "He's not just emotional about sad things either. He cried at his own wedding," Romero chuckled. "And most of my graduations or any picture-worthy milestones."

Isabel thought of her own dad and how cold and indifferent he'd always been. Romero's uncles weren't without their flaws but one thing she noticed right away was the way his uncle spoke of Romero. He seemed to rejoice in telling all those stories of him growing up. Each one he told was as if it happened just yesterday. All the funny things Romero had done over the years were still with him and she could almost feel just how much he'd enjoyed them. Even if the stories were mostly of Romero being a *knucklehead*, he obviously cherished the memories.

She leaned into Romero. "I like your uncles."

He pulled away to look at her. "You do?"

She smiled knowing how apprehensive he'd been the night she met them. He literally froze when his uncle brought up what happened at the bar. "Yes, I do. But tell me," she grinned. "Is their bar a stripper bar?"

She saw the surprise in his eyes. "Not a stripper bar but… the waitresses go topless." She could see he waited for her reaction.

"I had a feeling it was something like that." She looked straight into his eyes. "Just like you said before, so your uncles are a little rough around the edges. And reading up a little on what Ms. Manners has to say about dinner etiquette and the overkill of the F bomb wouldn't do them any harm." She laughed. "It might do them some good but they're good guys. They love you and *that* alone will make *me* love *them*. Don't worry about me judging them for the type of business they run or their mannerisms, okay? I'm not my sister. Please remember that."

Romero stared at her for a moment then smiled. He leaned in, kissed her once then stopped to stare into her eyes. "Izzy."

"What?"

"You're perfect."

Isabel laughed. "I *am* not."

"Yes. You *are*." Romero threw the remote on the floor and attacked her. The movie would have to wait until later.

Chapter 12
Man up

As it turned out Valerie came back only a handful of times to pick up more of her things. The girl had had the worst luck with guys during the time she'd stayed away from Alex. A nightmare ex-flame from her past came back to haunt her just as she and Alex were trying to make things work. He turned out to be a stalker of the worst kind, but when the chaos he ensued was all said and done he'd been arrested and to everyone's surprise, Valerie and Alex were married on a whim in Bermuda.

Isabel couldn't be happier for her and didn't even care that she'd be left holding the bill on Valerie's end of the lease. But Valerie had been adamant about paying her half still until the end of the lease was up. With Valerie gone now, Romero was at Isabel's place more and more. She liked it that way, but Pat was still at it, putting in her jabs about him.

Romero was in the shower and Isabel was making them breakfast when her phone rang.

"Good morning, Pat," Isabel said, as she whipped the eggs in a bowl.

"It's official!"

"What is?"

"Daddy is running for mayor!"

"Really? I thought he was leaning towards not doing it after all?"

"Well, he was over here last night and after talking

to Charles he decided to do it. Charles is going to have a dinner to announce it on the base and invite all the influential people he knows — and he knows a lot. This is so exciting. We're getting it all together as fast as we can. The dinner is two nights from today. Gina's flying in and Art already said he'd be there, too."

Isabel frowned. Her sister probably had Charles working fast and furiously before her Dad could change his mind. The last time she'd spoken with her dad he had his reservations about running. He wasn't sure if he was up for all the campaigning. But she should've known her sister would stop at nothing to get the chance to say her father was the mayor of San Diego. "Are you sure he really wants to do this, Pat? He didn't sound too enthused about it when I spoke to him last."

"Of course he does. He was just getting cold feet, but with Charles and me helping him, he'll be fine. You will be able to make it right?"

Isabel sighed. "Wednesday night, right?"

"Yes."

"I'll be there."

"Umm you may want to come alone because, we're having speakers and presentations and stuff. I'll need you to help me make sure everything runs smoothly. Then there's the family photo ops. The local papers will be there. They might even want to interview you or take statements. You're really not gonna have time to entertain anyone."

Isabel scooped the scrambled eggs onto two plates. "He's coming with me, Pat." Unless he *couldn't* go for whatever reason. Pat was crazy if she thought Isabel was going to allow her to continue dictating her life. Romero meant everything to her now and she'd be damned if she was going to make the same mistake twice.

"Isabel, can you think of Daddy for a second here? Art is coming alone."

"He is?" That surprised Isabel. The last time she spoke with Art he said he didn't give a shit what Patricia had to say about Sabrina anymore.

"Yes, *he* knows how important it is that this be perfect for Daddy."

Isabel rolled her eyes. "And how would bringing Sabrina make it *not* perfect?"

"Do we really need to get into that?"

Romero walked into the kitchen. He kissed Isabel then poured himself some coffee. "I'm gonna have breakfast now. Tell Daddy I'll be there Wednesday."

"Alone?"

"Nope." She smiled at Romero and pointed at the plate that was ready for him.

Pat exhaled exasperated. "I'll call you tonight. I wish you'd reconsider."

"Bye, Pat." She saw Romero's expression sour when he heard her name.

Setting her phone down she grabbed her plate off the counter and she sat down next to Romero, but not before planting a big one on him.

"Where you going Wednesday?"

"My dad is running for Mayor, after all. They'll be announcing it Wednesday night at a dinner on the Navy base. You think you can make it?"

Romero stopped chewing and stared at her. He still hadn't met her father. Because he was also in Alex's brother's wedding, the wedding and the events leading up to it had taken up a lot of their weekends, these past several weeks. And since his business had picked up so much work he'd been really busy lately. But she knew Romero wasn't anxious to meet him. "I have something going on late Wednesday afternoon. What time's the dinner?"

"I don't have all the details yet but she's calling me back tonight."

"I thought you said your dad didn't wanna run?"

Isabel got up and poured herself some milk. "He said he wasn't so sure he wanted to. But I guess he changed his mind." She wouldn't tell him she knew Pat was behind it all. He had enough reason to dislike her sister. She'd begun to notice how when Romero was bothered by something he'd stare off into space. He was doing it now. "What's wrong?"

"Nothing." He was obviously surprised that she noticed. "I just got a busy day today."

Isabel was actually looking at a day off. The district was making so many cuts lately they kept adding *collaboration* days to the school calendar. She got the day off but, of course, she didn't get paid for it. "Where are you working today?"

"I just signed a contract with the uniform distributor. They have several factories; they want us to drop in and do a surprise security inspection. Make sure they're covering everything the way they're supposed to, then I gotta meet with some dude that wants his girl followed around. He thinks she's cheating." He shrugged. "It's crazy how many people out there *think* their partners are fooling around. How do you *think* someone is cheating on you?"

The question confused Isabel. "Why not? If she's done something questionable or he's noticed something different about her lately."

"Exactly. If you think it so much you're willing to

hire someone to find out, you already know." He drank some of his coffee and continued. "You're just in denial, holding on to the miniscule hope that you're wrong."

"That's not fair though. Everyone deserves the benefit of the doubt. Their partner could just be having a bad week—month."

Romero shook his head. "I've yet to prove even one of these clients that thought their spouses or partners were cheating, wrong. I actually feel bad taking their money just to tell them something they already knew." His expression went suddenly hard. "I think I'd know."

In the relatively short time she'd known Romero, she'd seen that lethal expression several times now. Most memorably, the morning of Michael's call. She touched his hard arm. "I've always been a firm believer that cheating is inexcusable. I've seen it so many times on television and even read articles of people trying to justify it. I was lonely, felt neglected, my partner treated me badly—it's all B.S. If you're not happy and there's no working things out, you leave. Plain and simple, you don't sneak around. I just don't see the point. If someone else makes you happier, then you do the right thing and end the relationship you're in." She leaned in closer to his face that had somewhat relaxed a little. "So you'd never have to worry about me cheating, my love." She kissed him. "And if you keep me as happy as I feel now, I don't see how anyone else could *ever* make me happier."

He finally smiled. "I don't think it's something I ever wanna think about." He kissed her longer than she did then stood up. "I gotta go. What are your plans today?"

"Clean and grade some papers."

Romero glanced around with a smirk. "Clean what?" he laughed. "This place is spotless."

Isabel smiled, picking up her plate and glass from the table. "I'm cleaning out the fridge and the restroom could use a good scrubbing."

After putting his watch on and grabbing his keys off the counter he walked over to Isabel and pulled her to him by the waist, kissing her like only he could. "My perfect, Izzy," he whispered.

"Will you stop saying that?" She giggled. "God are you ever gonna be disappointed when you find out I'm not."

"Yes, you are. And you could never disappoint me." He patted her behind then let her go. "I'll see you tonight."

Romero hadn't slept in his own apartment in days. Strangely, neither he nor Isabel had addressed the fact. It's like neither wanted to bring up the idea of moving in together. It only made sense. Why pay two rents? Then she could stop taking Valerie's money for her half. But it felt too soon. And if he wasn't bringing it up, maybe he thought so, too.

*

The plans Romero had for Wednesday weren't anything that couldn't easily be rescheduled. It was just a meeting with another client who suspected her husband of cheating. Romero knew he could either reschedule or have someone else meet with her. It was no big deal, but he saw it as his way of getting out of having to meet Isabel's dad under these kinds of circumstances. Meet him during a dinner where he announces he's running for mayor, surrounded by a bunch of other snobs? Could there be a fucking worse time? Nope. He wasn't rescheduling shit. He'd just tell Isabel he'd have to meet her dad another time.

After the surprise inspections at the uniform factories, he met with the poor sap who suspected his girl of cheating. Before meeting Isabel, he didn't understand why these guys would bother. *Fuck the bitch* was what he'd always thought. No girl was worth this kind of aggravation and he most certainly wouldn't be spending hard earned money just to find out the obvious. *Now* what he didn't understand was how these guys could have the patience to wait around and wonder. Romero would get right to it if he so much as suspected Isabel might be doing something behind his back.

More than anything what he found so hard to understand now, were the reactions these guys had to seeing pictures and video of their girls with someone else. It was mind blowing. He hadn't thought much of it when he presented the last guy with pictures and he looked through them shaking his head and made a few comments about how he knew it. To see a picture of his Izzy so much as cozying up with another dude, would be beyond devastating. He didn't even want to think about what he would do. He was only glad she'd told him how she felt about the whole subject of cheating that morning. The very thought of her with someone else, before she said it, had made him furious.

He met with the guy at his office on a construction site. Romero was going to have to think about leasing a small office space. This driving around all over to meet with clients was getting old. He'd talk to Valerie soon about looking for a place for him. According to Isabel, she really knew her real estate.

The guy filled him in on why he suspected his girl-friend was being sneaky—same as always—increased amounts of out-of-town meetings, secrecy and caught in lies, but most telling and one he got a lot, were the texts and phone calls at odd hours of the night. He almost felt like telling him, "Dude, we both know she's cheating. Why do this?"

He stopped at his place before heading to Isabel's to pick up some more clothes. As long as she didn't object to him staying with her every night, he wasn't sure if he'd ever come back to his place. In fact, his lease was up soon. Maybe he'd casually mention that to her.

When she opened the door for him at her place she held her hands out as to not touch him, but she still leaned in to kiss him. "My hands are covered in to-mato, I was just dicing some. Maybe I should get you your own key."

"That'd be cool," he said, trying not to sound as excited as that made him. All right, he'd admit it. Living with her would be fucking awesome.

He started telling her about his day when she brought up her dad's dinner. "Oh, by the way, the dinner is at six but my sister wants me there early to help out."

Romero put on his best-disappointed face. "I can't, babe. I'm meeting that client *at* five." He couldn't help feeling like an asshole when he saw the discontent in her eyes. "I'm sorry," he said, coming around the counter. "We'll set up something with your dad another time. Okay?"

He kissed her. He was just getting going, thoughts of putting her on the counter and making it up to her entering his mind. Her loose shorts would make for easy access. Then her phone rang. "That's probably my sister," she said breathlessly, pulling away from him.

Well, damn.

He picked at the food in the different bowls she had on the counter. She wasn't kidding when she said she was cleaning out the fridge today. He bit in to a piece of carrot and leaned against the counter.

"No. I'll be alone. He has to work, but I'll be there early to help you." Isabel smiled at him and motioned for him to eat the food on the counter. He nodded with a smile of his own, checking her out. He could hardly believe she was all his. "When is Gina flying in?" There was a pause while her sister answered then, "And Art? Is he in town yet?"

Romero felt another twinge of guilt. This would've been the perfect time to meet the rest of her siblings. All of them in town at once—how often would that happen? Still, the thought of meeting them all under those circumstances was unsettling to say the least. He swallowed back the guilt.

Isabel wrapped up her phone call surprisingly fast. Her sister usually kept her on for much longer. Romero couldn't be happier. Just watching her in her soft shorts and tank she wore—obviously bra-less, made him forget about his appetite and how much he'd rather be doing other things with her.

She started to tell him about what her sister had to say, as if he cared, when he pulled her to him and devoured her mouth. Forgetting his thoughts about putting her on the counter he started her out of the kitchen. He wanted her underneath him *now*.

"Where are we going? Don't you wanna eat?"

"Oh, yeah I wanna eat." He smiled then laughed, when he saw her face go beet red in an instant.

By Wednesday morning, with all the talk about the damn dinner he'd heard and listening to how excited Isabel was that her brother and sister were both in town he could hardly fight the guilt anymore. Isabel wasn't the type to make him feel guilty about having to work. But she did say it sucked that neither Gina or Art would be in town until Wednesday afternoon. If they would've been she might've been able to set up something before then and have him meet them.

Still completely convinced that meeting them all tonight at that dinner was a bad idea, Romero had managed to finally shake off the feelings of guilt. Then he got a call from her just after lunch. "I'm so nervous about tonight."

"Why?"

"I don't know. I just saw something about my dad's upcoming announcement on the local news. This is pretty big. I've been trying not to think about it too much but... my dad's running for mayor! Holy cow! This is *huge*. God I wish you could be there with me tonight. But I know, I know, work comes first."

The hell it did. "Listen, babe. I gotta take this call on the other line but I'll call you right back okay?"

What the fuck was wrong with him? The girl he was crazy about wanted him there with her at one of the most important events in her family's lives and he was passing it up because he was *scared*? Just a few weeks ago he was pissed that she hadn't told them about him and now she wanted nothing more than for them to meet him. Time to man up. He called one of the guys on his payroll and arranged for him to meet with the client later that evening. Then he called Isabel back. "Izzy, guess what?"

"What?"

"That was the client I was supposed to meet to-night. They cancelled. I can go to the dinner." He didn't like to lie, but wasn't about to tell her the truth about how easy it was to get someone else to meet the client.

"Really?" The excitement in her voice only made him feel worse. "Yeah, really. You said you have to be there early. What time do I have to be there?"

"Dinner starts at six. I'll text you the exact address. I'm so happy you're going to be there."

Romero squeezed the phone in his hand. God he was an idiot. "Me too, babe. Can't wait to meet the rest of your family."

Chapter 13
Jacob

Hyped that Romero would be here tonight to help her with her nerves and excited now that the reality of what was happening finally hit her, Isabel walked into the restaurant. It surprised her that they hadn't picked something more upscale. Pat explained that Charles thought something more down to earth and less pretentious would appeal to a wider range of voters. So they'd chosen the buffet style restaurant, a favorite on the base known for its fair prices more than its food.

She saw him the moment she walked in, and her heart nearly gave out. At first, she was surprised but when she saw her sister approach Jacob with a huge smile, she was furious. How could she?

The news crews and the photographers for the papers were all over. She spotted her mom and Gina sitting with a few people she didn't recognize and walked toward them instead. She'd only been there a few minutes, just finished giving Gina a hearty hug when she heard Pat's voice behind her. "Isabel, guess who's here?"

She turned to see Pat and Jacob, who stood tall and very handsome in his heavily decorated naval uniform. He probably expected an, "Oh my God, Jacob!" And a big hug. Instead, she *smiled* big, she'd give him that. It *was* nice to see him after all these years. And their parting was an amicable one. There were no hard feelings, but the last thing she needed was for him to think she planned on spending any time with him tonight socializing. Romero would be there in an hour. After the Lawrence incident, she was certain he wouldn't be happy about her hanging out with her ex-boyfriend.

She held out her hand. "How are you, Jacob? It's been so long."

"Too, long," he said, shaking her hand. "Wow, the years sure have been kind to you."

Isabel felt her cheeks warm. "Thank you. They've been kind to you as well. I heard you're up for Lieutenant Commander. Congratulations!"

"Thanks. It's been a tough journey, but in the end it'll be worth it."

"Nothing worthwhile comes easy." Her sister agreed, then gave Isabel a look. "Mom, Gina." Pat walked Jacob around Isabel, to where they sat. "You remember Jacob, Bell's high school sweetheart. He's up for Lieutenant Commander in the Navy. Isn't that fantastic?" She turned back to Isabel, nudging her playfully. "And he's still single." She let out the stupidest giggle.

Isabel took a deep breath. Pat was relentless.

"Oh yes, of course I remember," her mother said, reaching out her hand to shake his. "How've you been, Jacob?"

After some small talk, Pat touched both Jacob and Isabel on the arm, who still hadn't taken a seat. "I'll go see if Charles or Daddy need me. This way you two can have a chance to catch up."

Isabel was going to kill her. "Didn't you need me to help?"

"No, I think we have it all under control. Stay where I can find you, though. The photographers will be taking some family photos in a little bit."

Oh, yes. Isabel was planning on sneaking away to some secluded corner with Jacob to *catch up*. God, she was infuriating. Isabel turned to Jacob. "So, how long will you be stationed in San Diego?"

"Until next year. But now my responsibilities are changing. Just because I'm stationed here doesn't mean I'll be here. I'll be flying out constantly."

Isabel nodded. "I can imagine."

"What about you, Bell? Your sister said you're a teacher now — middle school uh? You're a brave girl."

Isabel had forgotten that having dated him for over two years, he'd picked up on her family's pet name for her. It felt odd. This wasn't the same boy she'd gone out with in high school. This was a grown man now, on his way to be a Lieutenant Commander in the Navy no less, someone she'd slept with — calling her Bell.

She told him about her job and her plans to return to school in the fall, part time. He listened intently, asking a few questions. Photographers walked around taking random pictures. One stopped and took of picture of them without even asking, then nodded. "Thank you, Ms. Montenegro."

Isabel smiled then gave Jacob a look. "That was weird. How did he know who I was?"

Jacob laughed. "Get used it. From here on, everyone at events like these for your father will know who you are. Just wait until he makes mayor. It'll get even worse."

Pat rushed over to them, motioning to her mother and Gina who still sat at the table behind Jacob and Isabel. "It's time for the press family photos."

Isabel smoothed her hair. She hadn't even noticed Jacob watching her. "Don't worry you look beautiful, Bell." She glanced at him and he smiled. "I can't be-

lieve how much you've changed since I last saw you."
He placed his hand on his chest. "I mean you were always beautiful to me, but we were kids back then. You
look so put together now." He laughed. "Even in my
big tough uniform, it was still a little intimidating
walking up to you earlier."

Isabel smiled but said nothing more than, "Thank
you." He looked really good himself but she didn't
want to encourage anything. Her sister would be doing
enough of that on her own.

Art was already with her father and even as she
hugged him hello, she saw the camera flashes go off.
This was too weird. The family all stood on either side
of her father, smiling big for the cameras as they
flashed away. She tried her best to smile genuinely
even though this was all so strange to her. Pat had the
fake smile down. When it was finally over and she had
a moment alone with Pat, she pulled her aside.
"Patricia, why is he here?"

"Who?"

"You know what I'm talking about. My *high school
sweetheart*? What is wrong with you? Why would you
invite him to this and then so obviously leave us alone
to catch up?"

"Bell, it's not always about you. Remember tonight
is about daddy. Need I remind you Jacob will be a
Lieutenant Commander stationed in San Diego?
Charles knows a lot of people but he's always in Miami. Jacob's connections are mostly from around these
parts—people with lots of influence. He could be a big
help in this campaign and he offered to do whatever he
could to help." She turned and glanced at Jacob. A man
held a small notepad taking notes as he spoke with
him. "Besides I don't see the harm in you catching up

with an old friend. An old friend who's made a name for himself. It might remind you of what you're missing out on."

"You know what? I'm getting real tired of — "

"Belly Bell!" Isabel flinched when she felt fingers poke either side of her ribs. Art and Gina stood next to her smiling. By the time Isabel turned back to Pat she was already schmoozing with someone else.

"Isn't this crazy?" Gina's eyes were big with excitement. "Daddy? Mayor of San Diego?"

"Best thing about it," Art said. "If he pulls this off, he only has to do it for a few years, then he retires with a ton of perks. He's set for life." He stopped for a moment and checked Isabel out. "Wow, Bell. You look good. What did you do?"

Isabel smiled, feeling her face warm. Before she could answer, Gina answered for her. "Mom says she's in *love*." Well, at least someone was acknowledging it. "When do we get to meet this guy? Romeo?"

Isabel laughed. "It's Romero, and he'll be here tonight. You'll all get to meet him." That did something to her insides. She prayed Pat didn't do anything stupid. She hadn't even finished her thought when Pat walked over to them with Jacob again. "I invited Jacob to sit with us for dinner tonight." And there it was. Isabel was going to kill her.

*

Manny and Max had left Romero's room exactly as he'd left it. They told him it would always be his if he ever wanted to move back in. As usual Manny had been choked up about it and said there was no way he'd be able to take his things out.

Since his apartment was so small, he took very little with him when he moved out, figuring he'd be back often anyway. So most of his dress clothes were still there. He'd showered there and gotten ready. He told Manny and Max where he was going that night. They were about as impressed as he thought they would be. "Fucking, lying, thieving politicians."

"Hey!" Romero had warned Manny. "Don't ever say that in front of, Izzy. Politician or not, this is her dad we're talking about."

Max stuck his nose into Romero's bedroom. "Lookin' good there, Moe," he smiled. "You gonna be 'round a bunch of big wigs tonight, uh?"

"Yeah, I guess." The only one he was worried about was her dad. Isabel had never actually said it, but from the stories she'd told him about her dad, the man sounded difficult. That's probably where Pat got it from, because her mother was cool enough. All those years of literally judging people couldn't fare well for Romero. "This is the first time I'm meeting her dad."

Max winced. "Really?" He looked Romero up and down. "So you're wearing that?"

Romero eyed himself in the mirror, scrutinizing his long sleeved black dress shirt and his charcoal grey slacks. "What's wrong with this?"

"Nothing but this is his first impression of you. You want it to be one he won't forget. You know, make a statement."

"A statement?" Romero frowned.

"Oh, I know. I got just the thing." Max hurried away.

Yeah, that's what he needed—something out of Max's closet to meet Isabel's dad. Romero could already see the leopard tie or an oversized gold chain.

He shook his head, buttoning the cuffs on his shirt.

Max walked into his room holding a black fedora. It was actually kind of cool. "Here, try it on."

Romero did and looked in the mirror. "Not bad," he said, with a grin. "I've never seen you wear this."

"Never have. I just got it a few weeks ago and I was waitin' for a special occasion to wear it. Looks good on you. Now *that's* a statement."

Manny stuck his head in the door. "What are you two up to?" He watched Romero adjust the fedora. "Cool hat. You wearing that to the dinner?"

"I dunno," Romero said, still trying to decide. "Max says I should."

"Just remember to take it off during dinner."

Romero patted Max on the back. "Thanks. I think I *will* wear it."

He changed his mind about the fedora half a dozen times before he got there and finally decided what the hell and left it on. He texted Isabel to let her know he was there. She said she'd meet him at the door.

His jaw almost dropped when he saw her. He already thought she was sexy as hell but she wore a long sleeve black button down blouse that cuffed at the wrists tucked into a grey skirt that hugged her body perfectly. How the hell did he deserve her? "Oh my God," she smiled, covering her mouth as he got closer. "We match." He hadn't even noticed that part; he'd been so busy ogling her.

He saw her eyes go to his head and he touched the tip of the fedora with a smirk, "You like it?"

"No, I *love* it."

He kissed her. That perfume of hers, mixed with the sweet scent of Izzy, was going to be the end of him. "God, you smell good."

She giggled; then for a moment she seemed troubled. "Something wrong?"

"No." She took his hand. "C'mon. Everybody is just getting seated. It's a buffet so we'll serve ourselves." She turned to him and smiled. "You hungry?"

"I'm gettin' there."

Isabel introduced him to Art and Gina first. Funny, he liked both of *these* siblings right off. They were friendly and both complimented the fedora. Good ole Max came through.

She pointed to a tall, distinguished and stuffy looking man in a suit surrounded by other suits. "That's my dad. I'll introduce you just as soon as he gets a moment."

Exactly as he'd pictured him. "No rush," he smirked.

Her mother said hello and said she was happy he could make it. The only acknowledgment she got from Pat was a forced smile. Then she quickly looked at Isabel. "Daddy wants all the family sitting together." She pointed at the four seats left at the table where her mom, siblings and some other guy in a Navy uniform sat. Judging from all the fucking medals the guy wore, he was probably Pat's husband. "Daddy's next to mom. Charles and I are over there and this is you." She pointed to the only seat left next to the guy in uniform.

"That's okay. I'll sit at another table with Romero."

"Bell! Daddy wanted us all together."

Isabel glared at her. "I'm sitting with Rom—"

Romero squeezed her hand. "It's okay, babe. It's just for dinner. We can move around after." He didn't want her getting upset over something her stupid sister planned. Then he got a bad feeling. If the guy in the uniform wasn't Pat's husband, and she'd obviously made the seating arrangements, who the hell was he?

Isabel pulled him aside. "You're not sitting alone."

"I won't be alone," he managed a smile. "This place is packed. Just one question, who's the uniform you'll be sitting next to?"

She glanced away then back at him. "An old friend of the family. He'll be helping with the campaign. And I'm not sitting next to him, because I'm sitting with you." She gave him a look he wasn't going to argue with. But this wasn't a good way to start the evening.

They sat two tables away from her family. "You're disobeying your sister you know," Romero teased.

"Oh, she can go to hell."

"Izzy!" He chuckled. "I think you've been hanging around me too long."

"She can be such a pain sometimes."

Sometimes?

Romero rubbed her back. The guy in the uniform at her family's table came to their table. "Bell, you should sit with your family. I'll sit somewhere else."

Bell?

"That's okay, Jacob. We're fine." She turned to Romero. "I didn't get a chance to introduce you to my boyfriend, Romero."

"Nice to meet you, Romero." He shook Romero's hand. Romero nodded then Jacob turned back to Isabel. "C'mon, Bell." For some reason hearing him call her that made Romero cringe. "Your dad would want you over there. You really should be. I wasn't even going to sit there until your sister insisted."

That pissed Romero off. He knew Pat had something to do with the seating arrangements. But what made him even madder was that she arranged it so this guy ended up next to Isabel.

"Are you sure?" Isabel asked.

"Absolutely. I'll be sitting with my colleagues where I was planning on sitting in the first place."

Isabel finally agreed and they were back at the family table. He thought about how nicely this would've turned out for Pat if he hadn't come after all. Isabel's Dad finally made it to their table, along with Pat's husband. As expected, Pat's husband was in uniform, too. With just as many stupid medals as the other guy. Isabel introduced him to them both. Seeing how Charles held his military hat at his side reminded Romero to take off his hat and shake both their hands.

Her father nodded but barely flicked a smile. "I'm afraid tonight we won't get too much time to talk, but I trust Isabel will make arrangements for us to meet another time when we can speak more freely."

Neither Isabel nor Romero got a chance to answer before he was interrupted by someone with a clipboard and earpiece who knelt down next to him. Her father spoke to the guy for a while before turning back to the table and apologizing. "That's what I was talking about. It'll be like this all night."

Their table was the first asked to come up to the buffet. Since Isabel and Romero were the first back to the table, Romero took advantage to ask Isabel about Jacob. "Why does that guy call you Bell? I thought only your family called you that?"

Isabel glanced at him then down at the napkin she placed on her lap, positioning it just so. He saw her take a deep breath. "We go way back. I knew..." She cleared her throat. "I dated him in high school." Feeling a heat rise inside him, Romero stared at her but she wouldn't look at him. Instead, she reached for the salt. "Pat didn't think you were coming. I didn't get a chance to tell her." She stopped when Pat and Art reached the table with their plates.

Romero didn't care who heard. This was bullshit. He looked right at Pat. "You arranged for her ex-boyfriend to be here tonight because you thought I wouldn't be?"

Her sister looked scandalized, and Art smirked but said nothing, setting his plate on the table. Isabel put her hand on his leg. "Romero, not here. We'll talk about this later."

Pat gathered herself then said, "He is going to be a Lieutenant Commander in the Navy —"

"I don't give a shit what he is!" Romero sat up in his seat.

Isabel squeezed his leg. "Stop."

Romero tried his hardest to stay in control of his temper but he really wanted to tell the bitch off right there. She was fucking with the wrong person.

"You need to watch the way you speak to —"

"Pat," Art interceded. "You need to mind your own business is what *you* need to do.

Just then, Gina and Isabel's mom returned to the table. With her eyes and mouth still wide open, Pat put her plate down on the table and glared at Art. If Romero's expression was anywhere as intense as the anger he was feeling, her mother must have seen it. She then turned to Pat and asked. "What happened?"

"Nothing," Isabel said, quickly

Romero turned to her and she gave him a look that begged. He took a deep breath. Only for Izzy he'd let this go — for now.

Her mother pressed her lips together and placed her plate on the table then turned to Pat. "Do I need to remind you, all eyes are on us tonight?"

"I'm not the one who—"

"I really don't care, Patricia." Her mother spoke through a fake smile. "I'm sure you have something to do with the tension I'm feeling at this table right now. Just sit down and eat."

They all ate quietly, her father and Charles had obviously gotten sidetracked on the way back, but eventually they made it back.

Even after dinner and all the boring ass speeches they had to sit through, Romero couldn't even look in Patricia's direction without glaring. They started a slideshow of all the highlights of Isabel's dad's career as a judge. Romero excused himself to the restroom.

With one urinal broken and the other one occupied Romero stepped into a stall instead. He was nearly done when he heard someone step in the restroom talking. "I know, but I'm gonna be real busy for the next few weeks, so I can't make any promises." Romero was about to hit the handle to flush with his foot when he heard the next part and froze. "Yeah, but with her dad running for Mayor, this changes everything. This could open a lot of doors for me. I gotta stay close right now—be the ultimate sweetheart. Be patient and don't worry. If I play my cards right, this will all work out."

Romero stood there with one foot in the air and held his breath, trying not to make any noise.

"Okay, I'll call you and let you know as soon I make a few moves."

The door opened then closed and there was silence. Whoever that was, had left. Romero's foot hit the handle and he banged his arm trying to get out of there fast enough. He hadn't heard Charles speak too much, he'd hardly been at the table. He was too busy *network-*

ing as he put it. Romero had been too pissed most of the dinner to pay attention to him anyway.

He ran out so fast, he slammed into an older man who hit the floor like a brick. "Oh, shit! You okay?" He bent down to help him up but the old guy was dazed. "Give me a sec, son. I haven't seen stars like this in years." He shook his head and blinked hard, making Romero feel worse than he already did.

A woman who'd seen the whole thing rushed over to help. "Do you need help? Should I call someone? An ambulance?"

Great—just what he needed—for Isabel's dad's announcement dinner to make headlines for *this* reason.

"No, I'm okay," the old guy said.

Romero sighed in relief. Between him and the woman, they got the man on his feet. By the time it was over, he had no idea which direction the person on the phone in the restroom could've gone. "Damn it."

When he got back to the table, Charles wasn't there. He looked over to where Jacob had been sitting most of the night and he wasn't there either. He wondered if he should even mention to Isabel what he'd overheard. This could be something or it could be nothing. The guy couldn't have been talking about Gina. She lived in New York. If it was Charles, it could just be work related, but if it was Jacob...stay close? Be the ultimate sweetheart? What the hell did that mean? To *his* Izzy? The guy was out of his fucking mind. But Isabel *had* said he'd be helping out with the campaign.

On his way to Isabel's car, after the dinner was finally over, Isabel began to apologize. "Stop." He shook his head. "That was *all* your sister in there. You have nothing to apologize for. Has she always been that conniving? To have your ex show up because she thought I wasn't coming?"

"I'm not defending her, because when she found out he was making Lieutenant Commander and he was still single, I'm sure the idea of him and me reconnecting crossed her mind. But that wasn't the sole purpose to invite him here tonight." Romero held back all the sarcastic remarks that came to mind. He had no doubt that was *exactly* why her sister had invited him. "It's also *really* important to her that my dad makes mayor. Jacob has connections now. He could be a big asset to the campaign, so she's really counting on that."

The guy was going to be around for the whole damn campaign? "How long did you go out with this guy?"

They reached her car and she stopped at the door and searched in her purse for her keys. She was stalling and it irritated him. "Izz?"

"I don't remember. It was so long ago—high school, Romero."

"Was he your first boyfriend?"

She nodded, whispering, "Yes."

Feeling even more irritated now, he squeezed her hand. "Then you remember."

She lifted a shoulder and clicked the car opener on her keychain. "Just over two years."

"What!"

She turned to him and he pinned her against the car. "It was a long time ago. This was the first time I'd seen him or talked to him in *years.*"

The thought choked him, but he wouldn't put it past her sister. "Was he your first... *everything*?"

"Do we really have to get into this right here? Right *now*?"

That burned him up even more. "It's either a yes or

a no." Just like all those saps that hired him to find out what they already knew—he knew the answer just by looking in her eyes and it killed him.

"Yes, he was." She caressed his face. "But what does it matter? There's a reason why we didn't stay to-gether."

"And what was that?" He needed something—anything to keep him from walking back in there and telling her sister off. Pat had brought out the big guns tonight.

"There was no spark. *None*, and after talking to him tonight it only confirmed it."

"What do you mean?" He felt a panic he'd never felt before, thinking of all those fucking medals her family had such a hard-on for. "Were you *looking* for a spark?"

"No! Are you crazy?"

Damn. He was. For *her*. Romero hugged her bury-ing his face in her neck, taking in a deep breath of her—all of her. He was going to blow this. "You love me?"

"You know I do."

He breathed in deep, knowing he had *that* much. He only hoped he could remember that every time he had to be around or hear about this fucking lieutenant commander, Jacob—her *first*. "I love you *too* much, Izzy."

Chapter 14
Trouble

Since Isabel had an early morning staff meeting to attend, she was out of the apartment before Romero. He finished getting ready. Not wanting to eat alone he decided to stop at Moreno's for a breakfast burrito, maybe catch up with the guys. He hadn't hung with them in a while.

To his surprise, Sal was the only one of them there when he got there. He was leaning against the bar reading the paper.

"Don't act like you read."

Sal looked up and smiled when he saw him. "Funny you'd walk in. I was just reading about your future father-in-law. Alex had mentioned it but said Valerie told him it wasn't a for sure thing. I didn't know it was official."

When Romero got close enough he got a glimpse of the headlines. "It's already in the papers?"

"Yeah, front page. And they have a whole section about it on the inside." Sal tapped the paper. "You here to eat?"

"Yeah." Romero's eyes were still on the paper. "I'll take the usual."

Sal walked away from the bar to put in Romero's order. Romero turned the paper around and read the headline: *Superior Court Judge Arturo Montenegro III Announces Run For Mayor.*

Isabel and her family's picture had made the front

page. He skimmed the story and the few other pictures, flicking Pat's face with his finger before turning the page to see the rest of the article. There were more pictures including one of Isabel and Jacob standing alone talking. Feeling that inner heat that had become too familiar these days, he scanned the rest of the pictures. There was another of them in the background of one of her father. Fucking Pat stood with them with a big toothy smile. She sure as shit loved the up-and-coming Lieutenant Commander. Except for the picture where Isabel stood alone with him, Isabel appeared annoyed.

His eyes were back on the picture of Isabel and Jacob. Almost obsessively, he studied how they looked at each other. Was this the moment she'd been looking for the *spark*?

"Who's that with Isabel?" Sal asked.

"Her ex-boyfriend." It wasn't until then that Romero realized how tight his jaw had become and the words he'd spoke were through his teeth.

Sal laughed. "Is that why your eyes are nearly burning a hole through my paper?" He tugged at the paper. "Lemme see."

Romero shoved the paper at Sal. "Dude!" Sal smirked then examined the paper. "Where were you?"

"She had to be there an hour early, so I wasn't there yet."

The smirk on Sal's face was still there and it irritated Romero. "You gonna need a drink this early?"

"No, I'm not gonna need a drink this early," Romero said, reaching for the paper again.

Sal laughed again, but handed him the paper. "So what was her ex doing there?"

Romero filled him in briefly about her damn sister and her ex being a big shit in the Navy — in no way hiding his aversion to the whole situation.

"Heads of military are not going to get him far ahead in an election. He's better off sticking with the people he already knows. Being a judge, he probably already has all the connections he needs. City council members, legislators, and a bunch of city officials, who I'm sure owe him a favor or two." Sal took the paper Romero was still staring at and tossed it on the counter behind the bar. "Will you stop? She's with you now, not him."

"Yeah, but if it were up to her fucking sister, Izzy would be with *him*." Everything he'd felt the night before when he found out Jacob was her first, came flying back at him. "I'm no match for that shit, Sal. They all got their master's degrees, Izzy's gonna start working on hers soon — her dad's running for Mayor for Christ's sake!"

A waiter brought out Romero's breakfast burrito and placed it on the bar in front of him. "Thanks Julio," Sal said, and then he frowned, pouring Romero a soda. "First of all, it's not like you're *trying* to get the girl. You already have her. Right? And last time I saw you two together, she seemed really into you — shocker." He laughed. "I'm kidding, but here's my second point: I hope to hell you didn't sit there with that mouth of yours and talk the way you always do in front of her family and would-be in-laws. Did you?"

Romero chewed and covered his mouth, remembering Max the night Isabel met his uncles. "No! As a matter of fact, I've been trying to tone it down. Ever since I realized how much my uncles fucki—" He caught himself and Sal rolled his eyes. "How much they cuss."

"Try harder, dude." Sal tossed a few napkins in front of him. "No one's perfect. I'm certainly not, but why call attention to your imperfections with something so obvious as your overuse of the cringe-worthy language. From what you tell me, I can guarantee you her family doesn't toss around the F-bomb as much as you do, and especially not now that they'll be in the eye of the public. Everything they do or say from here on will be scrutinized. And if you're going to be rubbing elbows with all these big-shots, you don't wanna embarrass Isabel or do something that would taint her dad's campaign in *any* way."

That pissed Romero off. "Why would I do that?"

Sal raised his eyebrows and tossed the paper in front of him again. He knew exactly what Sal meant. He thought the same thing last night. Romero didn't look at it. Instead, he took a bite of his burrito and said nothing.

"These elections get ugly, Romero. His opponents will be looking for anything and everything to use against him. And your temper gets pretty ugly."

Romero stared at him but kept chewing. Needing to change the subject he finished chewing and asked, "What do you know about golf?"

Sal's eyebrows pinched. "Enough. I play a few rounds a week. Why?"

"Her dad mentioned maybe playing a round or two. I've never played. I told him I never have. He said I'd catch on." Romero shook his head. "I don't wanna make an ass of myself.

Sal lifted a shoulder. "I'm outta here as soon as Alex gets here. So I'm free for the rest of the day. We can go to the driving range and I'll show you the basics."

Romero shuffled his schedule around in his head, then swallowed the last of his burrito. "Let me make some calls. I can probably do that."

Sal was definitely the most patient of the three brothers. He laughed at times like when Romero was sure
Angel and certainly Alex would've been done with
him. But it was a give and take. Alex or Angel
would've just showed Romero how to stand and
swing. Sal explained the steps one by one, from the
proper way to shift your weight to the importance of
the back swing and the rotation of the shoulders. Then
there was the transition, the impact and finally the
through swing and finish. "I'm going for one round of
golf here, Sal. Not trying to take Tiger fucking Woods
down."

Sal wasn't laughing. "I thought you were working
on toning the language down?" He pulled on Romero's
arm, straightening it out. "And this isn't rocket science,
Romero. This is just the basics. "

Romero frowned, concentrating on his *transition*.
After about an hour of hitting balls, Romero couldn't
believe Sal was still completely committed to making
sure Romero had it right. "Remember to keep your
wrist locked when you're transferring your weight to
your left leg."

Romero did as instructed, huffing and sighing
through most of his *lesson*, but in the end, he was grateful Sal was so damned anal. He at least had the basics
down. "So what else do you know about politics?" he
asked, as they walked back to Sal's car. "'Cause I don't
know shit. All I know is they're a bunch of fucki... a
bunch of crooks."

Sal laughed. "That's your uncles talking. They're
not *all* bad. Some actually want to make a difference."
They reached his car and Sal opened his trunk. He

swung his golf bag in. "I wouldn't worry so much about that. Something tells me he'll be more interested in talking about you. What *you* want out of life. What *you* have to offer his daughter."

Romero frowned. Jacob and all his damned medals came to mind. *Fuck.*

"Don't sell yourself short, man." Sal closed his trunk and they both walked along either side of his car. "You're a good guy, and most importantly, you genuinely care about his daughter. That's what *really* matters. You just gotta watch that mouth of yours." They got in the car. Romero thought about his and Isabel's family ever meeting — what a nightmare that would be. Sal shoved Romero's shoulder just as he pulled the car out of the parking space. "What are you frowning about? You started your own business all by yourself and it's doing well. Not too many can say that. Hell, offer to do some security for him. He's gonna need it now. This may even open a few doors for you. Security in politics is huge."

That reminded Romero of the conversation he overheard in the restroom. *Open doors.* He still didn't know who had said it and which daughter he'd been talking about but he'd for sure be on alert from here on. "He's got security already."

"He's gonna need more. Trust me."

Romero stared out the window. It wasn't a bad idea. "Maybe I'll bring it up."

"One thing, dude and I wasn't playing when I said this earlier. You better keep that temper of yours in check. If her ex is gonna be around, you better be cool. Don't blow this. I'm telling you. The press will eat it up. The smallest of scuffles with this guy, especially at one of these events, and it'll be all over the papers the next day."

Romero squeezed his hand into a fist, taking a deep breath. Just the thought of this guy trying anything or her sister pushing to get them together again would set him off. "I know." He tapped his chest a couple of times with his fist and forced a smile. "I got this."

Normally he really meant it. This time he was worried.

*

It wasn't like Pat to show up unannounced, so when she did, Isabel worried. She opened the door quickly. "Something wrong?"

"No, not at all." She glanced into her apartment. "Are you alone? Or is *he* here?"

Isabel stepped back to let her in. "*Romero* is working late tonight. He won't be home until later."

Pat's head jerked back to face Isabel, the alarm screaming in her eyes. "He moved in?"

"Well… no but he's been staying here a lot." Isabel and Romero still hadn't talked about moving in together. She was beginning to wonder if they even had to. He was there all the time now anyway.

Pats mouth pinched to one side. "It's only been a couple of months, hasn't it? And he's already staying here *a lot*?"

It had been a week since her father's announcement and she'd gotten into it with Pat the very next day over the phone about her little Jacob stunt. She wasn't getting into it with her again, especially not about Romero, so she ignored her question. "What's going on? Why are you here?"

The expression on Pat's face changed suddenly. She

was up to something again. "We're almost all set up to start the campaigning full throttle. Charles found a great campaign manager — Gary Foster. He has an impeccable record of accomplishment." Pat put her purse down and took a seat on the sofa. Isabel sat across from her in the chair. "Daddy's friend owns several shopping centers in this area. He has a few vacant shops he'll donate temporarily to the campaign for us to run everything. The donations are already pouring in."

Pat filled Isabel in about all that was going to be done, from the signs and billboards to the radio interviews and finally got to the reason for her unexpected visit. "Everyone is doing their part. My firm will donate their time to look over all the legal aspects of what we can and can't do. What we need most is for people to get the word out. That's where you come in. Gary thinks you should let your union and the school district know that daddy has a plan to get more funding to the schools so they can stop making so many cuts. This way we can get their endorsements. And then maybe if you can commit to putting in a few hours a week to make phone calls and pass out flyers. It's gonna be a lot of work but if we *all* pull together we can do this."

Isabel waited for the catch. With Pat, there always was one. "That's it? Just get the word out and put in a few hours in a week?"

Pat nodded, smiling. "Can you do that?"

Isabel eyed her suspiciously. "You came over here to tell me that?"

"Well…"

Isabel knew it. She frowned. "What?"

Pat sat up straight. "I ran into Jacob again — "

"No." Isabel crossed her arms in front of her.

"You don't even know — "

"I know *you*, so no! I can't even believe you're still pushing this."

"Pushing what, Bell? All I was going to say was he asked about you. About you and Romero — how serious this *thing* with him is."

"And you said?"

"Well, I wasn't aware he was staying here so much and since it's only been a couple of months I said... I wasn't sure."

Isabel glared, undoing her arms and placing her hands on her thighs. "You *know* I wouldn't have invited him to daddy's dinner if it wasn't serious, Pat."

"Bell, please listen to me. I know you think I'm just meddling, but I love you and I'm worried. That's all."

"Worried about what? You don't know anything about Romero. You've never even given him a chance. The moment you heard the words '*he didn't attend college*' you made up your mind. An education and a bunch of medals aren't all that matter, Pat. I know to you it does, but not to me. He's a good person and he's good to me."

Pat nodded, leaning over and placed her hand over Isabel's. "I'll admit that at first that's the only thing I didn't like about him. But you were there. You can't tell me the way he snapped that night of the dinner wasn't a bit worrisome. If this is what he's like now, can you imagine how much worse he'll be with time? He glared at me the entire night. He has abusive written all over him."

"That's ridiculous." Isabel couldn't help but think of the heat in his eyes the day he heard Michael's message. And how Alex could barely hold him back the day after, when he looked ready to kill Lawrence. She'd seen that look in his eyes several times now, but not once had she felt threatened in any way. "He's not like that, Pat. Trust me, he would never hurt me."

"Not yet." Pat squeezed her hand. "Belly Bell, I work these kinds of domestic abuse cases all the time. The relationships all started beautifully. But they all say the same thing. The signs were there from the very beginning. The women chose to ignore them because they were so in love. Then when family members stepped in to try to help, these men turned them against their family. They're manipulative—"

"Jesus, Pat. You really think I'm that stupid? And what do you mean *these* kinds of cases? Nobody is abusing anyone in this relationship."

"These women are not stupid, Bell. They were in love and desperate to believe these guys could change—would change—for *them*. But some people just can't be changed. I have a bad feeling about him. Art said the same thing, too."

"He did?" That worried Isabel. Art was much less judgmental than Pat. Worse yet, he never agreed with Pat about anything.

Pat nodded. "Anyway, that's why I really came down here but I also was hoping you'd consider spending some time with Jacob." Isabel began shaking her head and Pat squeezed her hand again. "Listen to me, not in a romantic setting or anything. Gary asked me to draw up the schedules for the volunteers. You wouldn't even be alone with him. I could just schedule you on the same days. You'd be there with all the other volunteers making calls. He has so much to offer, Bell." Pat put her hand up before Isabel could protest. "Not that Romero doesn't. I just want you to be open to the possibility of staying friends with Jacob *in case* things don't work out with Romero." She gave Isabel a hopeful smile. "He said he didn't realize how much he missed you until he saw you again."

Isabel stared at Pat but didn't return the smile.

"And," Pat added, "I could've just done it without asking you first. You already knew he'd be helping with the campaign, but I wanted you to be with me on this."

"That's just it." Isabel pulled her hand away from Pat's. "I'm not. I'll do what I have to, to help dad. If Jacob is there when I go in to help, then he's there, but I won't be trying to develop any kind of *friendship* with him."

Pat smiled. "Fair enough." She patted Isabel's knee and stood up. "I'll start working on the schedules tonight and give you a call in a few days to let you know when your first shift is."

Isabel walked her chipper sister to the door, who said her goodbyes much too contentedly. On the surface, this little visit from her sister seemed to have gone Isabel's way, but somehow she couldn't help feeling like she'd been had.

Chapter 15
No one else

Waking up next to Isabel felt like something Romero had been doing forever. He couldn't even imagine not waking without her in his arms anymore. He spooned her closely to him, kissing her cheek. She didn't open her eyes but the corner of her lips rose ever so slightly. He smiled and whispered, "Don't wake up." To which she immediately opened her eyes and he frowned. "Izzy, you did just the opposite."

"I was already awake." She turned her body around to face him. "My eyes were just resting."

"But it's Saturday, you don't have to get up this early."

"Actually I do. Remember? I have to go in for a few hours and do some campaigning for my dad."

Romero tried to hide his irritation as she sat up. Thoughts of Jacob were immediately on his mind. She said he'd be helping out, but he knew there was no way she'd know when, where or how. He'd already told himself he wasn't letting Pat or Jacob be the cause of any friction between him and Isabel. They just weren't worth it.

He ran a finger down her bare back, wondering if even in the winter they'd still wake up naked. "I love waking up next to you, baby."

She turned to him. "I love it, too."

He stared at her, the words at the tip of his mouth. Then she said them. "Why don't you just move in already?"

Never in his life would he have imagined hearing those words from a girl would bring so much joy. He sat up. "Are you serious?"

She laughed. "You may as well. You're always here anyway." She caressed his face with her hand. "And I've been dreading hearing you say that you won't or can't stay some night."

He kissed her. God, she really was perfect. "Trust me. I wasn't planning on saying that ever again. I just wasn't sure how you'd feel about making it official."

She smiled widely. "Then it's official. You're now my roomie."

He pulled her down next to him, wrapping his arms around her warm naked body. "Oh, I'm way more than your roomie, and don't you forget it."

She giggled, squirming away. "No, no, babe. I don't have time right now. I'm already late." She pouted, obviously seeing the disappointment in his face. "But you're welcome to join me."

Romero knew exactly what that meant—*quickie*. He'd take it. When she got out of bed he chased her to the shower. He could hardly believe this is what life was going to be like from here on.

*

Gary Foster was a no-nonsense, let's get to it, type of man. Isabel saw it the moment she arrived at the campaign headquarters. His only response to her telling him her name was: "You're late."

Her shower with Romero had gone on a little longer than she anticipated, but it was oh, so worth it. Even if it meant getting the stink eye from Gary, her legs were still weak. "I know. I'm sorry, but I'm here now. What do you need me to do?"

He picked up a clipboard. "Lets see here... Isabel." His eyes scanned the paper on the clipboard.

Isabel glanced around and saw Jacob was already there. He was out of uniform, in a pair of jeans and wore a "Montenegro for Mayor" t-shirt. Everyone else wore the same t-shirt and she wondered why she hadn't been given one. Then she remembered. She was late.

He looked so different out of uniform. More relaxed. Jacob smiled when he saw her and she felt her cheeks warm because he caught her checking him out.

"Looks like you have flyer duty today." He flipped through the pages on the clipboard. "Now let's see where you're headed and who you're partnered up with."

As soon as he said that, she knew exactly who she'd be partnered up with. She should've seen something like this coming. "Why do I need a partner?"

Gary looked up at her then back at the clipboard. "We never send anyone out alone — safety reasons — *my* rule."

Isabel took a deep breath. She was sure her sister knew perfectly well about this rule of his, before she ever came over to talk to her. How was she supposed to get mad at her now? Her sister had made it clear what she was up to. Isabel just hadn't anticipated how cunning Pat would be about this.

Gary glanced around then motioned for Jacob to come over. She knew it. "You and the soon-to-be Lieutenant Commander are headed to the mall. Your sister hooked you up. At least you won't be in the hot sun. *And* you get a Navy man to escort your around all day."

"All day?"

"Well, just until you get all the flyers passed out." He pointed to a mountain of boxes full of flyers on a table. "You two can handle this." Jacob joined them and Gary turned to him. "Isn't that right, Commander?" Gary grinned. "You two can handle passing these little boxes of flyers out today right?"

Jacob smiled. "Of course. And call me Jacob."

"Alright, Jacob. You and Isabel here are headed to the mall."

Gary went over the mall's policy on passing out flyers, a do-and-don't list and they were on their way. "We can go in my car," Jacob suggested. "Why take two?"

Isabel hesitated. "Once we're done we can just go, right? If I take my car I can go straight home from there."

Jacob shrugged, opening the trunk to his car. "Which way do you live?"

Without thinking, she pointed.

"Well, then you'll have to come by here anyway. I can just bring you back to get your car."

With her mind muddled, Isabel couldn't think of an excuse not to fast enough. So she slumped her shoulders and gave in. Romero would be furious—knowing this was all Pat's doing again. But this was strictly business and he had to know he had nothing to worry about. She was crazy about him.

After hours of walking from door to door at the mall, requesting permission to post their flyer on the windows of their stores, Isabel was pooped. She never realized how big and just how many stores were in the mall. She was shocked at how rude some shop owners could be, too.

"You getting hungry?" Jacob asked.

She was, but she wasn't looking forward to sitting and talking to him. Up until then, their conversations had all been about the campaign. There had also been some small talk about her work, and how she had a meeting set up with the union to try to persuade them to endorse her dad. Lunch would most likely go a more personal direction. Even though she knew she was doing nothing wrong, she was certain telling Romero that she'd spent most of her day with Jacob was going to be uncomfortable at the very least. But telling him they'd also had a long lunch together would only make it worse.

One thing was for sure, she'd be talking to her sister about this again. The thought of spending time around Jacob had seemed harmless enough, but actually doing it felt much different. "Yeah, I could go for a bite of something."

They walked past Frisco's. Isabel didn't even look in that direction. No way were they eating there. She and Romero had gone back a few times since their first dinner together. As far as she was concerned, that was *their* place now. She didn't know it then, but in hindsight, that's the day she'd fallen for him. He'd melted her with his smile the entire night, but when he told her he'd been there two weeks in a row hoping to run into her, that's what did it. That's why the next night at the game, she was helpless to even try fighting off his kisses. She'd been putty in his hands ever since.

"I heard the Brazilian steak house here is pretty good."

No way was she doing a fancy restaurant with him. "I'd rather just grab something from the food court if you don't mind. It *is* Saturday and I'd like to get this over with and out of here as soon as possible."

He raised an eyebrow. "Big plans tonight?"

Not really. Even though she wasn't looking forward to telling Romero about who'd she'd spent her day with, she was anxious to get home to him. *Home.* She thought of their conversation that morning. They were officially living together.

"I'll take that smile as a yes."

Isabel felt her face flush as she broke out of her daze. "I'm sorry." God, she had to stop doing that. It was so embarrassing. "No, no big plans. But it *is* my day off. I'd like to spend some of it relaxing."

"I gotcha." He smiled.

When they got to the food court, he let her pick. She chose the fastest—a slice of pizza. Jacob seemed to sense her anxiety about being with him. He had to understand this was awkward for her. Even if it was for him as well, at least he wasn't in a relationship now. She appreciated that he kept the small talk at a safe level, but just as they walked out of the food court on their way back to finish passing out the flyers he asked, "Are you in love with him, Bell?"

She turned to him surprised by the out-of-nowhere question.

"I'm sorry. It's just that Pat said she didn't think you two were very serious, and to be honest I wasn't quite ready for what I felt when I saw you again. I was just hoping..."

Isabel glanced away. She was going to strangle Pat the very next time she saw her. "It is serious, Jacob, and I *am* in love with him. In fact, he's moved in with me now. Pat..." Isabel took a deep breath. "Well, she doesn't know too much about it—about him."

"She said he's a security guard?"

Isabel rolled her eyes. Of course Pat would tell him that. "He's a private investigator and he owns his own security firm." That's right. If Pat was going to go around listing everyone else's attributes she'd list Romero's. She was very proud of them.

Things were a bit uncomfortable after that. Pat had told Isabel that Jacob said he'd missed her, but she never expected him to mention how he'd felt when he saw her. Pat had set him up for that. Probably put it in his head that she might still have feelings for him as well. God, Isabel was going to let her have it.

Romero had texted her several times throughout the day, mostly to ask how it was going and to tell her he missed her. He had a few things he needed to take care of that day, but lately he'd been trying to leave her days off open.

She was on her way home—finally. He was already there waiting for her. She walked in to find him unpacking a few boxes. "I went by my *old* place," he said, with a smirk. "To pick up some more of my things."

She took her shoes off, remembering how Valerie used to fling hers off as soon as she walked in. Romero was her new roomie now. What a difference. One she never would have imagined.

"So how was it?" Romero asked, pulling out a pair of shoes from the box and examining them. "What did you do?"

"Passed out flyers… at the mall." She kissed him as she passed by him to put her shoes in her room.

"Zat right?" She heard him from her room. "You should've told me. I would've met you down there and helped you."

She squeezed her eyes shut just before she turned

the corner to walk back into the front room. "I wasn't alone."

He looked up from the box and their eyes met. The easygoing expression faded slowly. "Oh yeah? Who went with you?"

She swallowed and started toward the fridge like a coward, not wanting to face him when she said it. "Jacob and I were assigned to flyer—"

"You were with Jacob all this time?"

She turned back to him at the sound of his venomous tone. "We just passed flyers out, Romero. It's not like—"

"Did your fucking sister arrange this?"

"Hey! What happened to toning it down?"

"You know she did." He walked toward her that undeniable heat in his eyes again. "Just like she planned for him to sit at your family's table that night—next to *you*. Don't you see it?"

"Yes. I see it."

He stood right in her face. "So did you and *Jacob* get a chance to catch up, Isabel? Talk about old times?"

"Don't call me that. I already told you I hate hearing it from you."

"Why? It's your name."

She felt a lump forming in her throat. She hated to see him—hear him like this. The tears were already blurring her vision. "Because you only call me that when you're mad at me."

"Not mad at *you*. Alright what do you want me to call you? Bell? Oh wait, that's what *he* fucking calls you." He spun around and stalked back toward the front room. She saw him glance around almost panicked then he saw them—his keys on the coffee table. He grabbed them.

"Where you going?"

"Out." He glanced at his watch then back at her with a fury worse than earlier. "You know what? Fuck that." He slammed the keys back on the table, making her flinch. She saw him wince then, close his eyes for a second as if trying to collect himself. His now fisted hand almost shook and he spoke through his teeth. "You were with your ex-boyfriend *all* day, Isabel. So what *did* you talk about? I wanna know."

Seeing him so enraged and hearing him call her that again made the lump in her throat even bigger. "About the campaign, mostly."

"Mostly? What else? Did he bring up the past? You and him?"

"No!" Her voice cracked and she took a step toward him. "It was all business. I promise." She never wanted to be around Jacob again. Not if it upset Romero this much. She reached out for his hand and he recoiled but she grabbed it anyway. It *was* shaking. She looked into his eyes. They went from furious to panicked. Just like the night she'd told him Jacob had been her first. "What's *wrong* with you?"

"Tell me the truth, Izzy. Did you talk about anything personal? I *have* to know."

Hearing him call her Izzy, and *feeling* his scared eyes burn deep into her soul did something to her. "Yes."

He pinched his brows the panic gone now replaced with the heat again. "What? What did you talk about?"

"You." She brought his hand to her mouth and kissed it. "He asked if I was in love with you. And I told him *yes* and that you'd moved in with me."

"Why would he wanna know?"

She shook her head. "I don't know."

"You *do* know, Izzy." His tone, softened just a notch and again his eyes searched for something deep inside her. "Tell me, baby."

Hearing him call her that after he'd just called her Isabel twice had a hypnotic effect on her somehow and he seemed to know it. But it was working. She nodded, unbelievably hearing herself say, "Something about not being prepared for what he felt when he saw me again."

She saw his jaw clench. "And what was that?"

"He didn't say. I swear to you. After I told him I was in love and how serious my relationship with you is, we changed the subject."

"That's it? The whole day. That was the only personal thing you talked about?" He searched her eyes again. "No memories?"

"*No*. Nothing." She leaned in and kissed him. He barely moved his lips at first, but she continued to kiss him until he suddenly thrust his tongue in her mouth, kissing her *hard*.

Just as suddenly he pulled away. "I don't want you around him anymore," he said, bringing her to him by her waist.

"Okay," Isabel agreed breathlessly, without even thinking about it. What was he doing to her?

He kissed her again, deeper, then bit her lower lip hard, but not hard enough to hurt, arousing her to no end. She bit back. His breathing became heavier. "Tell that fucking sister of yours," he said, between kisses, "that I know what she's up to."

"Um hmm." Isabel was incredibly turned on, and she didn't even understand why. She didn't care anymore that he was disrespecting her sister. Pat had disrespected him, so she deserved it. She undid the top button of his jeans and yanked down the zipper.

They moved over to the sofa. Romero pushed his box of things onto the floor. He always did love her easy-access clothes and ever since he'd told her, she'd done her best to accommodate. She wore a denim skirt that he slid his hands up now, pulling her panties down roughly. "Get 'em off." He pulled his hands away to take his wallet out of his pocket and pulled a condom out. "I'm not playing, Izzy." Never once taking his penetrating gaze away from her, he pulled his jeans down and stepped out of them, then put the condom on. "I swear to God. If you don't tell her, I will. And trust me you don't want me to."

She nodded, transfixed in his eyes, not really caring about what he was saying. It was times like this she felt he had some kind of spell on her. She'd done as he asked and was ready for him when he moved on top of her. He kissed her just as he entered her — kissed her so deep and with so much passion, she felt it down to her curled toes. "No one else will ever love you like I do, Izzy." He moved faster and she moaned. "You know that, right?"

"Yes," she barely managed to say, feeling her body react in the usual way it reacted to him — crazy with excitement.

"Say it, baby. Say no one will ever love you like I do." Her entire body trembled and she moaned even louder. "I wanna hear it." His voice rasped.

"No one else." She could barely believe she'd complied so easily, but it was the truth. She wasn't lying. She believed him without a doubt. "Only you can love me like this." He stared deep in her eyes for a moment, continuing to *love* her like only he could. She held on to him, amazed at what he did to her. If what he wanted was to own her, he had from the moment he first kissed her. Not just physically but in every way imaginable. She was a sensible grown woman and if she stepped out of the picture for just a second, she might see something wrong with it, but there, that moment, nothing felt more right than being *his*, and she wanted nothing more than for him to know it—feel it.

He squeezed his eyes shut, finishing with a groan. "Only you, Romero," she panted, feeling the incredible pleasure rip through her body. No one could ever make her feel the unbelievable mixture of emotions he'd put her through this evening alone and she never wanted anyone else to. "I promise."

Chapter 16
The call

Never in his life had Romero felt the need to impress anyone. He'd always done and said as he pleased and if anyone didn't like it they could just go to hell. Now here he was carrying the golf bag Sal had lent him, ready to meet Arturo, Isabel's dad, for a round of golf and he was nervous as shit.

Sal had once again gone over the rules and showed him how to keep score, giving him tips then reminding him to watch his language.

Romero thought it was supposed to be just him and her dad but to his surprise and somewhat relief, Charles and her brother, Art were there also. At least it wouldn't be so one-on-one.

After greeting all of them and making some small talk about the weather, they all made their way on to the course. Romero didn't even care that he would most likely come in far last as long as he didn't make a total ass of himself. They all knew he'd never played before. What he didn't expect was for Art to be worse than he was.

"Maybe you should just watch," Isabel's dad said, disgusted, as another chunk of grass flew in the air and Art's ball rolled off to the side.

Art laughed. "Hey, I'm just here to spend some time with my old man. I couldn't care less about this stupid game."

Charles spent more time on his phone than engaging in conversation with them. When he wasn't talking he was checking his email or texts, then responding.

"I'm told you're in the security business," her dad said as Charles set up to take a swing.

Romero nodded. "Yeah. Security and private investigating, background checks—that kind of stuff."

"How long have you been doing that?"

Romero felt her dad's eyes sweeping over him, but nothing said he was impressed. He hated feeling like he was being scrutinized. He shook it off and answered as aloofly as possible. "I've been doing security for years but I only got the business off the ground this year."

It was her dad's turn to putt and as usual, he took his time setting up. Both Charles and Art were on their phones again. Romero stood a few feet from Charles who'd stepped away to answer his call. The entire time he hadn't paid any attention to any of their phone conversations until he heard a bit of Charles's current call that caught his attention. "I know, my love. I'll be done here in about an hour and then I'm all yours for the rest of the day."

Just hearing it brought a foul taste to Romero's mouth. How could anyone miss Pat? They continued playing and her father continued to grill him casually. "Is your family originally from La Jolla?"

Romero prepared himself to take the shot before answering. He swung and then watched as the ball flew through the air. He was getting pretty good at this. He turned to her dad who was still watching the ball. "Nah, I was born in Calexico, same as my uncles and dad. We moved up here a few years after they opened up their business. Said the schools and area in general were better for raising a kid. I was about four."

"What kind of business do they run?"

He knew it was coming and even though he always told himself he didn't give a shit what anyone thought. Annoyingly, he was beginning to realize that he did now, and maybe he always had. "A bar." He glanced at her dad then back at Art, who awkwardly set up for his shot. "The Silver Dollar, over on First Street."

Romero could tell just by the look her dad gave him, he'd heard of it—maybe even been a patron at one point.

"Never heard of it."

Romero figured that much. The uptight would-be Mayor was not about to admit to frequenting a topless bar. After shanking another shot, Art turned to Romero. "Your folks own The Silver Dollar?"

"Yeah, my uncles do."

Art wasn't judging like Romero had expected. "My buddies took me there for my twenty-first birthday."

Isabel's dad ignored Art. "What about your parents? What do they do?"

Romero set up for his next shot. Without looking at any of them he said, "Never met my mom, and my old man's in jail."

By the time he took his shot and turned back, he saw he had the attention of all three. Even Charles, who'd hardly looked up from his phone the entire time stared at him. Romero wasn't giving up anymore information than necessary. "Next hole." He stuck his club in his bag when he reached the cart.

When it was all over, he'd learned a few things about the men in Isabel's life. Art was surprisingly down to earth and had a desperate need to impress his father. Having two uncles who made him feel like he was the shits his whole life, even with his sometimes rotten grades, Romero couldn't relate to that, but he liked the guy so he felt for him.

Charles was a major kiss ass with Isabel's dad, something he'd never be. Sure, he'd gone out of his way to learn to play golf, but that's only because he didn't want to totally humiliate himself out there. And he'd looked up what her dad's stand was on some of the more major things, but again he just didn't want to inadvertently say something to open up a can of worms. He'd never cared enough to argue about politics.

But what surprised him most was as sweet and loving as Isabel was, her dad was as cold as a dead fish. Art tried the whole time to tell him about things even Romero was impressed with, like the fact that he was the youngest lawyer being considered as a candidate to run for District Attorney in Los Angeles's history. Her dad continued golfing as if he'd just been told the sky is blue.

Romero could see he wouldn't be impressing this man with his little security firm so he wouldn't even try. As long as her family didn't get in the way of him and Isabel being together he'd keep his business to himself.

They stopped for a drink at the clubhouse. On his way back from the restroom, Romero caught the tail end of Charles's phone call as he stood just outside, his back to Romero. "...I know I can't wait either. I'm almost out of here. I'll see you in a bit."

Somehow, it didn't surprise him that Pat was a pest. Isabel had only texted him once the entire time and it had only been three words. The only words he ever needed to hear from her.

I love you.

They finished their drinks and Romero was finally done with it. He'd done it and came away unscathed — hadn't dropped the F bomb even once. Sal would be proud.

He called Isabel as soon as he got in the car, placing the earpiece on as he drove out the driveway.

"How'd it go?"

"Good." He smirked. "I beat your brother's ass."

Isabel laughed. "Even I can beat Art at golf. He's always hated it."

Romero caught her up on how for the most part the few hours he'd spent with her dad had been uneventful. He told her about telling her dad that his old man was in jail and how he didn't ask much else. That seemed to surprise her. "He'll probably be asking me about it."

"You could tell him. I don't care." Since it was Saturday, Isabel's day off, Romero had taken the rest of the day off as well. "So what are you up to? Are you home?"

"No. Actually on my way to a late lunch with my sister."

"Gina?" Romero knew Isabel wasn't exactly on speaking terms with Pat, hadn't been for most of the week, ever since they got into it about Jacob. It had been exactly one week since her day with him at the mall and when Isabel asked Pat to not schedule any more of her time campaigning with him — the argument had ended with Isabel hanging up on her.

"No, Pat."

Romero thought about overhearing Charles on the phone. He remembered the last time Isabel told him she was meeting with Pat it turned out to be a blind date. After last weekend, he wouldn't put anything past Pat now. Maybe she set up some other kind of double date for them now. The heat was on again and he gripped the wheel. "Just the two of you?"

"Yeah, she wants to talk."

He remembered Charles's exact words. *After this, I'm all yours.* Something was up. "You're not lying to me are you, Isabel?" There was a silence on the other end and the heat he felt, now scorched through his veins.

"Why are you calling me a liar, Romero?"

"Is *he* gonna be there?" His heart pounded now like it had when he found out she'd spent the day with Jacob.

"He who?"

"Jacob!"

"No! Why would you think that?" She sounded almost exasperated. "It's just me and Pat."

He stepped on the accelerator, suddenly feeling the need to be with her. The need to look into her eyes when she said it to him. She'd lied to him before, but she'd promised she never would again. "Where are you meeting her?"

"Maxwell's on the base. What is the matter with you? Why are you so upset?"

That only enraged him further. "I'm more than fucking upset. Your sister's up to something. Why the base?"

"That's just where she was at today. So she asked me to meet her there. Jacob's gone, Romero. That's what she called to tell me. He left yesterday and he'll be out at sea for weeks so I don't have to worry about running into him at the campaign office."

Both relief and suspicion seeped through Romero, and he still felt the tension in his arms—his shoulders.

"Are you sure?"

"Yes, now will you tell me what set you off?" She lowered her voice. "Why did you call me Isabel?"

Romero still didn't understand why she hated that so much, but the only time he did feel compelled to call her Isabel was when he felt ready to explode. "Because anytime your sister's involved now, I don't know what to think. I don't trust her for shit."

"Yeah, well you need to start trusting *me*. I hate when you get like this."

As if she could see him, he nodded, taking a deep breath. "I'm sorry, Izzy." He really was. He didn't want her hating anything about him and he could hear it in her voice, she was losing patience with him and that made him nervous. Trying to sound much calmer he asked, "How long are you gonna be?"

The momentary silence made him even more nervous. "An hour, maybe... I miss you."

He exhaled slowly. Finally, something he could smile about but it reminded him of Charles's phone call on the golf course. Maybe Pat cancelled on him last minute to meet up with Isabel instead. Who knew? Who cared? All that mattered is that his Izzy hadn't lied to him. "I miss you too, baby. Hurry home."

He made a U-turn and headed back to the apartment. He'd started heading toward the base as soon as she'd said it. Visions of flipping over the table they all sat at when he got there had crossed his mind. Sal's words came to him suddenly. *The smallest of scuffles with this guy and it'll be all over the papers the next day.* Somehow, he was going to have to get a grip.

*

Pat waved at Isabel from her table. She was on her phone. Isabel made her way to her table. Pat was one of those people who talked as loudly as if she were in the privacy of her own home when on her cell phone. Isabel always walked away from crowds and spoke softly so that no one could hear her conversation. She could hear Pat even before she reached the table. "When will you know how long you'll be gone? Don't they tell you these things?" She paused, giving Isabel an annoyed look as she sat down. "All right, all right. Just let me know as soon as you know something. Okay, honey. I love you." She hung up, tossing her phone in her purse. "I swear I'm getting so sick of these surprise trips they keep sending him on. They expect him to just drop everything and go."

Isabel flipped through the menu, thankful that their first meeting after not speaking for several days didn't feel awkward. "Where are they sending him?"

"Miami. As usual. And then they can't even tell him for sure how long he'll be there. So I have no idea when to expect my husband back."

"That sucks." Isabel's attempt to sound sympathetic was weak at best. This is what her sister wanted after all. And to think Pat wanted Isabel to end up with Jacob who was headed in the same direction. No thanks.

"Bell, the last thing I invited you here for is to argue. But Charles just told me about Romero."

Isabel finally pulled her starving eyes away from the menu. "What about him, Pat?"

"Honey, his dad is in jail and his uncles own a topless bar?" Her sister's mouth hung open and she shook her head. "I-I don't even know where to start."

"Then don't."

"I *have* to. Daddy is running for mayor and his daughter is associated with, dating—"

"*Living with*," Isabel said, taking a sip of her water. "He moved in with me. We're living together now." She loved the way that sounded so she smiled.

Pat pressed her lips together. "Do you have any idea the amount of work that went into petitioning to get dad's name on that ballot? Any idea at all how much work, time and money is going to go into campaigning for him to win this election?"

As much as she was starving, Isabel was one second away from getting up and walking out. "What does any of that have to do with me?"

Pat leaned in and lowered her voice. "You are living with a man whose family runs an establishment that degrades women and whose father is in jail doing time for who knows what. You don't think the papers will have a field day if the word ever gets out?"

Isabel stared at her. She'd never looked at it that way. Would the press really care about her relationship with Romero? She shook her head. "How does Romero's personal life or family's life affect dad's ability to govern a city? You're being ridiculous. I came here to iron things out, but if this is what we're going to argue about then I'm leaving."

Her sister put her hand on her arm. "No, don't leave." She took a deep breath. "Fine. Lets talk about something else."

"Thank you."

"As soon as Charles gets back from this stupid trip of his, I want to throw him a party for his thirtieth birthday. It's not until next month, but since we're going to have so much going on with the campaign, I'll take whatever weekend works out best between now and then. I was thinking maybe you could talk to Valerie about getting me a deal at her restaurant. I understand they have banquet rooms."

Isabel peered at Pat over her menu. Funny, she thought she'd come here to get an apology for the way she'd spoke about Romero on the phone this week. Of course, this lunch was more self-serving for her sister than anything. She should've known. "Sure, I'll ask her."

"I hope the rooms are a good size because I'll be inviting *all* of his friends and fellow Navy mates." Her eyes met Isabel's for a second before continuing to study the menu.

"Oh, they're big enough. How many people did you have in mind?"

"A couple hundred, at least. This is why I wanted you to talk to Valerie for me. It's going to end up costing me a small fortune, so I'm trying to figure out where I can cut down a little."

As promised, the rest of the meal her sister never brought up Romero. Instead, she talked Isabel's ear off about the campaign, then the party for Charles and finally she grilled Isabel about the classes she'd be taking in the fall. She did throw in a few mentions of Jacob and how he'd been sent out as stand-in Captain while the Captain of the ship could recoup from an injury. "Charles says he'll make a great Captain someday."

"Good. I'm happy for him." She really was. "I remember that's all he ever talked about just before he enlisted."

Pat tilted her head. "You were so in love with him, Bell. You really don't feel *anything* for him anymore?"

"First of all, I really don't think I was *ever* in love with him, much less *so* in love."

"Oh, come on. You were with him for over two years and he was your first everything. How could you not be?"

"I dunno, maybe I *loved* him, but honestly, now that I know what being *in* love really feels like, I know I've ever been in love before." For a moment, she wished she could speak of Romero openly with her sister. "I've never felt what I feel for Romero for anyone—ever."

She saw Pat's mouth pinch to the side and she knew right there. That would be the most she'd ever be able to tell her about Romero. "I still think you were in love with Jacob. I *know* he has feelings for you. I also think that if you just gave him a chance—"

"Pat."

Pat lifted her hands up in front of her. "Okay, okay. I'm just saying."

"Well, don't."

On her drive home she thought of what Pat had said about Jacob. But she was one hundred percent sure about it now. Never, not even in the entire two years she'd gone out with Jacob, had she ever experienced what she had with Romero.

Chapter 17
Cici

This was the second time in a couple of weeks that Romero had wandered into a jewelry store at the mall. He'd gone there to check out the laptops at the home electronics store and just like the last time he was there, he ended up at a jewelry store. Just like last time, he told himself he was looking for a nice bracelet, maybe a necklace, something special Isabel could wear that came from him. And like the last time, he ended up looking at the engagement rings.

"Looking for anything in particular?"

He glanced up at the girl behind the counter. "Nah, I'm just browsing." His eyes went back to the rings under the glass.

"Browsing for engagement rings?" He brought his attention back up at the blonde girl. Something about her eyes was very familiar. "No, not really. Just curious, what does something like this go for?" He pointed at a square looking diamond.

When she didn't answer, he glanced up at her. She angled her head slowly to one side, then smiled big. "Oh my God. Is it really you? Moe?"

Romero studied her. He knew her from somewhere but he still couldn't place her face. Then he glanced down at the gold necklace around her neck with the name Cecelia, and it hit him. "Cici?"

"Yeah." She put her hand over her mouth.

"Holy shit!" He took a step back "Are you kidding

me? You look so different." She really did. The last time he'd seen her, *that* night, she had dark brown long hair. Now she wore it in a cute blonde bob. He would've never thought this was the same person.

"So do you! C'mere." She leaned over the counter and held her arms out. He leaned in and hugged her. Her perfume was as strong as he remembered her wearing it even back then.

An older woman walked out of the back. "Cici, you wanna take your lunch now? You've been here four hours."

Cici turned around. "Okay." She turned back to Romero then grabbed her purse from a cabinet inside the rows of glass counters.

He hadn't eaten anything since breakfast and it was almost three. For years, he'd been curious about what had happened to her. "Where you going for lunch?"

She walked out from behind the counter. "Umm, I'm not sure. I'm so sick of everything in the food court."

"How long you been working here? I come here a lot and I've never seen you."

She touched her hair. "Almost a year. You probably have. You just didn't recognize me. I still change my hair color and style a lot."

Romero smiled as they walked around the corner, his favorite restaurant coming into view. "How 'bout Frisco's. You can never get tired of eating there."

"Yeah, but compared to the food court, it's expensive."

"Let's go. I'm buying."

He hoped as much as her appearance had changed, everything else in her life had changed, also. Memories of that night came crashing down on him again. Never

one to beat around the bush, he asked her straight out
once they sat down at a booth. "So you still with that
asshole?"

The smile on her face disappeared and she shook
her head. "No. He's in jail."

That didn't surprise Romero. "Good—for hitting
you?"

"Well, having had two priors for domestic abuse
helped put him away longer, but that's not why he's
in."

She went on to tell him about how the idiot got arrested for assaulting someone at a nightclub and how
he'd pulled a knife so the charge was heavier. That
coupled with the two recent arrests for assaulting her,
he was looking at doing fifteen years minimum.

Romero didn't even realize he'd fisted his hands
until the waitress interrupted them to take their order.
He ordered his usual and Cici ordered a chicken salad.

"A salad? You don't come to Frisco's for a salad."

"Have you had their chicken salad?"

Romero shook his head giving her a disgusted look.

"It's the best. You're probably thinking it's this
dainty little salad but it's not. It's a monster. Watch,
you'll see."

After their food came, she told him about finding
out that she was pregnant just after Fred had been sen-
tenced. She'd been devastated, but there was no way
she was *not* having it. So she now had a two-year-old
boy. She showed him a picture. In it, the little guy wore
jean overalls and nothing else. He sat on the grass hugging a dog.

"His name's Moe."

Romero's eye shot up and met hers. "Your kid or
the dog?"

She laughed. "My son. I never forgot you, Moe." Her smile dissipated slowly. "You're the reason why I quit. I knew if I went back, I'd end up being with you eventually. I wasn't sure what I wanted back then but I knew what almost happened that night *would* happen, and I was afraid of what Freddy might do. He wasn't right."

Romero stared at her. "So you named your kid after... *me*?"

She nodded and he saw her face tinge with color. "I also liked the uniqueness of the name. Not too many Moes out there."

Romero didn't have the heart to tell her that wasn't even his name. But it's what she knew him by, so he supposed it's all that mattered. He glanced back down at little Moe again, feeling very strange about this news. "I'm flattered" is all he could think of to say. But he wasn't sure flattered was the right word to describe what he was feeling. She named her *kid* after *him*. She'd hardly known him.

"The moment I met you," she said, digging into her salad. "There was something about your eyes. Your uncles, they spoke so fondly of you. I had some of my best laughs listening to the stories they told of you growing up. Then that night..." She stopped moving her fork and just stared at her salad. "There was so much passion in your eyes. You were beyond concerned about my safety and me not going back home to Fred." She shrugged and moved her salad around again. "I dunno. You just stuck with me. They told me I was having a girl so for months I focused on all these girl names. Then when he turned out to be a boy, I was at a loss. My sister told me to think of people in my life that stood out for good reason. Then I thought of you and it just felt... perfect."

Romero took in everything she said. He thought about all the nights he'd spent thinking of her and beating himself up for not having reacted faster and maybe preventing Fred hitting her. It burned him up for months. Now after all this time he finds out she'd thought *that* much of him? He didn't even know how to feel about that. Half way through their lunch, his phone buzzed and he checked it. It was a text from Isabel.

Can't wait for this day to be over. Work is sucking today and I think I'm coming down with something. How's your day going? ... P.S. I love you.

For the first time since he'd decided to have lunch with Cici, it dawned on him that Isabel might not be thrilled about it. He'd certainly have issues with her going to lunch with a dude, even if it was just an old friend. And he wouldn't even classify Cici as an old friend. She was someone he once had every intention of banging. Those days seemed like another lifetime now. A time he never wanted to revisit.

His life had changed so much since he'd met Isabel. She was what had been missing his entire life. She grounded him—kept the ticking time bomb in him at a safe calm, something new to him. Although it'd been close to going off a few times, he'd never gone this long. If it weren't for his need to keep that side of him from her, he knew he would've had a major meltdown each and every one of the times he'd come so close. But *she* was the reason why he hadn't. He liked the new-found *somewhat* self-control he felt when he was with her. He was getting better at it, too. He'd never felt the kind of love he felt for Izzy, but he didn't just love her. He *needed* her.

"Something wrong?"

He glanced up when he realized he'd been staring at his phone—Izzy's text—that whole time. "I'm sorry. Give me a sec." He texted Isabel back.

Sorry you're having a bad day. Mine's been okay. I'll tell you about it tonight. I love you, too. Miss you.

"Nah, nothing wrong. The text just reminded me of something." That maybe he shouldn't be here—with her.

They finished their food. Cici hadn't exaggerated about the salad. It *was* huge. She hadn't even finished it. Cici had to get back to work and he had a sudden urge to be home. He walked with her halfway back to the jewelry store, but stopped when he reached the direction he needed to go toward the electronics store. He glanced at his watch. Isabel would be off soon.

"It was good catching up, Cici. I'm glad you're doing better now and I'm glad that dick's out of your life."

She smiled and nodded then to his surprise, she hugged him again, tighter this time and she held on longer so he had to embrace her. "I'm so glad I got to see you again." She finally pulled away. "I thought about stopping by the bar a few times. But then I'd always chickened out."

"I haven't worked there in years."

"That's right." She stepped back. He'd told her a little about his security firm over lunch. But mostly they'd talked about her and little Moe.

"I'd love for you to meet my son. You wanna take my number? My sister sometimes brings him to see me here at work." Romero pulled out his phone and programmed her phone number in as she rattled it off. "Send me an empty text just so I can program your number in mine." Romero did and she smiled when she pulled out her phone and saw the happy face he'd sent. "I'll text you and you know, if you're around maybe you can come by."

"Um…" He didn't want to make any promises. He didn't want to stir up any trouble with Isabel.

"Whatever, if you can you can. If not it's no big deal. At least now I know it's a possibility."

Feeling bad, he smiled. "Nah, text me. If I'm in the area I'll stop by. Sure—why not?"

"Oh and that ring you were looking at. It's pretty expensive. If you're seriously thinking about getting it, *please* come back and see me. I'll get you a good deal and I could definitely use the commission."

"For sure." He smiled.

They said goodbye and he went into the electronics store—the reason he'd gone to the mall to begin with, but with Cici and little Moe on his mind he couldn't even concentrate.

Isabel's car was already there when he drove into the parking lot of their apartment building. The whole ride home he'd gotten a little more nervous the closer he got. For a moment, he considered not mentioning Cici. But he'd never been one to lie or hold back anything. Most importantly, that's not how he wanted their relationship to be. He expected her not to keep anything from him, so he should do the same. Maybe if Cici hadn't told him about naming her kid after him, he wouldn't be so damn nervous. He was still trying to understand it so he was sure Isabel wouldn't.

She wasn't in the kitchen like she normally was when he got home around that time. "Izzy?" He threw his keys on the counter along with his wallet and sunglasses.

"In here." He heard her weak voice coming from the bedroom.

He walked in and she lay on the bed looking pale with a bright red nose. "What's wrong, baby?"

"I'm definitely coming down with something. A couple of the kids have been sick this week and I must've picked up something from them." He walked to the bed and she held her arm out. "Babe, maybe you should stay away. I'm sure I'm contagious, and I really feel like crap. I don't want you to get sick."

Stay away? "But I wanna take care of you. Did you take something already?"

"Yeah, I took some flu medicine and," she pointed at the water bottle on the nightstand. There was also a box of tissues. "I'm set."

"You need to eat, too."

"I'm not really feeling hungry." She told him about her day and the rowdy ass kids who sometimes said the most disrespectful things. He swore if he ever got them in a room alone he'd show them a thing or two about disrespecting their teacher—his girl.

Then there was the moment he wasn't looking forward to. Isabel wasn't like him. She'd likely not even care, but he hated that he'd stupidly open the door for her to think it okay to do things like that.

"So how was your day?"

"Same ole shit."

She pointed to the swear jar they'd started the week prior. He took the walk of shame and dropped a quarter in it. He'd asked her before if he could just put a couple of dollars in there for the next times he flubbed. But she said taking the walk of shame was part of the punishment.

He got right to it. "I ran into an old... employee of

my uncles at the mall and we had lunch."

He had her attention immediately and she sat up. "One of the topless waitresses?"

Okay, maybe telling her she'd been an employee of his uncles was not the best idea but she wasn't exactly a friend, and acquaintance sounded too suspicious. He should've put more thought into this on his way home, damn it. "Yeah, from a few years back. The last time I'd seen her, I was working the door at the bar, and her boyfriend showed up and slapped her around." He thought about it again for a moment. "I'd never been so fucki-... so mad in my life. She never came back after that and I always wondered what happened to her."

Isabel eyed him. "Why?"

He was surprised she'd let him slide on the swearing but she seemed more interested in Cici now. "I dunno. I guess I just wondered if she was even alive. You know being in that kind of relationship, you never know. She looked real different. I didn't even recognize her—works at Dan's Jewels at the mall."

"So you had lunch with her?"

Romero sat at the edge of the bed. "Yeah, it was her lunch hour and I hadn't eaten since breakfast so we grabbed something together."

Isabel's expression was a strange one. He could usually read all her expressions but he couldn't get a fix for this one. Maybe it was because she was sick. She did reach for a tissue and blew her nose.

Romero rubbed her leg. "You sure I can't make you something to eat?"

"No, make yourself something. I really don't have an appetite right now."

"Me either. I'm still stuffed. It was a late lunch."

She finished wiping her nose and threw the tissue in the wastebasket. "Whatcha have?"

He started taking his shoes off. "Frisco's." he kicked off his shoe.

She didn't say anything for a moment, then finally in a tone so unlike Izzy she asked, "You took her to Frisco's?"

He turned to her. Whoa — here he'd thought he'd seen all her expressions. He'd never seen this one, but it wasn't good. Her eyebrows pinched tight and there was an almost incredulous glare in her eyes. "I didn't *take* her there, Izzy. We were already at the mall. She said she was sick of the food court so I suggested — "

"*You* suggested it?"

"I like the food there. What's the big deal?"

"I can't believe you don't know what the big deal is!" Her eyes began to well up and he felt a weird panic creep through him.

He tried leaning closer but she pushed him away. "Why are you getting so mad?" She started to get up. "No, Izzy. Stay in bed you're not feeling well."

"I need to go to the restroom." She pushed his hand away again, walked out of the room and into the restroom, slamming the door behind her.

He waited and waited but after she'd been in there way too long, he knocked on the door. "Babe, you okay?"

"I'm fine." She didn't sound fine.

"Are you crying?"

She walked out and sure as shit her eyes were all red, making him feel that much worse. She tried walking past him but he pulled her to him. "Seriously? You're that upset about this?"

That seemed to make her even angrier then she

stopped and sniffed him. "Is that her perfume all over you? What *else* did you do with her?"

"Nothing! She hugged me goodbye." Damn Cici and her strong ass perfume.

"Get away from me!" She tried squirming away but he leaned her against the wall with his body and held her tight. "I'm sorry. Okay? I swear to you, if I would've known you'd be this upset I would have never—"

"Never what?" She slipped out of his hold and he let her. Only because he'd never seen her this angry. "Gone to lunch with another girl or taken her to *our* place?"

He followed her back into the room. "No, I wasn't even thinking about it like that."

"The way you are, I was under the impression that things of this nature were out of the question."

Romero felt himself heating up. "They are!"

She spun around. "Oh, really? But not for you?"

"No, it's just that Cici, well... she's different." Her eyes grew even wider. "No. I don't mean like—"

"Good to know. I'll make sure I only do things with guys who are *different*."

She started to walk but Romero grabbed her arm. "What the fuck does that mean?"

She glared down at his hand on her arm and he immediately loosened his hold. "Get your hand off me."

"First tell me what that means."

"Let go of me!" He did. "Get out."

He stood there unable to believe how his lunch with Cici had escalated into this. Her words still burned him but he was mad at himself for grabbing her arm like that. "I'm sorry."

"I said get out." Her tone softened but just a bit. "You don't have to leave, just get out of my room. You shouldn't be here anyway. I'll get you sick." She coughed before getting into bed.

He knew she'd only said what she did because she was mad, and hurt. But he hoped to hell she didn't actually act on it to prove a point. "Izzy, I get it. Okay? I made a mistake. I was stupid. I'm sorry. It'll never happen again." He got down on his knee next to the bed and touched her arm. "Please don't do anything just to make things even... you have *no* idea how crazy that would make me."

She rolled her eyes. "You really think I have no idea?"

"Promise me."

"I'm not promising anything right now, Romero." She grabbed another tissue. "And you really shouldn't be touching me. I'm telling you. You're gonna get sick." She shook her head after blowing her nose. "Go. You can sleep in Valerie's room tonight."

Romero noticed how her pink-rimmed eyes looked so dreary. She really was sick. He stood up and kissed her head. "Let me know if you need anything. Okay?"

She nodded and made herself comfortable in her bed. He walked out feeling like the biggest idiot on the planet. *Their place.* Of course.

Chapter 18
Suspicions

Falling in and out of delirium, Isabel didn't even know what time or what day it was. She turned to see Romero walk into the room. "Hey, how you feeling?"

She didn't respond. She remembered she was mad at him but she couldn't even remember why. "I'm still mad at you." She heard the rough words rasp out of her mouth, felt the burn in her throat and tightness in her chest.

Romero began to apologize, then his expression changed and he touched her forehead. "Izzy, you're burning up!"

"Huh?" In such a daze, she glanced around expecting to see flames.

Romero pulled the blankets off her. "But I'm freezing!" she said, trying to pull the blankets back on. Her clothes clung to her, wet with perspiration, and she began to shiver. She tried in vain to get the blankets back from Romero's hands. "Please! I'm so cold!" Just speaking scorched her throat and her entire body ached as Romero sat her up.

"I know." His voice was as panicked as hers was. "Baby, we gotta get this off you, *now*."

She didn't even realize she was crying until she heard her own whiny voice, "Why are you doing this to me?"

"Because I *have* to," he said, pulling her top off and then helping her up. "We gotta get your temperature down." He put his hand on her back. "Fuck, I should've checked on you sooner, you're on fire. I'm sorry, babe. I just wanted to let you sleep."

Her eyes burned when she blinked and her body shivered uncontrollably. Everything after that was a blur of her crying and trying to fight him while he held her under the cold shower as he tried frantically to calm her explaining why it was necessary.

Then there was a trip to the emergency room, her parents and sister arrived just as they were releasing her. Pat was angry that Romero hadn't contacted them sooner but he explained that in his haste he'd forgotten to take Isabel's phone. He didn't have any of their numbers. By the time Isabel was well enough to think straight and give him their numbers, they'd already been there for hours. "You're coming home with us," her father announced flatly. Pat nodded as Isabel held on tight to Romero.

"It's not pneumonia but the doctors said you're borderline. You need to be watched very closely." Her mother attempted to pull her away from Romero.

"I can watch her," Romero said.

"Don't be silly, the doctor said she'll be out the whole week. Don't you have to work?"

"I'll take the week off."

"I'd feel better if she was at home with us." Her mother's words were firm but cautious.

"You should go with mom and dad, Bell. Pneumonia is no joke. Don't take any chances."

Isabel just wanted to go home to her own bed. Her fever was finally down but she felt completely drained and her body still ached all over. Speaking alone, left her breathless.

"What do you want, Izzy? We'll do whatever you

want."

"I wanna go home." Her words were barely a whisper and she inhaled deeply, those four little words taking so much out of her.

That's all she had to say. "I'm taking her home. I'll take care of her this week. Don't worry."

Though they tried to argue, the decision had been made. Romero was by her side the entire week. Preparing her meals, bringing them to her in bed, making sure she took her meds on time. The only times he left was when her mother and sisters had stopped by to check in on her. He said he'd take advantage of them being there to go stock up on more meds and groceries but she knew his aversion to being in the same room with Pat was the real reason. The two had barely exchanged greetings but they'd both managed to be civil.

Isabel felt guilty about the amount of time Romero had taken away from his work, but even when her mother offered to stay with her for a few days so that he could go back to work he insisted on being there with her. She couldn't get over how devoted he was to taking care of her. She'd been a little surprised with the showers they took together. When he'd gently sponged her there was no sexual connotation at all. The only thing he was interested in was her well-being. Even when she teased him by touching him sensually in the shower, he'd warned it would be too much exertion for her.

His initial reaction to the doctor saying she may have pneumonia, before the chest x-ray, he'd gone white. But it wasn't until after the x-ray came back negative that he told her he'd heard of people dying of it.

By the end of the week when she was feeling better,

neither had spoken of Cici or Frisco's. His actions that whole week confirmed that there was no way he would ever deliberately hurt her. He'd made a mistake and she forgave him. However, the sting of knowing he tainted her memory of their first dinner together, still lingered.

Romero tried to convince her to take another few days off until she was feeling a hundred percent better, but she insisted she was. A week had been more than enough and she needed to get out.

Though she'd forgiven him, she still couldn't get two little words out of her head. *She's different.* What did that mean? Had he dated her? He'd probably slept with her. Valerie let her in on that much about him. Through out the years there had been no shortage of hussies willing to jump in bed with the big sexy bouncer. She was sure the women who worked at his uncles' topless bar didn't have qualms about casual sex, especially with someone who looked like Romero.

Isabel shook off the jealousy. He'd been wonderful — more than wonderful — this past week. She would just put it behind her.

Valerie left her a message about the deal she could work out for Charles' party so Isabel called her that evening when she got home from her first day back at work.

"Only thing is," Valerie said. "For a room that size all we have available in the next few weeks is either a Friday night or a Sunday afternoon. All Saturdays are completely booked for the next two months."

To Isabel's surprise, her sister wanted to book *that* Friday. "This week? That's so soon."

"No, it isn't. I already have everything planned. His gift, the band — they just finished telling me they're available for the next two weeks and it's perfect because Charles won't be back from his trip until Thursday. I can run around all week without him getting wind of it. Tell her to book it."

After calling Valerie, she told Romero about it and he frowned. "Babe, I don't think you're up for parties just yet."

"Trust me. It's not like my sister throws these wild parties. Think of my dad's dinner. A bunch of stuffy suits sitting around listening to a boring jazz band." She sat next to him on the sofa. He'd brought his plasma television over from his apartment and promptly hung it in her front room. It was his new favorite place to sit and relax.

He put his arm around her, his eyes still full of worry. "I can't be there that night. I gotta work some party over in La Jolla Shores."

"That's okay. My whole family will be there." She stroked his leg. "Not to mention Alex and Valerie. My sister invited them and Valerie said they'd go."

He touched her face. His expression reminded her of how he wanted to call 911 that first night, because her fever was so high. Somehow, she managed to convince him to just drive her to the emergency room. "Don't worry. I'll leave early. I'm sure it'll be boring anyway. But I have to show up for at least a little while."

"How you feeling?" The concern in his eyes warmed her.

"Great," she said, kissing him softly.

"You didn't get tired or feel weak all day?"

She smiled. "No, not at all." She kissed him deeper this time. "In fact." She stood up, tugging his hand. "C'mon. I think a week of not *exerting* myself has been long enough." She flashed him the most seductive smile she could.

"Are you sure?"

God, was she ever. "Yes, Dr. Romero. I think it's time to show you my appreciation for the past week."

Even as hesitant as he seemed, a week had been more than long enough for both of them. He seemed just as ready as she was.

*

That week she had another *collaboration* day and was off again—with no pay, of course. She planned ahead, making one of Valerie's favorite treats for lunch and invited her over. They hadn't had a good girl talk session in a while and Isabel was in need for one.

Thoughts of Cici's perfume all over Romero and those two little words still lingered. Valerie dug into the homemade pizza eagerly. "Oh my God, this is so good."

Isabel smiled. She missed sitting and talking to Valerie like this. Valerie gushed all about married life and how wonderful things were so far. "He keeps bringing up babies though, and I'm just beginning to adjust to managing an office on my own. I'm afraid to take time off right now. I know I'll have to if I have a baby."

"Well, why don't you just set up a date? Compromise—say two years from now or something."

Valerie shrugged. "He actually almost had me convinced. I had to switch my birth controls pills. I was getting migraines and the doctor said it might be because I switched brands a few months ago. I'm going back to the old ones but I had to give it a month to get these out of my system. Alex tried persuading me to just stay off them. Said we won't actively try," she laughed. "As if he can go even a day without *trying*."

Isabel laughed, then felt her face warm when she thought of Romero's sexual appetite. She was glad Valerie was too busy eating to notice her flushed face.

"So how are things with you and Romero? I think that was so sweet of him to take the whole week off to take care of you."

Isabel nodded in agreement and smiled. "Things are good. We've had a few intense moments here and there. And my sister hasn't exactly helped. But otherwise we're... good."

Valerie stopped and stared at her. "But..."

Usually it was Isabel who read Valerie well enough to know something was bothering her. In the last couple of years Valerie had become pretty good at reading Isabel, too. Isabel chewed the corner of her lip. "I dunno. It's nothing. I'm probably just being silly."

"You? Please. You're never silly. What is it?"

Isabel told her about Romero's run-in with Cici and her ridiculous outburst when he told they'd eaten at Frisco's.

"I don't think it's ridiculous. I would've been pissed myself. Personally, I think you let him off easy."

Isabel picked at her slice of pizza, thinking about it. "Thing is, when I called him on it, saying I guess it's okay for me to do things with my guy friends he said it wasn't but Cici was ...*different*. I don't know what that means."

Valerie's eyebrows pinched. "Did you ask him?"

"No, he took it back real quick, saying it wasn't what I was thinking and at that point I was so pissed and feeling so sick I told him to just leave my room. Then after that, I was so deliriously sick for the next whole week, we never brought it up again." She continued to pick at her food, her appetite deteriorating by the minute. "That's not even the worst part about it." Valerie had stopped eating, giving Isabel her full attention. "He reeked of perfume that night. He said he just hugged her goodbye, but it made me sick to my stomach."

Valerie touched her hand. "Ask him what he meant. I never heard of him having any serious relationships and I've never heard of a Cici. I'll definitely be asking Alex about it though. Still I wouldn't let this go and not that I think you shouldn't trust him, but if it were me, I'd raise an eyebrow the next time he mentions going to the *mall*."

After her lunch with Valerie, Isabel ran a few errands. Romero knew she was off and said he'd be home early. She thought of what Valerie said. She wouldn't even know how to bring up the subject of Cici without making things weird. But she knew one thing, if she didn't, it would eat away at her.

That evening after they'd eaten, Romero sat in the front room tinkering with the new laptop he'd purchased that day. Isabel finished cleaning up the kitchen then walked into the front room, noticing the bag he'd pulled the laptop out of. MicroTech—the electronic store—at the mall. "So you were at the mall again?"

Romero didn't even look up. "Yeah, I've been there almost every day this week. I finally had Sal meet me there today. I just couldn't decide what laptop to go with." He looked up and smiled. "Sal's too much. He actually brought papers he printed out from the research he'd done, comparing specs between the laptops I told him I was interested in. But he did help me decide." He turned back to the laptop on the coffee table.

"Now I just gotta get all the software uploaded and transfer all my files."

Flags had immediately gone up at the mention that he'd been there every day this week. This was the first she'd heard him mention it. "So did you see Cici this week?"

Romero looked up at her again and she searched his face for any signs of guilt or alarm. She saw something, but not guilt.

"No, I didn't." He held his hand out for her and she took it. He pulled her to him, making her sit and then kissed her. "I hope you're not still mad about that. I know we never got a chance to talk about it, but honest to God if I had known you'd be that upset about it, I would've *never* gone to lunch with her. And that whole Frisco's thing." He winced. "I swear I'm an idiot. I fucked up. I wasn't even thinking about that. I'm sorry. I really am."

Isabel noted how up until the very end he'd been doing pretty good about cleaning up his language. She tried to smile but something still gnawed at her. "What did you mean when you said she's different?"

Romero sat back and she brought her leg up under her. "I was just curious what her story was. For a long time I blamed myself for not having anticipated that fuc—" He pressed his lips together then cleared his throat. "Her boyfriend slapping her like that. He did it right in front of me."

"Did you two ever..." She couldn't even say it— didn't even want to imagine it.

"No. I told you she had a boyfriend."

Romero's guilt over Cici's boyfriend slapping her raised another question. "So why did her boyfriend slap her?"

That's when she saw it. It was so slight if she hadn't been staring in his eyes she might've missed it—guilt. She knew it. This wasn't just someone that worked for his uncles. There was more to it.

Romero opened his mouth then closed it as if he'd changed his mind.

"What? Just tell me." Isabel's heart rate had already picked up. She didn't want to have another outburst but this was stupid. "It's in the past. What difference does it make now? Unless you're hiding something from me."

"No. I'm not hiding anything." He squeezed her hand. "She was on her break. I was working the door outside. Her boyfriend showed up and saw her flirting with me. He was drunk and belligerent so he started going off on her. I actually had to pin his ass up against a car. I thought he'd calmed down and I let him go. That's when he slapped her."

Isabel saw his jaw clenched and how much that still upset him. She felt almost ashamed that instead of being warmed by Romero being so affected about a woman being abused, she was jealous. After all this time, something that happened to Cici brought out so much emotion in him. Remembering Cici's perfume all over Romero, she stared at him, wanting to tell him she didn't want to hear of him around her ever again, instead she asked, "So she's okay now? Did she marry the guy?"

"No, he's in jail now. Good thing, too. Otherwise her ass would probably still be with him."

And that would be a bad thing because he beat her. Isabel told herself—no other reason.

Romero pulled her to him and she leaned against his chest, inhaling deeply. Not a trace of Cici's perfume.

"I love you, Izzy." He rubbed her back. "I already messed up once. I promise it'll never happen again."

Isabel glanced up at his face and smiled. She wasn't that kind of girlfriend, insecure and suspicious. That's the last impression she wanted to give him, but something about this Cici girl rubbed her the wrong way. She'd let it go for now, but like Valerie said, she'd raise an eyebrow every time he mentioned being at the mall.

Chapter 19
Michael

It was early and the party in La Jolla Shores celebrating some real estate tycoon's eightieth birthday was winding down. Romero had a feeling when he saw the guests arrive. This bunch of geriatrics wouldn't be partying into the night. He'd already texted Isabel to tell her he would make it to Charles's party after all. Not that he was looking forward to spending time around Pat, but at least Alex would be there and he could probably stop and have a few drinks downstairs at the restaurant to help loosen him up before heading up to party with all the stiffs.

Once the party was down to a small amount of people and he knew his guys could handle it without him, he left. It was a good thing they'd asked for the security staff to blend in with the party goers. He didn't have to stop and change. He did, however make one stop.

He'd lied to Isabel earlier that week but only because he didn't want to ruin the surprise. If he'd admitted to seeing Cici earlier that week, she would've for sure have wanted to know why. He'd tell her tonight and hoped that once she saw the surprise, she'd understand why he lied.

His heart sped up as he neared the jewelry store. He'd almost gone with the earrings—diamond studs. Cici was actually the one who talked him into getting the ring. Talk of marriage hadn't even come up between him and Isabel. Even though they were living together now, he still liked the idea of giving her something that gave their relationship that much more validity. He hated to admit it, but having her family see just how serious he was about Isabel had a lot to do with his decision as well. He'd called ahead to let Cici know he was stopping by to pick up the ring.

Cici had explained giving her a ring didn't have to mean they were getting engaged. People bought rings for all sorts of reasons: promise rings, anniversary rings or just to say I love you. He still wasn't sure what his exact reason would be, he just couldn't wait to see it on her. "Is it ready?"

Cici looked up and smiled, her perfume heavier this time than it'd been all week as if she'd just sprayed herself. "You're gonna love it."

He'd picked out what Cici referred to as a princess cut diamond. He'd seen plenty of women wearing round diamonds. He liked that it was square. He had to be sneaky and snag one of Isabel's rings from her jewelry box to get the right size. If he'd gone with the one carat he could've paid in cash, but once he saw what a two carat looked like, he had to have it. Only now, even with Cici hooking him up, he'd still be paying it off for the next year. It didn't matter. His Izzy was worth it.

Cici had been more than ecstatic. Apparently, this was one of her biggest commission earnings to date.

She brought out the small box from the back and came all the way around the counter to hand it to him. He'd already paid the down payment and the paperwork was all done. Only reason he hadn't taken it home yet was because it had to be sized and Cici had them give it an extra polish. She opened the box. The ring sparkled brilliantly. It was perfect. He'd made the right choice. Isabel was going to love it.

After handing it to him, Cici hugged him again, and though he almost didn't, he felt bad not hugging her back, so he brought his arms around her waist and hugged her. "You have no idea," she whispered, her arms still around him, holding him tight. "How much this commission is going to come in handy. Thank you for coming back to me. I really, *really* appreciate it."

He told her she was welcome but still, she didn't let go. "My sister's always going on and on about how we all have an angel looking out for us." She squeezed him even harder. "If you had any idea what this money means at this time in my life. You'd know why I'm calling you my angel right now." She kissed him on the cheek and finally pulled away slowly.

After hearing and seeing how grateful Cici was about her commission he was glad now that he'd gone back to her to get the ring. Since Isabel had been so upset about the whole Frisco's thing, he'd actually considered going to another jewelry store and avoiding Cici altogether. But knowing she was a single mom, and since she *had* asked him to, he knew now he hadn't made a mistake going back to her.

The whole way to Moreno's, Romero kept sniffing himself to see if he smelled of Cici. Even sick, Isabel had smelled the perfume on him and it wasn't even as bad that day as today. But the smell had penetrated so badly into his nose he couldn't tell anymore if he smelled or not.

When he got to the restaurant, he placed the bag with the ring in the trunk of his car. He wanted to give it her later when they were alone. He stopped at the bar before going up. Sal was there micro-managing some of the newer bartenders. "Will you stop and have a drink with me, ass?"

Sal frowned but walked over to where Romero sat. "I don't usually drink while on duty but you've always been such a bad influence." He grabbed two beers and handed one to Romero then popped one open for himself.

"Good," Romero said, dropping a twenty in front of him. "And I'm gonna need something stronger than a beer before heading up there."

"Your money's no good here, Romero." Sal shoved the twenty back at him and pulled out a bottle of tequila. Romero frowned. Ever since he started his security business and now that the restaurant was so busy, they'd asked for his services quite a few times. Romero always complied but when it came time to pay him he took but a fraction of what he normally charged his clients. These guys were like family to him—no way were they paying him his regular rate. So now, he was never allowed to pay for his damn drinks.

"I heard you played doctor all last week?" Sal placed the shot of tequila in front of Romero.

Romero downed the shot, remembering the sheer terror he'd felt when he realized how bad Isabel was. "Yeah, Izzy got pretty damn sick there for a minute—scared the shit outta me."

"So what was it?"

"Bronchitis, bordering on pneumonia." Romero tapped the bar with the empty tequila glass and took a swig of his beer.

Sal stared at him for a second. "Don't you think you should take it easy? Isn't her whole family up there?"

"I ain't looking to get a buzz, I just wanna relax the muscles a little before I have to be around her fucking sister. I can't stand the bitch."

Sal frowned and glanced at the lady sitting next to Romero. "Will you tone it down? I thought you said you were working on that?"

He had a few more shots and a couple of beers when his phone buzzed in his pocket—a text—from Alex.

Where are you? This is boring as shit.

Alex had texted him earlier asking if he was going to be there. Seems he wasn't exactly a willing participant either but since Valerie wanted to go to this thing, he said he was taking one for the team.

Romero laughed, feeling a lot more relaxed than when he got there. "Get me one more for the road." He tapped the shot glass on the bar.

"I really don't think you should," Sal warned.

Romero tapped it again ignoring the warning and texted Alex back.

Already here. Be up there in a minute.

When he got off the barstool, he realized that maybe he *had* had a little too much. He smiled—he'd be fine.

As he walked through the restaurant, he began to regret that last shot but he was no lightweight. He'd been hammered plenty of times in the past. This was nothing. He noticed the couple at the bottom of the stairs from the other side of the room. They appeared to be arguing—always so much fucking drama.

That's why he loved his Izzy. Only reason she'd given him a hard time about Cici that *one* time, was because she wasn't feeling well. But the last time she'd brought it up, she was cool about the whole thing. And why? Because she was perfect—that's fucking why. The man tried to kiss the girl but she jerked away from him and walked off. He followed after her as she stormed out the restaurant. Romero chuckled.

By the time he reached the stairs, he'd acknowledged that maybe he was a little drunk. It dawned on him just then, that since he'd met Isabel he hadn't been drinking like he used to. It'd been a while since he'd been this juiced.

He walked upstairs taking in deep breaths, then made a beeline to the restroom before going into the banquet room. He splashed some water on his face. "You're fine," he whispered at himself in the mirror. A few more minutes passed, then he splashed his face again and dried off, fixing his hair a little.

Feeling well enough, he walked back out to the hallway. The same guy who'd been arguing with his girlfriend was out there on his phone. Romero recognized the suspenders and the rust orange shirt. As he turned in Romero's direction, he saw it was Charles. Romero did a double take. Okay, maybe there was more than one guy here with suspenders and that same shirt.

Charles hung up and smiled at him, reaching out his hand. "How's it going, Romero?"

"It's going good. How's the party?"

"Good, good. She really got me. I had no idea."

As they walked in together, Romero glanced around casually, curious to see how many other guys in suspenders and an ugly-ass orange shirt were in there. But the first thing that caught his eye was Isabel's table. Valerie and a very bored-looking Alex sat with her. The band played some sleeper jazz music. Romero almost chuckled. That is, until he saw Pat walk up to her table with a guy in a Navy uniform. Isabel seemed to know him. Romero started toward them.

What the hell was her sister up to now?

Isabel smiled at him when she saw him coming and then turned to Pat and said something. Pat's eyes were immediately on him, her expression hardened the second their eyes met. "Yeah, I see you, bitch," Romero said under his breath. "Did you think I wasn't gonna be here again tonight?"

Pat walked away with the guy before Romero reached the table. Romero patted Alex's shoulder as he passed him. "'Bout time," Alex said.

He hugged Valerie, before sitting down next to Isabel. She slipped her hand into his and was about to kiss him, but he pulled back a bit. "Who's that guy your sister brought over?"

Isabel's brow pinched slightly. "A friend of Charles."

"Why'd she bring him over to you?"

"To say hello. I hadn't seen him in a while." She searched his eyes. "What's wrong with you?"

The heat he normally felt about Pat doing this kind of shit was more intense this time. He was *so* sick of her. "Nothing's wrong with me. What's wrong with you?" Isabel almost pulled her hand out of his but he held it. The waiter came by and Romero asked for a beer then brought his eyes back to Isabel.

"Hey, what took you so damn long?" Alex asked, then lowered his voice and leaned in closer to Isabel and Romero adding. "This party is a real sleeper."

Valerie shushed him. Romero didn't take his eyes off Isabel. "I was downstairs with Sal, having a couple drinks."

"A couple?" Isabel's face soured. "Your *breath* is giving me a buzz."

Romero ignored the comment. "When's your sister

gonna stop playing her fucking games?"

"Nice. So you have a few drinks and you forget all about trying to clean up your act?"

Romero took a deep breath in an attempt to calm himself, but it was so much harder when he'd had a few. For him alcohol was a toss up, it either calmed him or did just the opposite and if he'd known what he would be walking into, he would've never had that last shot. He squeezed her hand. "Your sister does that to me."

She must've seen it in his face because she touched his cheek with the back of her hand. "Please stop," she whispered. "*He* asked *her* about me. She mentioned I was here and he's the one that wanted to come over a say hello. That's it—nothing more."

Was she kidding? That only pissed him off more. "Why was he asking about you? Who is this guy?" Romero glanced around. He spotted the guy by the bar and sure enough he was looking in their direction. "Is he someone you went out with?" Romero stared him down. He had to get hold it together. If the guy didn't stop looking their way he was but one breath away from standing up and asking if he had a fucking problem.

Isabel's fingers touched his chin, turning his face back to her and looked him in the eye. "*Please* don't do this now. I'll tell you about it later."

"Tell me what?" He was done. If her sister had pulled another stunt, he wasn't holding back this time. "Is this another ex-boyfriend?"

Isabel stood up and held her hand out for him to take. He stood but turned back to the guy who had finally stopped looking their way.

"Where you going?" Alex asked as they walked

past him.

"We'll be back," Isabel answered for him.

For the first time Romero noticed just how sexy the dress Isabel wore was. He'd never seen her in it. Here she didn't even think he was going to make the party until he texted her earlier. The heat inundated him. "Babe, why are you wearing this?" he said, as he caught up to her and walked next to her.

"Why not? Don't you like it?"

"Yeah, but I wasn't gonna be here." He stopped right in front of her. He knew he was being obnoxious. But this whole thing was making him crazy. What was Isabel going to tell him about this guy later and why was she dressed like this if he wasn't supposed to be here? "So why the fuck would you wear something so..."

Her expression went hard and this time *she* spoke through her teeth. "You texted me you were coming before I left the apartment. I thought you'd like it. I bought it for *you*."

He stared at her, his heart still thudding against his chest. All he could think of was how much he hated Pat. "Oh."

She started walking again and he followed her. They walked out of the banquet room and she took him to a corner, near the stairs. "What is the matter with you? How can you just blow in there like that and start a fight?"

"I'm not fighting with you. I'm just sick of your sister."

"She didn't *do* anything."

He held her face in his hands and kissed her but his heart was still hammering away. "I'm sorry. Okay? Just tell me one thing."

"What?"

He knew he had to stop. She was going to see him for what he really was. He already saw that she was losing patience with him. But he couldn't. "Is that an ex-boyfriend?"

"No!"

"Then why was he asking about you?"

Finally, he saw the irritation in her eyes weaken and he knew he had good reason to be suspicious. "That's Michael."

Romero stared at her. "Michael?"

"Yeah," She put her hands around his wrists. His hands were still on her face. "The guy she set me up on the blind date with."

It suddenly came to Romero. "Is that who that is?" He took his hands off her face. "She invited a guy she's trying to set you up with here tonight?" *Fucking bitch!*

Before he could walk away, she grabbed his hand and pulled him back. "Romero, he was Charles' friend before he was the guy she set me up with. This *is* a party for *Charles*, remember?"

She was irritated again and he stared at her exasperated eyes, trying to calm down. She walked closer to him and to his surprise, hugged him. "Baby, you have to stop this." She stopped then pulled away. "What do you — *Who* do you smell like?"

Ah, hell. "I stopped at the mall."

She took a step back, her expression just as fierce as the night he told her about Frisco's. "To see *her*?"

"No, not to see her." Shit he didn't want to tell her now. The whole damn thing would be ruined. "I'll tell you about it later."

"You stopped at the mall and you're now covered in her perfume, then you come in here and blow up at me because some guy asked to say hello?"

"A guy your sister is trying to set you up with."

"You're unbelievable." She walked away back toward the banquet room and he went after her. "Maybe you should leave," she said, as he caught up to her.

Like hell he was leaving. "I went there to buy *you* something, Izzy. At the jewelry store."

She turned to him but kept walking. "And that's why her perfume is all over you?"

"She hugged me—"

"She does that a lot. Doesn't she?"

Except for the time he'd told her about Frisco's and her efforts were weakened because she was so sick, he'd never seen her like this. They reached the table and Isabel sat down next to Valerie. He sat down next to her and put his hand on her leg, leaning in to her. "I can explain it all. I swear."

She pulled away from him. "Can you not sit so close to me? You reek of *her*. It's disgusting."

Romero pulled back. He'd almost forgotten about Michael until he heard the laughter coming from the bar behind him. Michael was looking their way again, and if Romero didn't know any better, the smirk he wore was directed at him. Romero straightened out in his chair and stared right back at him. If this fucker was calling him out, he was more than ready to take him on.

Chapter 20
Hell Hath No Fury

The fact that Alex and Valerie were there tonight was somewhat of a relief. Isabel could barely stand sitting next to Romero, and she didn't know how much longer she could take smelling the scent of another woman on him before breaking down. She was so incredibly hurt that the touch of his hand on her leg nearly burned her. How dare he? And he had the audacity to walk in there and make a huge deal over Michael talking to her while he was with this girl doing God knows what that had him completely slathered in her smell now.

The more she thought about it the more it infuriated her. She pushed his hand off her leg. "Please don't touch me right now, okay?" she whispered.

"Izzy, please. I'm telling you I can explain. You'll understand. I promise."

Feeling on the verge of tears, she whispered back. "Not here. Not now." The last thing she wanted to hear was his lame reasons why Cici just had to have her body all over his. Isabel had smelled it all over his neck, too.

When both Alex and Romero made a trip to the men's room, she prayed he'd at least try to wash some of the disgusting smell off of him. Valerie leaned over with a knowing, but sympathetic expression. "Everything okay?"

Isabel rolled her eyes, but felt a distinct knot that had been building in her throat the moment she realized who it was she smelled on him. Her heart had dropped to her feet and she'd been overwhelmed with jealousy. She reached over for her glass of wine. "He had the nerve to be pissed that Pat brought Michael over to say hello to me; and Valerie, he stinks of that girl again. He admitted he stopped to see her at the mall. He claims he went to buy me something at the jewelry store and she just hugged him, but why the hell is he *drenched* in the stink of her perfume?"

Unlike Romero, Isabel saw Valerie's eyes widen at the mention of Michael. Valerie knew exactly who she was talking about, but her jaw had dropped when she told her of Cici's perfume on Romero "Are you kidding? I thought his cologne was a little weird when he hugged me. And why did he have to go back to *her* store to get you something? There's like twenty jewelry stores at the mall."

Isabel told her about him admitting being at the mall several times that week, and how he'd had claimed it was because he was buying a laptop.

"Oh, hell no." Valerie squeezed her hand, reinforcing the fact that Isabel wasn't overreacting. "I'd demand to know everything about his relationship with this girl. Not only that, think about it, Isabel. What would he do? I seriously doubt he'd be sitting here holding it all in."

Isabel thought about him asking her not to do anything that might make them even. The gall he had was maddening. To storm in there like he had, knowing full well where he'd just come from. If she hadn't already seen his fiery reactions to some of the incidents that involved her with other men, she might be tempted to give him a taste of his own medicine. None of those other times he'd been infuriated were her fault. What she felt now was entirely his doing.

"Absolutely," Isabel agreed. "He nearly blew a vein when I explained who Michael was, and mind you, this was just after that girl obviously rubbed all over him." Isabel nearly growled that last part out.

Valerie looked around. "Is Michael still—" She turned back to Isabel. "Maybe we should leave."

Isabel saw the worry in her eye. "Why?"

Valerie glanced back again, to where she'd stopped cold the first time. "He's standing over by the bar with a bunch of other guys and keeps looking over here. Sounds like they're getting loud, too. That's never a good sign."

Isabel heard loud laughter from the direction Valerie had glanced at. She dare not even turn around to look. Michael's cockiness after he'd had a few drinks came to mind. She'd told Valerie about that after her date that night. She was surprised Valerie remembered. Her stomach was one big knot now.

The guys made it back to the table. If Romero had tried to wash some of the stench off he hadn't done a very good job of it, because it hit her as soon as he sat down. At that moment, she really wanted him gone. She couldn't stand it anymore.

Sudden bursts of laughter continued from behind them, with Romero and Alex glancing back a few times.

"What's with all the guys in uniform?" Alex asked, taking a drink of his beer.

Isabel pushed Romero's hand away again and tried to answer sounding normal and not as hurt as she was feeling again. "My brother-in-law is a Lieutenant Commander in the Navy."

Alex raised his eyebrows. "Is that right?"

Valerie nudged him. "I've told you so many times."

Alex kissed her, with a smirk, "Yeah, you did, babe." Isabel caught him giving Romero a look as if he hadn't the faintest. "So how come your brother isn't in uniform?"

There was more laughter again from the men at the bar. It seems they were getting even louder. Isabel gulped, feeling herself becoming more emotional by the minute. "He didn't know about the party. It was a surprise."

The band started another slow tempo song and she almost jumped when she felt a tap on her shoulder. "Dance with me, honey."

Relieved for the excuse to get away from Romero she smiled at her father and stood up. "I really don't know how to dance to this, daddy."

"I don't either. Just go with it."

She didn't even look at Romero as she walked away. It wasn't until she was on the dance floor and saw a few flashes go off that she realized the press was there — of course. She should've known Pat would take advantage of any opportunity to get her dad's name in the papers.

Her stomach nearly dropped when she saw Romero and Alex headed toward the bar. Her eyes darted to the bar area where there were still herds of uniformed men standing around but thankfully, Michael wasn't one of them. She let out a relieved breath. "Something wrong?"

Her eyes met her dad's and she smiled, shaking her head. "No."

"Smile that way, honey."

She turned to where her father was looking, in time to see a camera flash in her face. "Leave it to your sister," he said, through his smile, "to turn her husband's party into part of the campaign."

Once the photographer walked away, Isabel leaned into her father, trying to think of something other than Romero and what he'd been doing with Cici today. "Daddy, are you sure you wanna go through with this? You don't have to, you know? It's not up to Pat and Charles. I get the feeling they talked you into this."

Her father smiled. "I don't mind running, even if I don't win the election. It's a good experience and I'm meeting a lot of people I wouldn't have otherwise. I just don't like all the extra media attention. And your sister seems to revel in it." He nodded his head in the direction where Pat stood with Charles and someone who took notes and appeared to be interviewing them. "She and that damned campaign manager have interview after interview lined up for me all this week."

"Well, you don't have to do them all, Dad. You tell them what you can and *can't* do." Her sister made her so mad. She knew her dad, but even more so her mom, were looking forward to him retiring. Now he was going to be busier than ever.

"Speak of the devil."

Isabel turned to see her sister waving them both over to where she and Charles were standing. Isabel glanced back at Romero. He and Alex were already back at the table with Valerie. She saw that rather than look concerned about having upset her, he was laughing about whatever Alex was telling him.

She and her father made their way over to where her sister and Charles stood with what Isabel could only imagine was a reporter. "Daddy, this is Scott Price with the La Jolla Sun. He just wanted to ask you a few questions."

Isabel gave her sister a look, which Pat quickly ignored. The reporter wasted no time asking her dad about his plans to improve San Diego's legislation.

Isabel and Pat stepped aside to where Charles stood, texting something. "Can you put that thing away for at least five minutes?" Pat scolded. "Isn't everyone you know already here?" Without waiting for him to respond, Pat took a few steps away to stand by her father as if he needed her there for moral support.

"Hey bud, having fun?" Michael put his arm around Charles' shoulder.

His words were a little slurred and Charles laughed. "Not as much as you, obviously."

"Well, let's do something about that. You're the birthday boy." He laughed, then sized Isabel up blatantly. "Ms. Isabel, umm, umm, umm." He put his hand over his chest. "I'm sorry but my heart is breaking here."

She felt her face warm and she casually glanced back at Romero. He was still engrossed in an obviously hilarious conversation with Alex. She wondered why the hell he was in such a good mood all of a sudden. Was it his little visit with the ex-topless waitress that had him so cheery? She'd never considered herself a jealous person but the thought of him touching another woman like he touched her made her want to scream.

"Ga-damn, Charles. Why didn't you introduce me to your beautiful sister-in-law sooner?" He stepped up closer to her. "You can't be serious about this guy right? Your sister said he's not exactly a winner." He stood so close she could smell the rancid liquor on his breath. "You haven't been with him very long. You think I might still have a chance?"

Her face was very hot now but she was also annoyed. As mad as she was at Romero, she wouldn't allow anyone to put him down. "My sister knows very little about him, so she's not exactly qualified to be passing judgment."

Charles walked away to answer his phone. Michael took a swig of whatever putrid liquor he was drinking and stepped even closer to her. "You didn't answer my question." He smiled wickedly.

She glanced over to Romero whose eyes had locked on them now. Feeling the lump suddenly in her throat again, she made a hasty decision. Romero may've gone crazy a few times because of her sister's doing, but he'd never felt the hurt she was feeling at that moment. As stupid as she knew it was, she smiled back at Michael. "The future is always uncertain."

"I knew it." He smiled even bigger. "I'm a bit of an expert in body language and I could tell you weren't having the time of your life over there, earlier."

She lifted a shoulder and continued to smile but felt the tears begin to fill her eyes.

Suddenly Michael looked concerned. "What's wrong, honey?" He put his arm around shoulder.

She couldn't believe she was going to let herself fall apart now, in front of Michael. "Nothing," She breathed in deeply, willing the emotion to pass. "I'm fine."

"Isabel, what the hell's going on?"

She and Michael turned at the same time to see an infuriated Romero charging toward them. Alex was right behind him. He had everyone within hearing distance's attention, including her father and the reporter.

Michael didn't pull his arm off her. "She's venting. Can you give us a moment?"

She saw the shock in Romero's eyes then the rage.

"Fuck no! I won't give you a moment with her!" He turned to Isabel. "What are you venting about?"

Without thinking, her own angry words shot out. "Us!"

His eyes opened wide. "You're telling this fucker about *us*?"

A crowd had begun to gather, including the reporter who now seemed more interested in them than in her father.

"Hey, watch your language." Michael held her even closer and now that Romero was close enough, the smell of the perfume still on him assaulted Isabel, making her even angrier.

Romero's eyes were immediately on Michael's arm and Isabel could see it was a struggle for him to not lose it completely. He spoke through his teeth. "Get your fucking hands off her."

She didn't turn to see Michael's expression but she could hear the smile in his words. "Maybe she wants them there."

She tried to smile when Romero turned to see her response to that, but the tears nearly blurred her vision. She was done with this game. It hadn't made her feel any better. Knowing she made a huge mistake she tried moving Michael's hand off her shoulder but he stupidly wouldn't let go. "Stop, Michael," she said still trying to move his hand, as he stubbornly held her to him. The next thing she saw was Romero's fist flying into Michael's face.

Alex pulled her away and what followed was pure chaos. Romero was like an enraged animal. There was no stopping him. With her hands at her face, she gasped. She'd seen him angry before but never like this and this was all her fault. "Stop, Romero. Please!" She turned to Alex. "Stop him!"

Alex watched as Romero got a few more punches in before making a move. There were already other bodies attempting to stop the brawl, but so far they had been completely unsuccessful. One guy even got Romero's elbow to his face as Romero cocked it back to pound Michael again.

Valerie was suddenly next to Isabel and squeezed her arm.

"Oh my God. This is all my fault."

"No it's not!" Valerie tried convincing her. "C'mon." Valerie pulled her away from the crowd of men trying in vain to stop Romero's rampage.

Isabel couldn't pull her eyes away. Alex had finally pulled Romero away but she saw what a huge struggle it was to contain him. Michael's face was already a mess and Romero wanted more?

She didn't think it possible but her heart sunk even further when she saw the uniformed police rush in and make their way through the crowd. Within seconds they had Romero shoved against the wall. Isabel covered her mouth with her hand. "What did I do?"

"This. Is. Not. Your. Fault." Valerie insisted.

"I want that fucking animal arrested!" Michael yelled at the officers patting Romero down.

The cops that stood in front of Michael, tried settling him down. Belligerent, loud and obviously humiliated but trying to play it down, Michael scoffed at the officer who asked if he needed paramedics to look at him. "Nah, I'm fine. This ain't shit, son! I've been in wars. He didn't do shit to me. But it's enough to throw his ass behind bars where this loser belongs."

Romero was already being handcuffed and Isabel fell apart. Valerie put his arm around her. "It's gonna be okay."

Michael's mouth was still running and Isabel wanted to scream at him to shut up! "You blew it, you idiot!" Michael taunted as they walked Romero past him. "Probably the only chance a loser like you had with someone like Isabel."

"Shut. Up!" Isabel finally yelled.

Romero wouldn't even look in her direction, but she saw how tight his jaw was.

"Sweetheart, I'm just agreeing with what you said. Your future with him *was* uncertain." Michael continued and at that, Romero glanced up at her. "Now I think the choice is pretty obvious. You can come back over from the dark side."

Her sister was trying to get everyone back in their seats. Valerie suddenly hurried away from Isabel toward Alex who was now stalking toward Michael. Isabel rushed after her. She'd never forgive herself if they arrested Alex also because of her.

"I want him out!" Alex yelled to the cop trying to interview Michael. Valerie reached him just in time and held him by his arm. "This is my restaurant and I reserve the right. Get him out or I'll throw his ass out myself."

The cop gave Alex a bored look. "Alright, sir. Calm down. We'll walk him out just as soon as we're done here."

Sal was there now. Like Valerie and herself, he probably spotted Alex charging in Michael's direction and rushed over. Isabel hadn't even noticed he was right behind her. "What happened? I saw them take Romero away."

"Romero beat the shit outta this guy," Alex said loud enough for Michael to hear, though if he did, he pretended not to.

Isabel walked away from the group when she saw her mother and father approaching. Her mother looked at her sternly. "Isabel, I want you to tell me the truth."

Isabel sniffed, and the tears still dripped from her eyes. But she stared at her mom. "The truth about what?"

"Is he on drugs?" her father asked.

Isabel turned to her father. "No!"

"Then what was the matter with him?" Her mother demanded. "No one in their right mind does that—no matter how angry."

"No..." Isabel thought about the liquor she'd smelt on his breath. "He had a few drinks but that's it. Look, this was my fault—"

"That he turned into a crazed lunatic?" Up until now, her mother had been accepting of Romero, even though Isabel knew she wasn't thrilled that he had no education beyond high school, but she was furious now. "Is that what you're gonna say when you make him mad and he turns on you? That it was your fault?"

"He'd never turn on me." For an instant, the memory of him holding her arm the night she insinuated she might turn the tables on him came to her. But he'd let go when she asked him to. "He wouldn't."

"Isabel this is not the time or place." Her mother glanced around and lowered her voice. "But we need to have a serious conversation about this. Your father and I are extremely concerned for you. You know I don't care about his career choice. I was willing to give him the benefit of the doubt, even if had chosen to skip the education, but this... this is unacceptable."

Feeling all the emotion she'd felt over the evening come to a shattering peak and now hearing this, Isabel could barely speak. "Well, I'm a grown woman, mother. You can't ground me anymore and refuse to let me see him."

"He's no longer welcome around the family, Isabel. And that's final," her father said, adding to her already battered heart.

Without saying everything she wanted to, because after tonight she didn't even know if her and Romero would still be together. And because she could feel that at any moment she was going to fall apart completely, she walked away without saying a word. They called after her but she ignored them, hurrying as the tears came even faster now, burning down her face.

Chapter 21
Aftermath

Romero was past the hurt and the anger. All he felt now was numb. He lay there in his old bed at his uncles' house staring at the ceiling like he'd done so many times in the past when he'd felt let down or just pissed. Only now, the only person he was pissed at was himself. He'd lain there the entire night since his uncles and Alex had bailed him out.

Alex had obviously filled his uncles in on what happened because all Manny had said when he got out was, "What I am I gonna do with you?"

His uncles had already been in contact with their lawyer and Romero knew this much: he was looking at felony assault charges. If convicted, he'd not only do time, but he'd lose his P.I. license and his right to carry a gun, which was necessary to run his business. His temper had finally cost him dearly. Not only was he looking at possibly ruining what he'd worked so hard to get, he'd lost the one thing he didn't know if he could live without — Izzy.

He closed his eyes and for a second an image of Isabel in Michael's arms flashed before him. He sat up in a violent jerk. Suddenly he felt the deep ache again. The one he'd felt for hours as he sat in the jail cell. Isabel had gone over to talk to Michael about *them* — to vent — to tell him her future with Romero was *uncertain*.

He knew every one of her expressions now and

when he'd glanced at her in hopes that he'd see anger at Michael's lies, he saw guilt instead. She'd already admitted what she'd done. What he'd tried so desperately to hide from all this time was out there now. If there was any doubt before yesterday, it was gone now. He was beneath her.

What an idiot he'd been to think getting her a ring could seal the deal. As if that's all it took to hold on to someone like Isabel. It was just a matter of time before she figured it out for herself and turned to someone like Michael, a fucking commander or whatever the hell he was — someone more at her and her family's level than he ever would be.

Manny was at his door holding the newspaper in his hand. "You made the front page."

Romero stared at him but said nothing.

"Pretty bad, too." Manny shook his head. "Get dressed. We're going to see Nick. He normally doesn't see clients on a Sunday but he's making an exception for us."

Nick had been their attorney for years. He was actually a long-time customer of his uncles' bar before becoming their attorney. People always assumed only scum frequented titty bars, but they'd be surprised how many doctors, lawyers and even politicians were regulars there.

Romero went through the motions, numbly, taking a shower and getting ready. The entire time he replayed the events of the night before. His mind jolted when he got to the moment he spotted her with Michael. Michael had been close enough to kiss her and she was smiling about it. The hurt had outweighed his anger by a ton, but it only escalated his emotions to the point of no return. Every punch he landed he wanted it to be harder than the last. Never in his life had he wanted to kill another person and last night he had. He thought of his dad and squeezed his eyes shut, fisting his hands. He was *not* his father, damn it.

He checked his phone again for any possible missed calls or texts from Isabel—none. Obviously, their relationship had met its fate last night. What hurt most, was that she was already unsure about things between them even before he blew it. He should've backed the fuck off when he'd sensed her losing patience.

Although he knew just the thought of his Izzy with anyone else made him insane, he really thought he'd be able to keep that side of himself from her, push come to shove—for the sake of not losing her. Last night was proof there was no way. Even now, he hoped he'd never run into her with someone else because he'd only prove to her without a doubt, once again, how wrong he'd been for her. All the trouble he was in now, all the heartache he'd have to endure because of what he did last night—none of it mattered. He knew he'd do it again in a heartbeat if he ever saw her in someone else's arms. He was hopeless.

The attorney didn't tell them anything they didn't already know. Basically, Romero was screwed any way you looked at it. Since it was still the weekend, formal charges had yet to be filed, but based on the facts there was no doubt the DA wouldn't file.

He explained to Romero what he might want to consider. If he was charged with felony assault, which was more than likely, they usually offered a deal that would save time and money. Plead no contest to a lesser charge like simple assault. It carried a smaller fine and less jail time. Since Romero had no priors, and he'd cooperated with the police at the time of the arrest, Nick said he'd probably be out in a month, but would be on probation for at least two years. That meant no carrying any weapons during that time.

Romero listened, his mind wandering back and forth, to what Nick said and what Isabel probably thought of him now. As serious as this was, his life — his *career* — was on the line here, all he could think of was what was he going to do without her?

"Will you pay attention?" Manny nudged him.

Romero snapped out of it, frowning. "I *am* paying attention."

"I *am* paying attention," Manny mimicked him. "He just asked you a fucking question."

Romero stared at Nick blankly. "Say again?"

"Is there anyone that could testify on your behalf that this assault was provoked in any way?"

Isabel immediately came to mind. He'd already decided staying away from her would be the only way he'd survive not being able to be with her anymore. He was going to have Alex pick up his things for him as soon as he felt up to talking to anyone about it. "No."

"Are you sure?" Max asked.

"Yeah, I'm sure. The guy pissed me off so I clocked him. Everybody there saw it. It's why they arrested me."

"That's just it," Nick said. "Why *did* he piss you off? If it's a good enough reason it might be permissible to use as having been provoked. You might get off with just a fine, and paying for damages. And from what the report said this guy insisted when asked several times that he was fine. The judge could dismiss it all together. Stranger things have happened."

Romero stared at him, the memory of last night coming back to him. He felt the heat rising in him again. "He was being an asshole."

"The guy had his hands on Moe's girl." Manny glanced back at Romero. "Alex told us." Manny turned back to Nick. "My boy has anger issues as it is. God forbid you so much as say anything bad about his girl, and the prick last night had his fucking paws on her." Manny shrugged. "What are you gonna do?"

Nick jotted a few things down. "We might have something. You'll probably be required to take a few anger management classes. But I may just be able to pull something off here. Not making any promises, but we'll see."

Manny and Max both smiled. When they got outside Romero turned to Manny. "Why do you do that, uh? Why do you tell people I have anger issues? You've done that my whole life."

"Because you *do*. Look at the mess you're in because of it. And if I hadn't mentioned it in there it may not have sparked whatever idea he got. I helped you out, you fucking ingrate." Manny shook his head and tossed Romero the keys to the car. "You drive, and you're buying breakfast. After the night you put us through, it's the least you could do."

Romero took a deep breath. His whole life he'd been hearing his uncle talk about his anger issues like it was some kind of handicap. A handicap he'd hoped Isabel would never find out about. She'd witnessed it first hand last night, and just like he'd known she'd do all along—she ran the hell away.

*

Valerie came right over after Isabel broke down on the phone with her. Isabel insisted she didn't have to but

Valerie wasn't having it. Isabel had been there countless of times when she gone through her roller coaster
relationship with Alex. She even showed up with food
from the restaurant.

"I had a feeling you probably haven't eaten. I know
you don't when you're depressed."

As good as the food smelled, Isabel really didn't
have an appetite. Valerie had called her last night to
tell her Romero was out and she'd waited for him to
call. She couldn't bring herself to call him. She remembered how possessed he'd been last night. She shuddered to think of what might've happened if all those
people had not been there to stop him. He was probably still furious with her, and she didn't blame him.

Last night had been horrendous. When she wasn't
lying awake crying, she was having a nightmare. In
one of them, she'd seen Romero at the mall embracing
and kissing another woman. She'd charged at them
ready to attack the woman, but Romero had pulled the
woman behind him and told Isabel he no longer loved
her and to let them be. The entire dream, the woman's
perfume was everywhere, and so strong, it nearly suffocated Isabel so much so she coughed until she woke
herself up.

"Do they know anything yet?"

Usually Isabel was the one that prepared the food
but this time Valerie pulled out two huge burritos and
fresh tortilla chips from aluminum containers of food
she'd brought and poured them both soda. "Sit down,
Isabel. You have to eat. I'll tell you while we eat."

Isabel sat down with Valerie at the small table, surprised that Valerie had anything to tell her. She
thought Valerie would say she didn't know anything it
was too soon. "The last thing Alex told me today about

it was that Romero was going to meet with his uncle's attorney today. But his uncle called the guy last night and let him know what was going on. The attorney told him he could most likely be facing felony assault charges."

Having a father who was a judge and siblings who were also attorneys, Isabel knew enough about the law to know that if convicted it would carry jail time. This could ruin him. She felt the wave of tears coming on again. Valerie rubbed her arm gently. "Isabel, they don't know for sure. It all depends on the judge and he could try to fight it. Everyone there saw what an asshole that guy was. He obviously instigated it."

"*I* instigated it." Isabel didn't fight the tears anymore. "I knew he'd react violently and I still went along with Michael's flirting, because I was mad at Romero. Now he's probably ruined his life." Isabel buried her face in her hands.

Valerie stood up to hug her while rubbing her back. Suddenly Isabel had a thought and lifted her head, wiping her face with both hands. Her dad knew people. Maybe he could help. She knew he was mad last night but he'd never refuse to help his own daughter, especially if she begged. "I gotta call my dad."

She stood up and rushed to the counter where her phone was, grabbing it. Valerie stared at her but sat down then began to eat.

Her dad answered on the first ring. "Daddy, I need your help."

At first, her dad refused. They went back and forth for a while, and he was steadfast about not wanting to do anything for Romero. He said he deserved whatever they slapped on him. "Maybe it's for the best if he goes away for a while."

Isabel hadn't even thought that far ahead. She was still holding out hope that they'd be able to somehow work things out and they'd be together again soon. She already missed him dreadfully. What if he did go to jail—for years?

"Oh, Daddy," she sobbed. "I don't know what I'd do."

There was a silence on her dad's end, then she heard him breathe. "Please don't cry, honey."

"You have to help him. It was all my fault. I'll never forgive myself—"

"First of all," his voice was strong and deliberate again. "if I hear you blame yourself for his actions ever again, I'm definitely not helping."

Isabel breathed in deeply, feeling a sudden hope. "Okay, I promise I won't anymore. What can you do?"

"I really don't think I can do much. If the plaintiff, in this case Michael, insists on going forward with this, the DA has no choice but move forward and prosecute. You saw how angry Michael was last night, and although he didn't want to admit it, his injuries were extensive." Her father stopped and took a deep breath. She knew he must've been thinking about how crazed Romero had been again. "Honey, I can't do anything about it unless Michael files an affidavit of non-prosecution. Normally, I would never advise anyone to this. It's irreversible once filed. But most importantly, the DA could turn around and press charges on him for bringing false charges against someone to begin with. That's where I'd be able to help. I could make sure that doesn't happen. But the impossible part is going to be getting Michael to agree to something like that. He'd be a fool *not* to press charges."

This time Isabel took a deep breath, once again regretting the decision she'd made last night on a stupid angry whim.

"I'm sorry, honey. Even though, I still don't want that man around you or the family. You know I'd do anything for *you* but my hands are tied here."

She thanked him, hung up and turned to Valerie. She thought about it before saying it but this might be the only answer. "I'm gonna have to go out with Michael again."

Valerie's jaw dropped. "You can't be serious."

"I have to, Valerie. It's my only hope."

*

After speaking with her father and finding a tiny glimmer of hope, Isabel had been able to finish at least half the burrito Valerie had brought her. Not surprisingly, Valerie had inhaled hers in its entirety.

She briefed Valerie about her plan to try and convince Michael to cancel the charges and made her promise not to tell Alex. Her only hope was Michael's ego. It was as big as the ship he'd sailed in on. The papers had already reported that he'd been beaten to a pulp. For as much as he protested last night that he Romero hadn't hurt him, she was sure he was none too happy about those headlines. Not only that, she was sure he'd love nothing better than to take another stab at Romero. And what better way than to steal his girlfriend?

As soon as Valerie left, Isabel pulled out the answering machine from a drawer in the kitchen. Since Valerie had moved out she didn't need it anymore so she'd put it away but she'd never erased the message Michael had left her. After sifting through several messages before finally finding his, she fast-forwarded it not wanting to relive that horrible morning and how God-awful it felt to listen to him go on about their fantastic date while Romero's accusing eyes burned a hole through her. She got to the part with his number and jotted it down.

She was beginning to think he might not answer, but then he did. She cleared her throat after hearing him say hello. "Hi, Michael."

He was quiet for a moment. "I'm sorry, who is this?"

"It's Isabel. I wanted to see how you're doing."

"Isabel." She could almost hear the smile. "I'm great. Couldn't be better."

Purposely trying not to sound demeaning she asked, "How's your face? It looked pretty bad last night."

This time, *he* cleared his throat. "It always looks worse than it feels. But I can assure you, I'm fine. I'm glad you called though. You seemed pretty upset last night. I can't say I blame you. Is he always that violent?"

Isabel closed her eyes. This was going to be harder than she'd thought. She had to make Michael believe she didn't care for Romero anymore. "Sometimes. It's why I'm considering breaking things off with him."

"Considering? After last night, I would've thought you'd all but washed your hands of him. The man's dangerous." He paused before adding, "I mean for you, that is. You're really selling yourself short with this guy, Isabel. You don't deserve that."

As tempted as she was to end the call now, her decision had been made. She wouldn't back out now. Romero could go to jail because of her. She had to do this. "I don't know. I'd been sort of considering it for a while now, then after seeing you last night... well I was thinking maybe we could get together and... talk."

Michael jumped at the bait. "Absolutely. As a matter of fact, I was just thinking about what I could do tonight. I took the whole weekend off for Charles' party so I have a free night."

Isabel gulped. "Tonight works for me."

After hanging up, Isabel stood there in the kitchen contemplating what she was about to get herself into. She wouldn't even think about what Romero might say or do *when*, not *if* he found out. She only prayed this worked out so he'd understand why she *had* to do it.

Chapter 22
Little Moe

Nick said it may take a few days before they knew anything for sure. In the meantime, he was getting everything ready and told Romero to just go about his business, and stay out of trouble.

Romero took his uncles to Moreno's for their Sunday brunch. He needed to talk to Alex. First of all, he wanted to find out if there had been any damage he needed to pay for. Then apologize for any trouble he may've caused.

Alex wasn't there, only Sal and Angel were. He sat with his uncles for a while and ate, but he wasn't feeling very hungry. Halfway through eating he walked over to where Sal was at the bar reading the paper again. He looked up at Romero from the paper and shook his head. "How you feeling?"

Romero shrugged. "Alright I guess."

Angel walked up from behind Sal. "Dude. I heard about last night. How's Isabel feel about all this?"

That dull ache had been present the entire morning. Even when he'd tried not to think of her. Romero wondered if it would be there permanently. It sure as hell felt like it. "I dunno. I haven't talked to her."

Sal lifted an eyebrow. "She's that mad, uh?"

"I guess. Listen, I'm sorry about last night. I didn't mean to cause any trouble for you guys here. I just snapped. Let me know if you need me to pay for anything."

Sal's face screwed up then he laughed. "Only thing broken was that guy's face."

Angel laughed. "Yeah, I heard you fucked him *up.*"

As much as Romero wanted to smile about that, the consequences from it were too dire. At this point going to jail and losing his PI license came a distant second and third to his main concern. He was already feeling the withdrawal effects of being away from Isabel. Not wanting to talk about it anymore, he changed the subject. "Where's Alex?"

Sal smirked. "He had a rough night last night, too. He'll be in later today."

"I need to talk to him." Romero turned to Angel, remembering his wife Sarah was Valerie's cousin. "Maybe you can do it for me."

"I need to get all my stuff from Isabel's place. But I don't wanna do it myself."

Romero saw the expression on Sal's face go somber. "Seriously, that bad? You two can't work this out?"

Feeling the ache even deeper Romero gestured toward the paper still in Sal's hands. "That shit ain't gonna blow over, Sal—not with her and especially not with her family. They didn't like me to begin with." He looked down and flexed his badly bruised knuckles, feeling a tightness in his throat he'd only felt a few times in his life. "I'm no good for her."

A customer on the other side of the bar caught Angel's attention and he walked over to see what he needed. Sal stared at Romero. "I think you're wrong. Have you talked to her since last night?"

Romero shook his head, unwilling to speak, fearing the emotion he was feeling would betray him. He still stared at his knuckles; not wanting to even look at Sal.

"I'd talk to her, man. So you blew up. Alex said you

had good reason." Sal chuckled. "But then coming from another hot-head that doesn't hold a lot of weight." He seemed to wait for a response but Romero said nothing—he couldn't. He was busy trying to swallow the softball-sized knot in his throat. "For what it's worth," Sal continued. "I think you two are good for each other. You balance each other out. And hey." Romero finally looked up at him when he realized Sal wasn't going to continue until he did. "Alex told me about all the bullshit that guy was yelling. You gotta know that's all it was, right? He *had* to say something to try and make you feel as stupid as he felt. You beat his ass in front of all his Navy buddies. He knew he ended up looking like the pussy who got his ass handed to him. I wouldn't believe a word he said."

Romero wondered if Alex had also told him Isabel had admitted to venting to him. And he'd seen the look on her face. Even if Michael had taken her words out of context, there was some truth to it. He didn't even blame her. What kind of future could she look forward to with him?

Sal would never understand. No one would. His whole life he'd dealt with the inability to hold back what was on his mind, especially when he was mad, but with Isabel everything was magnified a million times over. All his emotions for her, including what he was feeling now, were so overwhelming there was no way he would get a hold on them. He stood up and glanced at Sal. He had to get out of there. "Thanks, man. Tell Alex I'll be calling him."

He walked away leaving Sal staring at him. The sympathy in his eyes made Romero feel even worse. Romero needed to distance himself from Isabel and the sooner the better or this whole thing was going to kill him. The only thing he cared about getting from Isabel's apartment was his laptop. Everything else, he didn't give a shit about. Even the laptop could be replaced, but there was client information on it that he needed secure.

Once he had that he'd walk away forever. Having the willpower to stay away from her was not going to be easy. Already he was tempted to go see her now. Maybe being locked up wasn't such a bad thing after all.

*

Taking the chance of Romero showing up while Michael picked her up was out of the question. So she agreed to meet Michael at his hotel room. Originally, she'd planned to meet him somewhere safer and far less intimate, like at a restaurant where there was no chance he'd try to make a move, but he finally admitted that he wasn't really feeling up to going out yet.

She knew meeting with Michael alone would be bad enough in Romero's eyes. Meeting him in his hotel room might be the final straw, but she had no choice. She'd never be able to live with herself if Romero had ruined his life because of her stupidity. She had to at least *try* to fix this.

When she got to his room, she realized why he hadn't wanted to be seen in public. She wondered why he would even want *her* to see him this way. His face was one giant raw wound. Her heart sunk. How in the world would she convince him to drop the charges? Every time he looks in the mirror, he must be cursing Romero.

She couldn't help herself and she brought her hands

to her mouth. "Oh my God, Michael."

He smiled. That alone had to hurt. "I told you, it looks a lot worse than it really is." He took a step back, opening the door even wider for her. "Come on in."

She walked into his room. The room service he told her he'd be ordering had already arrived. His suite had a front room and a small kitchenette. There was a tray of cheese and crackers on the coffee table. A bottle of champagne and two empty glasses sat on the counter of the kitchenette.

Michael poured them each a glass and asked her to have a seat on the small sofa in the front room. He sat next to her but not too close. "So did you have anything in particular you wanted to talk to me about?"

She couldn't help staring at his banged up face. Both eyes were swollen and purple. The blood vessels in one of them had popped making the whites of that eye completely red and the other one had a big gash under it. His lip was ripped on one side and there was a knot on his forehead the size of a golf ball. As egotistical as he was, she still couldn't understand why he would be okay with her seeing what her boyfriend had done to him. "Michael, I'm really sorry about last night."

"Oh no. I already told you. *You* didn't do anything. He did, and he'll get what's coming to him."

Isabel bit her lip. "Did you see the paper this morning? They made a pretty big deal about it. And I saw it on the news. They were talking about how badly he'd beaten you." So the last part was a lie. It hadn't actually made the television news. Not that she knew of anyway. But it was working. She had his attention and he was frowning.

"Really? I saw the paper but didn't see the television reports."

"Yeah, and it wasn't just the local news either. I guess because my father was there and someone got wind that it was his daughter's boyfriend who had been arrested. I felt terrible when they kept repeating how bad your injuries were." She took a sip of her champagne taking in his how rigid his expression had become. "The worst thing is my sister was telling me this will probably be all over the news at least until the election. My dad's opponents will no doubt take the story and run with it. Making the Mayor's daughter's boyfriend out to be a monster who tore a poor Navy commander to shreds."

The rigid expression was now an all out scowl. "Is that what they said? The paramedics weren't even called. I wonder where they're getting their facts from."

"Probably the police report. I don't know, or witnesses," she sighed. "I can just see it now. The cameras and news crews will be there at every court appearance repeating the story over and over. This is a nightmare. My family is so upset with me about this."

He sat up straighter, visibly disconcerted. "They shouldn't be angry with you, Isabel. You didn't do anything."

"But they are, especially Pat. This may cost my dad the election. I only wish there was some way to fix this."

Michael stood up and brought the champagne bottle from the counter. He filled his glass and refreshed hers. She could see his mind was working then he changed the subject. "Can I ask you something?"

She nodded cautiously. "Yes."

"Where'd you meet this guy?"

"At a wedding shower." She'd give him as little information about Romero as possible.

"I don't mean to be out of line here, but I don't understand how someone as obviously intelligent as you could get involved with the likes of him."

Tempted to defend Romero, but knowing she was there to convince Michael she was now having second thoughts about him, she refrained. Instead she lied. "I really don't know." But she did throw in a jab. "I think maybe I was just taken in by his good looks and his tough guy persona. A lot of women are attracted to that."

Immediately, his face turned to stone. "Fighting dirty isn't tough. It's what cowards do."

"Fighting dirty?" Anger almost overtook Isabel but she caught herself. Even though she didn't understand how a one-on-one fight with no weapons and no one else jumping in could be construed as dirty, she nodded. "You're right. He is a coward." It almost hurt to say it. Romero might be a lot of things, but a coward certainly wasn't one of them.

Seemingly content with her response, Michael's expression morphed into a smile. "So does that mean you've made up your mind? You said you were *considering* breaking things off."

Isabel sipped her champagne. "I need to talk to him. I haven't today at all. I'm still too upset about it."

"What's there to talk about? The man is a raging monster. You saw him last night. He had no self-control. Don't you ever worry that..." He stopped and his eyes opened a bit wider. "Has he ever gotten that way with you?"

Isabel shook her head, but she was purposely unconvincing. "No."

"You sure? You aren't lying to protect him. Are you Isabel?"

"Can we talk about something else? I'm trying not to think about him today. That's why I'm here."

Even with his face so messed up, Isabel was able to see the satisfied undertone of his smile. "I *thought* we'd made a connection on that first date your sister set up for us. That's why I was so surprised when you didn't call me back."

Isabel resisted rolling her eyes. *So surprised*. Really? Instead, she decided to stroke his ego. "When my sister started the whole set up, I still hadn't met Romero. By the time it finally happened I was already seeing him. But believe me." She lowered her eyes and smiled. "I was really tempted."

That puffed his chest a little. "I'm glad to hear it. When I saw you last night, my jaw nearly hit the floor. You looked even more amazing than I remembered. And trust me, you left quite an impression."

He told her about how he'd watched her most the night and how by the time she'd walked over to talk to Pat and Charles he was convinced that boyfriend or not, he should make a move. "Even though things turned out the way they did. I think I made a good call, because look who's come to pay me a visit already?" He reached over and clinked his glass to hers. "Let's eat. I put the shrimp cocktail in the fridge."

He stood up and went to fetch them. Isabel walked over to the small table by the kitchen. She used the time they ate to ask about his work and threw in a few questions about what his colleagues would think when they saw how badly he'd been injured. Each time she noticed how it irked him and he attempted to change the subject.

Casually, she'd come back to the subject of his *horrendous* injuries, at times wincing when he spoke and she'd stare at the rip on the corner of his lip. A couple of times she asked if it hurt to eat or chew.

Eventually she brought the conversation back to her father's campaign. She hoped to plant the idea that dropping the charges would lessen the amount of airtime the story of her boyfriend beating him to a pulp got. But by her being so concerned about her father's campaign, he could use the excuse that he was doing a noble thing for her and her father by letting it go. "I just hope the trial is a speedy one. Because you know, these campaigns can get vicious. And the media loves to milk these kinds of stories." She shook her head. "My brother called this morning to tell me it's already made the local news in Los Angeles." Another white lie but she had her fingers crossed under the table.

Michael wanted them to head back to the sofa in the living room for some more champagne after dinner, but she declined, saying she still had papers to grade and an early meeting in the morning. She was getting pretty good at lying. It was easy when the person didn't know you well at all. She would never be able to look in Romero's face and lie.

He walked her to the door and thanked her for coming by, then touched her arm. "I really hope you decide to do the right thing and drop that loser. Your sister mentioned she was worried about you being with him, and after last night, I have to agree with her completely." He came close to her face. "But that's not my only reason, Isabel. I really would love to give us a chance." He lowered his lips to hers but she turned her face and he kissed the corner of her mouth.

"I'm technically still with him, Michael. It just

doesn't feel right." She touched his lip with her finger. "Besides I wouldn't want to hurt your lip. It's ripped so bad."

He pressed his lips together and he saw the annoyance in his eyes. "I'm fine. I promise." He ran a finger down her cheek. "But I really hope you do make that decision and soon."

She nodded. "I will. Good night, Michael. I'll call you."

"I'll be waiting."

Isabel smiled and turned away. Even though he hadn't offered to drop the charges, she'd definitely been right about him hating the idea of the story being reported that he'd gotten his ass kicked. She felt evil giggling. How could he look in the mirror and still keep saying he hadn't?

It was late and she knew the mall closed early on Sundays but she was driving right by it and it was still ten minutes before they closed. She couldn't help herself and turned in, parking by the entrance she knew was closest to Dan's Jewels. Chances were Cici wasn't even there, but Isabel just had to check.

Her stomach churned as she walked in the mall entrance. She could see the jewelry store from the entrance. There was only one person behind the counter. She was young and blonde and busy arranging something on the counter so she didn't look up. Though she couldn't see her face one thing was for sure, she was well endowed. Certainly something that would garner extra tips at a topless bar.

Isabel got closer but she didn't plan on going in. She just wanted a good look. She wasn't even sure this was Cici or not.

A little boy ran past Isabel and into the jewelry

store. "Mommy!"

The girl looked up and Isabel could see she was young and damn it — attractive. Still, the little boy gave her hope that maybe this woman was married.

"Cici!"

Isabel's head jerked to see that another girl, a brunette just behind her was who had called out for Cici. She turned back to see that the blonde in the jewelry store was in fact Cici. She was looking straight at the brunette, but still running her fingers through her son's hair.

"I'm gonna run into Sears real quick before they close," the brunette said. "Moe, come with me. Let Mommy finish up her work."

Isabel froze feeling the strangest numbness overtake her. Moe? Cici had a son named *Moe*? What were the odds? Is this what made her so *different*? She'd had his baby? But why wouldn't he tell her he had a child? Romero had no secrets. It was one of the things she loved most about him most. He put it all out there. *Like it or not — this is who I am.* Moments passed before she realized she'd stopped in the middle of the mall and stood there as people walked around her.

She began her slow walk back to the exit of the mall. Last night she'd decided to give Romero at least a week to cool down. If he hadn't called or attempted to reach her by then, she'd call him. Now she wasn't sure she'd be calling him at all. If in fact he did have a son with Cici, she wasn't sure she could deal with him needing to continue his relationship with her. It was obviously a close one if it involved embraces that left her scent lingering on him for hours.

Chapter 23
Broken

Four days—that's how long it'd been since Romero had seen or talked to Isabel, and he was going crazy. Monday, Alex and Valerie had dropped by to pick up his laptop. He'd changed his mind about making things so final after only one day without her so he'd told Alex to only pick up his laptop—nothing else. But Valerie had called Isabel ahead of time, and she had all his things packed and ready for them when they got there. She asked Alex to come back when he had time to take down his plasma T.V. There was no question about it. She was done with him.

Romero sat miserably, staking out a house where a client's husband had entered over an hour earlier. The guy's car still sat in the driveway. The house was being rented by two women. He knew that much from running the records on the house. He already had pictures of this guy with one of the women that lived here in all kinds of compromising situations. Ever since he'd picked up more employees, he usually left this work to them, choosing instead to be home with Isabel but all week he'd been out here every night. He had enough pictures of this guy to hang him dead with his wife. But still, he was out there getting more.

He thought of Charles and the woman he saw him with at the restaurant. Was he really *that* stupid? His wife had been right upstairs. If Romero didn't do this kind of shit for a living he might question that what he'd seen, maybe it wasn't what it looked like. He'd forgotten all about it since then.

It had been a hell of a week so far. Getting little to no sleep at all, mindlessly going about his days. Nothing mattered anymore. Not even when he got the call that morning from Nick to tell him the charges against him had been dropped. It should've been uplifting news—his uncles were happy enough. Yet, it didn't even feel like it mattered. His life was still wretched.

The only thing constantly on his mind was how the hell he was he going to survive without Isabel. It was just a matter of time before her fucking sister finally set her up with someone who interested her. Maybe she'd even give Jacob another shot—or worse—he squeezed the camera he held—she'd go out with Michael again.

Sitting up straight, he felt that familiar heat inundate him. That same heat he had so little control over, especially when it involved Isabel. He took deep breaths and closed his eyes, counting down from ten. Just one of the stupid tips he'd read on the internet the other night on calming techniques. He'd learned from trying it earlier that he had to count *super* slow or he'd get down to one *way* before he was even remotely calm. He did what the article said. *Identified* what was causing the *tension* and removed it from his thoughts so that he could *diffuse* the issue.

He smirked when he realized it was actually working. Finally, after several minutes of this, he felt calm enough to open his eyes. He opened them slowly, smiling triumphantly, then glanced over to the driveway only to see the car he'd been watching was gone. "Aww fuck!"

Well, hell. He'd wasted all that time sitting there for nothing. He turned the car on and decided he had no choice but to call it a night.

On the drive back to his uncles' house, he got to thinking about Charles again. Maybe he could do a little digging and find out what he was up to. If anything, it would give him the satisfaction to know Pat's husband was cheating on her. Who could blame the sap? He was stuck with her. Pat wasn't ugly. In fact, irritatingly enough, she looked a lot like Isabel only she had shorter hair. But it was like in that movie *Shallow Hal*. Her personality was so nasty it made her ugly.

His uncles were both still at the bar when he got home. Aida was in the kitchen cleaning up and closing it down, as she put it. Anyone who ate after she closed it down had better put their shit away or there would be hell to pay.

He said hello to her as he walked through the kitchen into the hallway. He grabbed the laptop from his room and brought it out into the dining room. Some of the software he had should be illegal. It dug so deep into peoples' private lives it was scary. He didn't even need to know Charles' last name. He typed in Isabel's name taking a deep calming breath from just seeing her name. It immediately brought up all her next of kin, her extended family, even employers. He clicked on Pat's name bringing up all her info and there it was.

Romero laughed when he saw Charles' given name was actually Carlos Castro. He'd changed it to Charles years ago, no doubt because he thought it sounded more sophisticated. "Alright Carlos Castro, lets see what you're up to."

He sat back to wait the few minutes to bring up Charles' latest credit card activity. He had several but there was one in his name only from the same bank where he had an account in his name only as well. Always a revealing sign.

Aida answered her phone in the kitchen and it immediately caught Romero's attention. "What? Slow down, Manny. I can barely understand you."

Romero turned away from the laptop to listen.

"Oh my God!" She shrieked. "Who shot him?"

Romero jumped from his chair and rushed into the kitchen. Aida was already crying. She shoved the phone at Romero. "Max was shot!"

"What?" Romero took the phone feeling his heart drop. "What happened?"

"The bastards shot my little brother, Moe!" Manny sobbed.

Hearing his uncle sob had Romero choking up. "Who did? Where? Is he still alive?"

"I don't know! I don't know! The ambulance took him. I'm on my way to the hospital now."

Romero managed to get the hospital information from his hysterical uncle. He and Aida ran out the door and into his car. Aida tried to make some sense out of what Manny was still trying to tell her on the phone. "Tell him to just wait 'til we get there. He's hysterical enough, he shouldn't be on the phone while he drives, too."

"Honey, we're almost there. You can tell us when we get there. Okay? Just try to calm down."

Romero was nearly hit by a car in the hospital parking lot as he ran through it to get to the emergency room. Manny was already there sitting in the waiting room bent over, his face buried in his hands. Romero and Aida rushed over to him. Aida sat next to him. Without getting up, Manny wrapped his arms around Romero's waist and sobbed against his shirt. "What if we lose him, Moe? What are we gonna do?"

Suddenly Romero felt the tears in his own eyes drip down his face. He didn't even remember the last time he cried. His voice cracked. "What happened? Who shot him?"

Manny moaned, unable to compose himself. "Some stupid bastards got in a fight at the bar. Shots were fired and Manny caught one in the chest." Manny moaned again, his body shaking as he continued to sob against Romero.

Romero hugged him, his own tears coming in mass now. This was hands down the worst fucking week of his life.

*

There was nothing left to clean. The pantry, the fridge, even the linen closet, had all been cleaned out this week. The grout on both the kitchen and bathroom tile were thoroughly scrubbed and now looked good as new. Every crevice in the apartment had been vacuumed and cleaned. Isabel lay there on the sofa smelling the pine cleaner scent that filtrated throughout her apartment. Her muscles ached. Her knuckles were raw. She'd done everything she could to keep herself busy all week and still she felt the warm tear run down the side of her face as she lay there desperately trying not think of the one thing she'd avoided thinking about all week. Romero.

She missed him terribly. Sunday night after getting home from the mall, she'd decided she just didn't have it in her to deal with Romero's relationship with Cici. If he had to continue seeing her for his son's sake, it would kill her each time he came home with her scent all over him. The thought of him spending any time with her even if it was only for his son's sake would be too painful. Now she couldn't decide what would be worse, that or this. Lying here wishing with all her might that she could feel his arms around her, just one more time. It was all she'd thought of every night since that horrible night.

She'd been so sleep-deprived since then, and now she felt her body giving in to the exhaustion. Normally, she'd get up and brush her teeth, get into her sleep-wear, make sure her clothes were ready for the next morning. Now she let herself give in to the exhaustion. Let her body call the shots until it slowly shut down and slipped into an abyss of nothingness.

Far away in the distance, there was a ringing. A ringing she'd been hearing the entire time she'd floated in a chasm of weightless reflection. Images of happier times with Romero floated through her semi-consciousness. Making love through the night, laughing as they enjoyed their dinner, kiss after glorious kiss then the ringing stopped. Along with it so did the images.

Panicked, Isabel shuddered. Then the ringing started again. This time she opened her eyes and realized she'd been dreaming, but the ringing continued. The lamp in the front room was still on but it was dark out and Isabel sat dazed wondering what time it was. It finally dawned on her that it was her cell phone ringing in the kitchen.

She stood up feeling groggy. One glance at the clock on the microwave gave her the chills. It was four in the morning. Who would be calling at this hour? She hurried to her cell and saw it was Valerie. Clearing her throat, she answered it, her anxiety growing by the minute. This couldn't be good.

"Hello?"

"Isabel, I'm sorry to wake you, but I thought you should know."

Isabel clutched her chest. "What?"

"Romero's uncle Max was shot last night." Isabel's heart nearly stopped and she held her breath as Valerie continued. "Alex overheard someone at the restaurant talking about a shooting at the Silver Dollar but he couldn't get a hold of Romero. Romero finally returned his call late last night. I've been trying to get a hold of you ever since."

Isabel wanted to tell her she'd fallen asleep on the sofa. That she hadn't heard the phone ring until just now, but she couldn't speak. Finally, she got her mouth to function. "Oh my God. Is he dead?"

"No, he was still alive the last time I spoke with Alex. He's been at the hospital with Romero ever since Romero called him last night." Valerie took a deep breath, her voice sounding very strained. "Honey, I know you're mad at Romero. But I really think he could use your support right now. Alex said he's in bad shape. Maybe... maybe you could at least call him."

"What hospital?"

Isabel nearly ran right out after she hung up with Valerie but she felt so dirty from all the cleaning she'd done the night before that she decided to shower first. With her heart at her throat the entire time she got ready to go she didn't know what to think. What would she say to him? What if Max died? Valerie said he was in critical condition. What could Isabel possibly say to Romero to make his pain any less?

Slipping into a pair of denim shorts and a cotton

tee, she fumbled the neatly aligned flip-flops in her closet finding the army green ones that matched her top. She had no time to worry about make-up or her hair so she pulled her still wet hair into a ponytail and slathered a little face lotion on and a dab of lip-gloss.

A myriad of thoughts swam through her head as she drove to the hospital. It was only Thursday, but already this week felt like the longest of her life. Each day that passed got worse. Now this.

She hadn't heard from Michael since Sunday and she still had no idea whether he was going forward with the charges against Romero, but then she *had* said she'd call *him*. She'd give it until the weekend and see if she heard anything between now and then.

As she pulled into the hospital, she was overcome with emotion. For all she knew Max could already be dead. Her heart ached for Romero—for Manny. She walked through the parking lot, her heart thudding even harder when she saw Romero's car.

Alex walked out of the sliding door to the emergency room looking very grim just as she walked up to him. Isabel brought her hand to her mouth. "How is he?"

"So far, he's better than he was last night. He got out of surgery about an hour ago." He shrugged. "He was critical when he got here, now he's critical but stable. So it's touch and go."

That was somewhat good news but Alex still looked worried. "Are you leaving?"

"Yeah, I gotta go check on Valerie."

Suddenly feeling yet another troublesome concern Isabel asked, "What's wrong with Valerie?"

"I don't know. She was fine last night, but I just called her right now and she's not feeling well at all.

She sounded terrible."

Come to think of it, Isabel had noticed something in Valerie's voice when she'd spoken to her earlier. The shock of hearing about Max had overshadowed it. She also thought Valerie was just upset about Max. Alex started to walk away. "Romero is right inside."

"Alex, have Valerie call me, or I'll worry. Okay?"

He nodded and rushed off. The dark sky was beginning to take on a bluish hue with soft rays of pink and orange as the sun began to crest. Isabel stared at it, taking a very deep breath before stepping inside. The first thing she saw was Manny in a corner seat, eyes closed, leaning against Aida who had her arms around him. Romero sat two seats away in the near empty waiting room. He was hunched over, his elbows on his knees and his hands in his hair.

She gulped, trying to be strong. Even though Manny's eyes were closed, she could see the area around them was red and swollen. She remembered Romero telling her how Manny was not ashamed to cry and she could only imagine all the crying he'd done tonight.

She walked over and took the seat next to Romero. He didn't move at all and she brought her hand up, stopping just before it touched his back, afraid of what his reaction would be. Did he hate her now? Was he still angry at her? Finally, she let her hand touch his strong back and he lifted his head. His eyes widened when he turned and saw her.

"Izzy?" he said it as if questioning if it was really her.

She smiled trying to hold it together. "How's Max?"

His eyes began to flood, but he was without expression. He hugged her. At first softly but every breath he took, he hugged her even harder. He didn't say a word and she didn't ask anything else, just ran her fingers through his hair until his breathing began to calm. Without letting go of her or even pulling away to face her he finally whispered against her ear, "Please don't leave me. I promise I'll try harder." Slowly he pulled away and their eyes met. "I'm nothing without you, Izzy."

She stared at his wet, worried eyes, not sure how to respond to that. Then she remembered Cici. Now wasn't the time to discuss that. "We can talk about this later. Right now I just wanna be here for you."

The worry never left his eyes but he took her hand and sat back. She sat back with him. "Do they know anything yet?"

Just as he was about to respond a door to the admitting room opened and a doctor walked out. They all sat up at once. Manny stood. The doctor walked up to them. He explained Max had been very lucky. The bullet had only nicked the top of his lung and had missed any vital arteries. "However, we'll need to monitor him very closely for the next few days because anytime a lung is punctured in any way the patient runs the risk of developing fluid in the lungs very quickly which can then develop into pneumonia."

Isabel saw the alarm in Romero's eyes at the mention of the word and he stood. She stood with him.

"I don't foresee that happening, everything looks good right now, but it's always best to be cautious, so he will remain in the ICU for the next couple of days. The pain medication he's on will keep him out for most of the day. I'd suggest you all go home and get some rest. Come back later tonight. That's probably the earliest he'll wake." Seeing the apprehension on both

Manny and Romero's faces, the doctor added. "We'll call you if there is any change. But I can assure you the worst is over."

"Thank, God. Thank *God!* " Manny said.

Aida hugged Manny and Isabel squeezed Romero's hand.

Once outside a very drained looking Manny turned to Romero. "We're going to grab some breakfast before heading home. You two wanna come with?"

Romero and Isabel exchanged glances then Romero shook his head. "Nah, you go ahead. I'm not feeling real hungry right now."

Romero and Isabel walked silently through the parking lot. Finally, Romero spoke up. "The charges were dropped."

Isabel turned to him wide eyed. "They were?"

The corner of his lip lifted, though he didn't seem very happy, but then under the circumstances that was understandable. "Yeah. We have no idea why. Nick, my attorney, was getting ready to file my paperwork when he was notified the charges had been cancelled."

Isabel couldn't believe her plan had actually worked. It was the first good thing that had happened that week. They stopped at her car.

"Izzy, I'll do anything to make this better. I'll change. I promise. Just please tell me it's not over." He kissed her hand.

"I don't want it to be over either, Romero."

His face brightened a bit but there was still apprehension. "So we'll work on it? *I'll* work on it. I'll do whatever you ask."

Isabel stared at him. Her heart full of hope but two things still nagged at her terribly. Cici and Michael. She was going to have to tell him eventually. She wouldn't run the risk of him finding out some other way. All that mattered now was that the charges had been dropped and Michael could never file them again. "We have to talk."

Chapter 24
BREATHE!

The ride from the hospital to Isabel's apartment wasn't even that long but it felt like an eternity and of course Romero hit every ga-damn red light there. When he pulled into the parking lot of her apartment, he saw her car was already there. Unlike him, she'd obviously missed all the red lights.

He hurried to her front door. The adrenaline of being with her again had given him a much needed second wind. With the night he'd had, he should be ready to pass out. Instead, he felt completely charged and ready to go. The door was open and he smelled the coffee the moment he walked through it. She was making breakfast, too.

Her comment about needing to talk, although somewhat promising, felt a little staid and it made him nervous. But he'd been serious when he told her he was willing to do anything. So whatever it was she wanted to talk about they'd get through it. They had to. After this week he knew, without a doubt, there was no way his life would ever be complete without her.

She smiled when she looked back from the stove where she stirred something around in the pan. Cautiously, he approached her from behind. He hadn't even tried to kiss her at the hospital, though he nearly crushed her in his arms again before letting her get in her car.

He'd felt something. He couldn't be sure but she

held back and he didn't want to push. Unable to help himself he brought his arm around her waist from behind and rested his hand on her belly. He leaned his face against the side of hers kissing her temple. "I missed you so much," he whispered.

"I missed you, too." For a moment she seemed to give in, leaning back into him, even turned her face allowing him to kiss her lips softly. But then she stiffened and straightened out again. "We need to talk." Her tone turned sharp, just like that.

Even though he knew he should, he couldn't pull himself away from her. "So talk."

She pulled away to reach for a couple of plates and he had no choice but to let go. Then she dumped scrambled eggs onto each of them, sprinkling salt, pepper and cheese. "Nothing fancy today."

"That's okay, I'm not even hungry."

They sat at the kitchen table and she wasted no time. "Tell me about Cici, and I mean the truth. All of it."

Romero stared at her. He hadn't even taken the jewelry bag out of the his trunk yet, afraid just looking at it would be too painful. "I bought you a ring. I was going to give it to you Saturday night after the party. I stopped at the jewelry store before the party and she hugged me because she got a good-sized commission out of it." He reached out and touched her arm when she looked away. "She wears a lot of fuc..." He winced. "A lot of perfume." Damn it he was going to have to try harder.

She moved the egg around on her plate. "What else?"

"That's it."

Her eyes were back on him again and they were full

of emotion. "You never did *anything* with her?"

Alright, he said he'd do whatever it took, so he took a deep breath. "I was different before, Isabel." Her eyebrows creased as if she was expecting to hear the worst. "I never slept with her if that's what you're thinking... but I would've. If her boyfriend hadn't shown up that same night he slapped her... it probably would've happened. He slapped her because he caught us making out."

Understanding swept over her face and she nodded. "Is that why you never forgot about it?"

"Yeah, I knew she had a boyfriend. Manny even warned me that he was a crazy asshole and I should stay away from her, but I didn't. I purposely set out to nail her because it's what I did back then. I was an asshole, too." He pulled his chair closer to her and leaned in. "That's not me anymore, Izzy. I swear to you."

He saw she was trying to make sense of everything he said then she blew him away with her next question. "What about her son, Moe?"

He pulled back. "How do you know about him?"

Isabel pulled her arm away from him. "Is he your son?"

"No. Who told you about him?"

"I went to the mall Sunday. I saw her there with him. He called her mommy and his name was Moe."

He dropped his head back. "Listen babe, I don't know why she named him Moe or..." he changed his mind. It was best to just come clean. "Yeah I do." He told her the story Cici had told him at Frisco's, leaving out the part about Cici saying she never came back because she knew they'd end up finishing what they hadn't the night her boyfriend slapped her.

"So do you think she has feelings for you?"

"No." He reached for her hand again. "I don't know and I don't care. She knows the ring I bought was for my girlfriend. Izzy, *trust me*. You have *nothing* to worry about. I won't ever go back to that jewelry store again. I won't even go to the mall without you, if that's what you want. I told you. I'll do anything you ask."

Her face flushed a tiny bit and for the first time that morning, he saw a hint of a smile. "You don't have to do all that."

Romero moved even closer to her. "Just tell me you haven't given up on me. You don't know what it did to me when Alex dropped off all my stuff."

She ran her fingers through his hair. "I thought you had a son with Cici."

That was it? She wasn't running from him because of his *temper issues*? He couldn't hold back any more and he kissed her. Damn he'd missed her lips. "You forgive me for Saturday?"

She nodded and he kissed her again. "Me packing your stuff up had nothing to do with Saturday. That was my fault."

Romero pulled back and looked at her. "Your fault? I'm the one that lost it."

"Yeah, but you wouldn't have if I hadn't purposely flirted with Michael to make you mad. It was stupid. I was still so mad about the smell of Cici's perfume on you."

Michael's words came back to him along with the same sting he'd felt that night. "Did you really tell him you were questioning your future with me?"

This time she kissed him, then looked him in the eyes. "Something like that, but it was all part of the stupid state of mind I was in. I wanted him to think that so he wouldn't question why I was being so nice to him. I wanted you to hurt as much as I was hurting. But trust *me*. I'll never do that again. I'm sorry."

All week he kept going back to that, certain that if she had already questioned their future together what he'd done that night had only confirmed her doubts. Hearing her reason for why she actually said it now, although it wasn't the greatest feeling to know she'd *meant* to hurt him, was still an enormous relief. "Wait here."

He startled her when he stood suddenly. So he leaned over and pecked her before walking away. "I'll be right back."

He ran out to his car and took the bag out of his trunk. Feeling the nerves start up in his stomach he tried pushing them away. He hurried back to her apartment and walked inside. She was pouring herself a cup of coffee, but curiously eyed the bag.

"Okay, don't freak out. This could be whatever you want it to be. I just wanted to get you something nice."

Isabel leaned against the counter holding her coffee mug with both hands as he pulled the box out of the bag. Romero couldn't make out her expression, but he did catch how her eyes grew wider when he took the box out. He walked over and held it out for her.

She stared at him biting the corner of her lower lip then put her mug down on the counter. She took the box from Romero and opened it very slowly as if something might jump out at her. Now her eyes really opened wide. "Romero," she whispered, bringing her hand to her mouth. "It's beautiful. But I can't accept this."

His heart dropped. "Why?"

She finally took her eyes off the ring and looked up at him. "It looks so expensive."

"It is." He smiled, feeling slightly relieved. "But you're worth it, baby."

Isabel looked back down at the ring and then up at him again. "I don't know what to say."

"Just say you'll wear it." He pulled the ring out of the box and slid it on her left hand's ring finger. Just as he imagined, it looked perfect on her. He kissed her. "And that you forgive me." He kissed her again even deeper. "And that you love me."

"I love you," she said, wrapping her arms around him. "God, I love you."

He groaned because he felt the sincerity in her kisses. She really did love him. Now that he had his second chance, he'd be damned if he was going to blow it. "C'mon." He tugged her hand, pulling her behind him and practically sprinting to the bedroom.

*

Last night hadn't been the only night Romero had gone almost the entire night without sleeping during the past week. Isabel told him she'd been deprived of any sleep herself all week. So it wasn't surprising that after only an hour of making up for the time apart they were both out. Apparently, he'd been more tired than Isabel because she was already up when he woke. He hadn't even felt her get out of bed.

He could hear her talking softly in the front room when he walked into the restroom. Obviously, she was on the phone because he heard no other voices. The sun was already heading south. Holy shit, how long had he slept? He had to admit it felt good. Everything felt damn good now.

He ran into Isabel in the hallway. She held her

phone in her hand and he attacked her against the wall, kissing her neck as she giggled. "Why didn't you wake me?" he asked in between kissing her neck.

She squirmed. "You were sleeping so soundly, I didn't have the heart to. I've only been up a little while myself. The phone woke me."

"Who was it?" he said, nibbling on her ear.

She didn't answer and he pulled his head up to kiss her when he saw her unnerved expression and he immediately thought of Max. "What's wrong?"

"It was Michael."

Romero stared at her, trying with all his might to slow the waves of heat that begun searing through him. "What did he want?"

"To let me know about him dropping the charges against you. But..." Her eyes went down to her phone and stayed there. "I need to tell you something."

Her tone and the fact that she couldn't look at him when she said it only made it harder for him to stay calm but he took deep breaths, hoping she didn't notice just how deep. "Okay, tell me."

She told him about talking to her dad Sunday and how he said it would be up to Michael to drop the charges. "I called him the day after you were arrested."

He felt his eyebrows jump up along with his heart rate. "You called Michael?" It was becoming increasingly impossible to remain cool but he was determined to not blow it again.

"I had to do something, Romero. I was desperate. I felt so guilty because it was all my fault."

Aware that he'd pressed up against her a little harder than he should, he pulled back but just a little, and he placed his hand against the wall above her head. "So what happened?"

She glanced at him again but looked back down at her phone immediately. "I played nice. I told him I was calling to see how he was doing and I said I was hoping we could talk."

Romero swallowed hard, remembering how stumped he and Nick had been that the charges had been dropped. His heart was really going now and the hand above her head fisted. "What did you do?"

"I went to see him."

"Did you now?" He tapped the wall with his fist, but not as hard as he really wanted to. "Where at?"

"He didn't want to meet somewhere in public because he said he still wasn't feeling well enough. This was only a day after it had happened."

Romero almost didn't want to ask. The whole breathing shit had gone out the window several questions ago. "Where'd you meet him?"

She didn't answer at first, then in almost a whisper she finally said, "In his *hotel room.*"

His fist banged the wall and she flinched. "You went to his hotel room?" His insides were completely lit now and he panicked, moving away from the wall trying to hold it together.

He felt her hand on his arm. "Nothing happened. That's not what I went there for. I just wanted to talk to him."

Romero took a few steps away from her, both fists at his hips. *Fucking breathe!* He commanded himself. "So what did you do? Why'd he drop the charges, Isabel?"

There was a pained look in her eyes at the sound of her name, but she spoke fast, explaining how she'd laid it on thick about the news reports and how worried she was about it affecting her dad's campaign. And then she told him about how she'd pretended to be considering breaking things off with him in hopes that if Michael thought she was available, he might drop the charges as a way to get on her good side. "We just had dinner and some champagne. Then I left. That was it. It was a long shot but it worked. I hadn't heard from him until now."

Romero walked back to her flattening his hands against the wall on either side of her face and leaned in. "And he didn't try anything?"

"He tried to kiss me goodbye but I didn't let him. I said it didn't feel right since technically I was still with you."

His heart still hammered, even though he felt just tiny bit more in control. Still, he had to know. "What else did he have to say just now?"

"He asked if I'd broken things off with you yet."

"And you told him?"

She placed her open hand on his bare chest. "Don't get mad but I still played it off like I'm unsure." Romero clenched his jaw. "Only because I want to make absolutely sure he doesn't change his mind about dropping the charges."

"You know even if he does change his mind you're not going back to see him again. I'd rather do the fucking time."

She nodded, then smiled almost guardedly. "I don't think he can. At least that's what my dad said. Once the charges are cancelled, it's irreversible — unless you assault him again."

Romero leaned in and kissed her, feeling the tension in his muscles begin to settle. "Yeah, well make sure you don't even think about meeting up with him again or that just may happen." Even though she smiled at that, he had to wonder if she knew he'd never been more serious.

She ran her hands up and down his bare back. "So tense." Her hands moved down to the waistband of his briefs and she tugged on it. "Let's go do something about this."

Finally, she'd said something that didn't make him want to punch a hole through the wall.

*

Neither of them had exaggerated when they said they'd hardly got any sleep that week, because after Isabel finished relieving Romero of the tension he'd worked up, they fell asleep again.

When they woke again, it was early evening and they were ravenous. They showered, grabbed something to eat and headed back to the hospital.

Isabel stared at the ring on her finger. Romero had said it could be whatever she'd wanted it to be, though that wasn't exactly a proposal. At this point, she wasn't sure she would've wanted it to be. There was still the matter of her father saying Romero wasn't welcome around the family.

Pat had also made it a point to call her that week just to remind her how worried the family was about her safety, calling Romero unstable and insinuating she was delusional for thinking he would never unleash his wrath on her.

Isabel had seen it today. She couldn't think of a single thing worse than telling Romero she'd gone to Michael's hotel room, and though she'd seen and felt how difficult it had been for him to not explode, she'd also taken note of the effort he made not to. Something like that would be hard for any man to hear, but she knew how much stronger things of this nature affected Romero and he'd done it. He got through it. He may not always but in her heart, she knew they couldn't be more wrong about him. There was no way, no matter how angry, that he would ever harm her.

Her phone rang just as they reached the hospital. It was Art. He didn't make it to Charles' party and Isabel hadn't been surprised. Even before the party, Pat had mentioned to Isabel the comments she made to Art about his fiancée, Sabrina and as usual, in very off-handed Pat like style, they were rude.

"Hi, Art."

"Bellie Bell, you busy this weekend?"

Isabel thought about it. She didn't have plans but after the week she'd spent away from Romero, she was hoping to spend the entire weekend with him. "Not really, why?"

"Me and Sabrina were going to drive down there on Sunday. I was hoping to get everyone together for brunch... we have an announcement to make."

Isabel smiled. "An announcement? Oh my God did you guys set a date for the wedding?" As excited as she really was, Art had always said they'd wait until Sabrina was done with school. The last time he'd mentioned it she still had at least a year to go.

"I'm not saying, Bell. You have to wait. But I'm calling to make sure you leave the day open. I know it's kind of last minute, but that's just how things worked out."

He sounded excited and that excited her as well. Finally some good news, even though to some, mainly Pat, it would be anything but good. "Sure. Let me know where and when and I'll be there."

Romero took her hand after coming around the car in the hospital parking lot. Just like that, the good vibes she was feeling deflated. Either she told Romero he couldn't come with her Sunday, that he'd been banned from all her family functions or she took him, going against her family's wishes.

"Your brother's gonna be in town?"

Isabel nodded, smiling. "This Sunday. He's got an announcement to make, I think he and Sabrina set a date for the wedding. And it must be soon if he wants to get us all together so fast."

"Really?" Romero smirked. "This should be interesting."

Isabel took a deep breath. Romero didn't know the half of it.

Chapter 25
Lies

The next morning Romero drove back to his uncle's house to pick up some of his things, most importantly his laptop. His battery was completely dead. He'd left the laptop on when he got the news of Max and forgot all about it.

Max was doing a lot better now. There were no signs of fluid in his lungs, and he was able to talk a little the night before. The unlucky bastard had been the only one hit that night, but they'd at least arrested the guy who'd fired the shot. It appeared to be unintentional. A stray bullet and Max was just in the wrong place at the wrong time, but they were still investigating.

Romero plugged in his laptop to let it charge while he showered and got ready for the day. Isabel had left early to work. He felt bad that she'd called in sick the day before on account of him. Since he didn't have anything at her place he left with her in the morning and decided to get ready at his uncles'. By the time he'd finished getting ready and made himself something to eat, his laptop had a good enough charge. It had saved his work and took him directly to the last thing he'd been working on, reminding him of Charles.

He logged back into the software and it went directly to the last records he'd looked up—Charles's secret bank account. There were an awful lot of hefty deposits in the last few weeks and suspiciously large amount of transfers to another bank account. Romero clicked on the account the money was being transferred to. The account was registered to a Nicole Herrera in Miami, Florida. Interesting.

He got caught up snooping for about an hour. In that time he uncovered the hefty deposits to Charles' account all matched the same amounts of withdrawals from another account Charles had only that account was registered under the LLC name Montenegro for Mayor Campaign. Could Charles be stupid enough to be taking campaign donations and funneling them to his girlfriend's account? Didn't he know all this shit could be traced? Unless he really thought that no one would ever suspect.

Romero remembered Pat bragging at the announcement dinner about how most of the donations to the campaign were coming from Charles' connections. If that was the case, Charles could be reporting smaller donations than were actually being made and pocketing the rest. All he had to do was deposit the actual amount and withdraw the difference, but it was still a risk.

Deciding this was just too interesting to not look into further, Romero put in a few calls to some of his own connections.

Pissed that he'd wasted an hour on this, he got his stuff together and headed out to meet a client.

By the end of the day, he was anxious to see Isabel again. He called her on her way to her apartment but she hadn't answered. As he drove in, he noticed more cars in the parking lot than usual. If he wasn't mistaken, one of them was Pat's car. *Fuck.* He hoped she wasn't there.

The door to the apartment opened just as he walked

up to it. Isabel walked out and closed the door behind her. "What's going on?"

"My family is here."

"Why? Something happen?"

"No, they just decided they wanted to speak with me... alone."

Romero stared at her confused. "About what?"

"About what happened with you and Michael, among other things."

"What's there to talk about?"

The door opened behind Isabel and Pat stood there hand on hip. "Bell, we're waiting."

Romero caught a glimpse of who was there. Both her parents, even Charles, and then he saw him— Jacob. Immediately it spiked his senses. Fucking Pat. She was never going to give up.

"What's he doing here?" His question was directed to Pat not Isabel.

"He's here as a friend who's as concerned about Isabel as we all are."

Romero glanced at Isabel, who closed her eyes for a moment, then back at Pat. "Concerned for her? Why?"

Then it hit him and he almost laughed, though he wasn't amused at all. It was so stupid but it didn't surprise him that Pat would do something like this. "Are you fucking kidding me?"

Her father was at the door now, behind Pat. "Is there a problem, Isabel?"

Romero stepped back but glared at Pat. "You put an intervention together to get Isabel to drop me?"

"You're dangerous," her father said. "We're just looking out for one of our own. You'd do the same."

"And what does bringing her ex-boyfriend along, have to do with me being dangerous, Pat?" He practically spit her name, feeling the anger begin to take over. Before she could answer, he turned to Isabel. "Are you seriously buying this shit? Do you really believe for a second that I could ever hurt you?"

"No!"

"Be reasonable, Bell," Pat insisted. "He says he won't now but look how quick he is to get violent. Believe me I know the signs."

"You don't know shit!" He turned back to Isabel. "Are you really gonna do this Isabel? Go back in there and listen to all her bullshit and have your fucking ex-boyfriend tell you why I'm no good for you? Don't you see what she's doing? "

"I don't think I like the tone you're taking with either of my daughters." Her father stepped in front of Pat. "This is why we're concerned, honey. If he speaks to you this way now how can we trust that he won't get worse?"

Charles stood behind Pat now. Romero smirked. "No disrespect, sir." His eyes met Charles'. "But I'd say Isabel is not the daughter you should be worried about."

"How dare you!" Pat moved herself in front of Charles.

"Romero!" Isabel finally spoke up.

"It's okay," her father said, putting his hand on Pat's shoulder. "I think I know exactly who I need to be concerned for and it's not Pat."

Charles hadn't stopped staring at Romero. "Go back to your little intervention, Isabel — back to Jacob."

Isabel called out for him as he walked away. He had to, and he wasn't looking back either. If he stayed there even a minute longer, he might help Pat prove at least one part of her points. Things could get violent very quickly and he wasn't about to put on another show for her sister to use against him.

It didn't even bother him so much that they think he wasn't good enough for Isabel. What bothered him the most is that they would think he could ever hurt her. He'd throw himself in front of a bus for Isabel before he'd hurt her.

He'd only been at Moreno's for about twenty minutes venting to Sal about Isabel's intervention when his phone rang. It was her.

"Please come home." Her voice broke as she continued. "I made them all leave. I didn't want to have to choose but if they're gonna make me then I choose you. I love you."

Romero stood up and waved at Sal, walking back toward the exit. "Baby, don't cry. You don't have to choose. I'll just... I'll just stay away when they're around."

"No, if they won't accept you then they lose me, too. I told them that."

Damn it. This wasn't what he wanted. As big a pain as her family was, he knew Isabel would be miserable if they were out of her life. He'd seen how excited she was about seeing Art this weekend. "I'm on my way, babe. We'll talk when I get there."

*

After hearing Romero speak to both Pat and Isabel the way he had, her father told her the family would never turn their back on her but they'd also never accept Romero and that was final. More than just his language, he was convinced that he one day would get the tragic news that Romero had unloaded all that anger he seemed to be carrying, on her.

For the first time, he brought up the fact that Romero's father being in jail must have a lot to do with it. He'd seen the vicious cycle time and time again. A father convicted of a violent crime more than likely would have children who followed in their footsteps.

Isabel insisted Romero's father had not been convicted for anything violent, but it was futile. Her father had already taken it upon himself to look into Romero's dad's case and knew that he'd nearly killed a man with his bare hands while incarcerated. He'd given Romero the benefit of the doubt, but after seeing what he'd done to Michael he was convinced that it was just a matter of time before he became violent with her, too.

No one was more adamant about it than Pat, and she'd taken great offense to Romero insinuating her father needed to worry about Charles. Isabel wasn't sure what *that* had been about but she could only assume he was looking for any way to offend her, though smearing someone who had nothing to do with it was probably not the smartest thing to do.

The only thing Jacob had said was that he would always be there for her if she ever needed an ear and for her not to hesitate to call him.

In the end, none of them were able to convince her that Romero could ever hurt her. Not once in all the times she'd seen him angry had she ever felt threatened. She was tired of them trying to demean him. If any of them would just take the time to get to know him they'd understand why she was so in love with him.

Romero tried to convince her Friday evening when he got back after they left that she should be there with her family on Sunday for Art's announcement. He said he didn't mind not being there, he'd use the time to work out, something he'd been neglecting lately. At first, she refused but he was able to convince her when he pointed out that Art had nothing to do with the intervention and he could probably use her support, since Pat would more than likely do or say something to sour his big announcement.

They'd made love for hours after that, with Isabel wanting to show him how little influence her family's worries had on her. Even if they didn't, she believed in him — in them — categorically.

Saturday, Romero told her he had to work most of the day. He'd cut down significantly on the weekends but she knew in his line of work, weekends had to be busy for him. She was a little disappointed she'd looked forward to spending the entire day with him since part of Sunday she'd be busy with Art's brunch, but she didn't complain. How could she?

On her way to meet Valerie at the mall for lunch she got a call from Jacob. She sighed, remembering the intervention and wondered if he had more to say.

"Hi, Jacob."

"Hey, Bell. You busy?"

"I'm driving but I have my earpiece on. What's up?"

"Listen I just wanted you to know, that yesterday I didn't feel real comfortable about the whole intervention thing. Your sister sort of caught me off guard when she asked me to be part of it." He was quiet for a moment. "I don't want you to think for even a second that I don't think you smart enough to come to your own conclusions, especially one as big as this one. Your family made a lot of good points yesterday but bottom line is the guy has a short fuse, and from what it sounds like, mostly when it comes to anyone coming between the two of you. Who could blame him right? So he blew up and he has, as your sister put it, a filthy mouth." He chuckled a little, making Isabel smile. "Being in the Navy, I'm around a lot of guys like that. And I know it doesn't mean they're bad. I know you, Bell. If you feel it in your heart—you truly believe he would never hurt you. Then go with your gut. Forget what everybody else says. I wanted to say this last night but I had a feeling I'd be mauled by your family. So I just wanted you to know I wish you only the best, and I know you don't need anyone helping you make these kinds of decision for you. Least of all me."

Isabel's felt her heart swell. Despite things not having worked out between her and Jacob, she remembered now why she'd been with him for such a long time. He was a good guy through and through with a heart to match. "Thank you, Jacob. That means a lot to me. I had a feeling my sister's persuasiveness had more to do with you being there yesterday than you thinking you needed to convince me Romero was bad. Thanks for this. It's nice to know someone has faith in my ability to make a judgment call."

"I *know* you do. That's why I wanted to make sure you didn't think I didn't."

She wished him the very best as well before hanging up and felt even better about standing her ground against her family's wishes.

*

Isabel reached across the table at lunch and squeezed Valerie's hand. "I'm glad you're better; the last couple of days have been so crazy for me I'd forgotten to call you."

Valerie called Isabel Friday morning letting her know she *was* feeling better but wasn't up to talking. With the stupid intervention waiting for her when she got home, she hadn't had a chance to talk to her. But last night Valerie called her and invited her to lunch today. "I was feeling better last night. That's why I called you, but I almost cancelled because I woke up feeling like total crap this morning again."

Still eyeing her menu for anything that sounded good, Isabel didn't look up. "What do you think it is?" The Crab Shack wasn't one of Isabel's favorites but Valerie really liked it.

"Hmm, I dunno." It was odd to hear Valerie sound playful about being sick. "For the past few days I've been throwing up my guts every morning."

Isabel lowered her menu to see Valerie smiling. "Oh my God. Are you…"

Valerie laughed. "I'm not sure yet but it's a definite possibility. I've been off the pill for almost a month now. Only problem is my period's been all screwy because of it." She put her menu down and grinned. "The best part about it is Alex is totally clueless. He really thinks I have some kind of stomach virus. I wanna keep it that way so I can surprise him."

Isabel couldn't help but smile giddily then stopped. "You're not upset about it are you? I know you said you wanted to wait a little longer."

"I did but now that I might be, I'm actually getting excited about it. I just don't wanna say anything to Alex until I know for sure. He's been pushing for this for a while now. I'd hate for him to get his hopes up and then have it be a false alarm."

"I won't say anything to Romero until it's a sure thing and Alex knows." Isabel reached across the table and a squeezed Isabel's hand. "I'm excited for you. I really am."

Isabel filled Valerie in on everything that happened the last couple of days and everything she'd cleared up with Romero, including his relationship with Cici and her son, Moe. Valerie nearly swooned when she saw the ring he'd bought her and said she didn't care what anyone said. It was definitely an engagement ring.

They'd almost made it through their entire meal when Valerie had to leave the table suddenly, feeling sick. Isabel was about to get up and check on her when she saw a very pale looking Valerie walking back to the table. Isabel felt so bad for her.

"Maybe it *is* a virus. This is the first time it's hit me in the afternoon."

Isabel smiled, tilting her head. "It's only called morning sickness but it can hit at any time of the day. I'm even more convinced now that you are pregnant. I'm only sorry you didn't get to keep your lunch down. You were in there for a while. You probably threw it all up."

"*All* of it." Valerie made a face. "And just looking at the rest of this food makes my mouth water, but now in a good way."

Isabel finished and Valerie paid. They walked out of the mall and hugged goodbye just outside the entrance. "Promise me you'll call me as soon as you know something."

"I will," Valerie said, lifting her sunglasses and looking past Isabel's shoulder. "Is that Romero?"

Isabel turned in time to see Romero pulling out of a parking space and turn toward the exit of the parking lot. "Yeah. Hmm. He said he was working today."

When she turned back to Valerie, her expression matched what Isabel was feeling. She'd mentioned to Valerie Romero's promise to not return to that jewelry store again or even the mall without her. Not that she'd taken him up on it but she hadn't exactly turned the proposition down. What's more, the entrance closest to where he had parked was the one closest to the jewelry store.

Valerie changed her expression quickly and shook her head. "Don't jump to conclusions. Just ask him as soon as you get home, or better yet call him and tell him you saw him here. Ask him what he was doing."

Isabel preferred to see his expression when she asked him. He hadn't lied to her yet, and she had no reason to think he might start now. Not after everything they'd just gone through. She smiled trying to appear unfazed by it. "No, I'll just ask him when I get home. He goes to MicroTech a lot for all his camera and computer stuff."

That seemed a good enough reason for Valerie. They said good-bye again and Isabel headed home.

As much as she told herself it was probably nothing and to stop jumping to conclusions, Isabel gave in and called him on her way home. She may as well get the simple explanation now before she began to make herself crazy. He might not be home until later that evening and she'd be ready to throw him out with all the stories she was sure her imagination would come up with by then.

She stared at the beautiful diamond on her finger as she sat at the red light, waiting for Romero to pick up. "Hey, Izzy."

His voice made her smile. "Hey, what are you up

to?"

"Working. It's been a busy day."

"Oh, yeah. Where at?"

"I met a client over by the marina. Then had to install some telephone bugs at an office where some paranoid ass, thinks every one of his employees is out to get him. That took a while. I just got one more place I have to stop and take some pictures then I should be heading home."

Isabel held her breath waiting for him to mention the mall. "Hmm. I had lunch with Valerie at the Crab Shack at the mall." She hoped that would elicit him mentioning his own stop at the mall.

"God that sounds good. I haven't even had a chance to eat."

Now she was mad. "So you were no where else today? Except for the places you mentioned."

He was quiet for a moment and she knew her tone had taken him by surprise. "Yes."

"I saw you, Romero. Just now—at the mall. Why are you lying to me?"

She heard him exhale. "Babe, we gotta talk."

She had no idea what he could possibly have to tell her now but it was enough to garner an incredibly annoying lump in her throat. "You're damn right we do."

He must've heard the strain in her voice. "I know what you're thinking, babe but…you know what? Fuck the pictures, I'm going straight home. Meet me there. There's something I gotta tell you."

Even after she'd hung up with him, the lump remained in her throat. She'd been through too much this week. She wasn't sure how much more she could take.

Chapter 26
BIG mistake

This was not how Romero planned on breaking the news to Isabel about Charles. He didn't even have all the facts yet. It had started out of sheer curiosity. He'd come to realize through his line of work, that there were two types of people when it came to cheating spouses. The ones who demanded to know the truth and would end things accordingly when they got it, and those who chose to look the other way, living blissfully in ignorance as long as their perfect lives remained unscathed on the surface.

He figured she was so unlike Isabel, Pat most likely preferred blissful ignorance. In that case, there was no point in trying to enlighten her with the truth. She probably already knew or at the very least suspected. But things were beginning to take an unsettling turn.

At first, he'd done this for his own personal guilty pleasure. It'd be nice to have one up on stupid Pat, knowing her life wasn't as perfect as she liked everyone to think. The very reason why he hadn't planned on telling Isabel. But now he wouldn't feel right keeping what he knew to himself. He just wished he could've waited until he knew everything before having to tell Isabel.

He got to the apartment before she did. He was just putting his wallet and keys on the counter when the door opened behind me.

"Okay, just tell me. Why were you at the mall? Why

did you lie to me?"

Romero turned and walked to her, surprised that she looked ready to cry. "Babe, relax. I wasn't there to see Cici. I know that's what you're thinking."

"Then why *were* you there?"

He took her by the hand and led her to the sofa in the front room. "I was there to see a friend who works security at the mall."

He backed up and told her about seeing Charles with another woman at the birthday party, then about the bank accounts. "My friend at the mall and I go way back to when we were both working bouncer gigs at clubs. He's now head of security at the mall. But he does some stuff on the side." He hesitated to tell her the next part because he knew her family must've fed plenty of shit to her about the kind of person he must be. "He used to hack into computers back in the day, and though he doesn't do it so much anymore, I can still count on him to do things for me here and there." Isabel stared at him, her eyes wide, but at least she didn't look upset anymore—not at him anyway.

"If I'm right, Charles is having an affair, babe. It's with a woman in Miami. And he's been embezzling money from your dad's campaign and transferring it to her account."

Both of Isabel's hands were over her mouth now. "You know this for sure?"

"I know for sure he's been taking money from the campaign account and putting it into hers. And I know he stays with her whenever he's in Miami. What I don't know is what he's planning on doing with all that money and if she's actually someone he's having an affair with or just an accomplice, but it looks bad. I don't know if your sister knows about this either."

"Of course she doesn't."

"Well." Romero didn't want to sound condescending but it was hard to believe she was completely clueless. Charles hadn't exactly covered his tracks too well. "You never know, but his other girl knows about Pat. She's been giving him a hard time lately, which is the reason why I think he may be considering making some kind of move. I'm just not sure what, but I think that's what the money is for."

Isabel started to get up. "I have to tell her."

Romero reached for her hand. "No, Izzy, not yet."

"Why?"

"Because it's still not clear-cut what this relationship with this girl is. It looks likes she might also be married, but there's something weird about it. I'm still checking things out. Although that doesn't mean anything. She could be having an affair herself. But he could still say she's just an assistant. He has several. And the whole transferring money to her account he could probably come up with something relating back to the campaign and just deny the whole damn thing."

"But—"

He squeezed her hand gently. "What do you think your family is gonna say when you tell them *I'm* the one making these accusations? Without proof whose word do you think they'll take?"

She stared at him, taking a deep breath.

"Just wait. I should know this coming week. My friend at the mall is gonna... look into his computer and see if he can get some personal stuff between Charles and this woman. And I've made a few other calls. I should be hearing from them soon, too."

Isabel shook her head. "How am I supposed to face this lying bastard tomorrow without slapping him?"

Romero laughed. "Just think of what your sister will do to him when she finds out. He'll get what's coming to him. Don't worry."

Isabel leaned in slowly. "I'm sorry I was thinking the worst about you."

Romero lay back pulling her onto him. "No. I'm sorry I kept anything from you. I just wanted to have everything down before I told you." He kissed her. "I told you, you have nothing to worry about. But I get why you might've jumped the gun this time. I probably would've myself." He chuckled. "Only I wouldn't have handled it quite as calmly as you did."

"No, you handled hearing about me going to see Michael just fine. I was proud of you."

Romero let his head hang back. "Don't remind me."

He filled her in on a few more of the minor details he'd uncovered, but he didn't have a whole lot more to tell her. He only hoped this wasn't something that looked and smelled bad, but was actually nothing. That happened a few times when he was following a potentially cheating spouse. Isabel's family already didn't like him and him flinging false accusations like this, certainly wasn't going to buy him any points. As long as Isabel could keep this under wraps until he knew for sure, everything should be okay.

*

Art and Sabrina were already there when Isabel arrived at the restaurant Sunday. She hugged them both eagerly. "So what is it?"

They both laughed. "You have to wait until everyone is here," Art said kissing her on the cheek. "Where's Romero?"

Isabel rolled her eyes. "Don't get me started."

"What happened? Did you break up?"

"No." She took the seat across from Art. "After last week's nightmare he's been banned from coming around the family. They all say he's dangerous for me, but we both know who's the most adamant about it. They actually had an intervention for me on Friday."

"Get the hell out of here."

The waiter came by and filled their champagne glasses. Isabel took the pitcher of orange juice on the table and poured some in her champagne glass. She loved mimosas. "No, I'm not kidding. Whose idea do you think that was? They even brought Jacob along to put in his two cents."

Art laughed. "Well, Pat's in for one today. I don't give a damn what she says anymore."

Isabel downed most of her mimosa and nodded her head. "Good for you." Maybe if Pat spent less time worrying about other people's relationships, her own wouldn't be such a mess. "Did you really tell Pat you agreed about Romero being dangerous?"

Art finished sipping his champagne making a face. "No, she said I did?"

"Yeah," Isabel nodded. She should've known Pat was full of it. "She said you'd agreed the night of dad's announcement dinner."

Art then laughed. "I said she better watch her ass, because Romero didn't seem like he'd be one to take her shit."

Isabel had to laugh, too. Of course, Pat would find a way to turn that around in her favor. She then eyed Sabrina, remembering how Pat had made it sound like Art purposely hadn't brought her to please Pat. "And why weren't you there the night of my dad's dinner?"

Sabrina's eyebrows lifted and she looked as if she felt guilty. "I'm sorry." She glanced at Art. "I thought he'd told you. My mom had surgery that week.

She was in no condition to be left alone. So I stayed home to look after her."

Isabel shook her head. "Oh, no worries. I was just curious." God, she should've known better. Pat had always had a way of manipulating everything to her advantage.

After asking Sabrina a bit more about her mother's health, the waiter came by and refilled Isabel's champagne glass nearly to the top, leaving little room for the orange juice. Her parents arrived together with Pat and Charles. Art, Sabrina and Isabel all stood to greet them. Pat's standoffish attitude toward Sabrina didn't go unnoticed by Isabel.

Isabel reached out and gave Charles a quick handshake instead of her usual hug and kiss on the cheek. She could barely stand to look at him. Her parents sat next to her, leaving Pat no choice but to sit next to Art and Sabrina. The bad part about that was Isabel would now be facing Charles through entire brunch.

"Well, are you going to tell us why we're here now?" Pat asked as she placed her napkin on her lap.

Art pulled out his phone and Isabel took another big gulp of her mimosa. She was nervous for him. Whatever it was, she'd be behind him all the way. She didn't want Pat squashing their news. She was so good at that.

"Let me get Gina on the phone. I promised I'd put her on speaker so she could hear it at the same time as you guys did."

Pat rolled her eyes, already disparaging whatever he was about to tell them. The waiter walked around the table, pouring more champagne all around, as Art placed the phone in the center face up on speaker.

"Hey. Art." Gina answered, sounding excited.

"Hey, Gina. You're on speaker. Say hi to everyone."

She did and everyone greeted her back. Isabel's insides were beginning to turn. She was sure Art would be announcing his wedding date and she was terrified that Pat was going to say something stupid.

"Alright, you ready for this?"

"Yes!" her mother said. "I'm dying. Just tell us."

Isabel took another drink of her mimosa and waited, holding her breath.

Art and Sabrina exchanged glances then addressed her parents. "You two are going to be grandparents."

Pat's jaw dropped. Gina squealed on the phone, making Art reach for the phone and turn the volume down. Before Pat could say anything, Isabel stood up and rushed around the table. "Oh my God. I'm gonna be an aunt?"

Art smiled and nodded pleased that Isabel seemed so happy. Her parents followed, hugging them both, apparently happy about the news also. Even Charles stood to shake Art's hand and hug Sabrina. Pat was the only one who remained seated. "Art, you two are not even married. Weren't you guys using protection?"

Leave it to Pat to ask such a thing at a moment like this. Isabel wasn't sure if it was the mimosas she'd drunk so fast or just the fact that Pat could be such a witch that made her speak up. "It doesn't matter, Pat. They're obviously very happy about this and so am I." She turned and smiled at both Art and Sabrina.

"Actually we did use protection," Art said then turned and smiled at Sabrina. "But sometimes these things happen."

"Mistakes?"

"Pat." Her mothers tone was forbidding.

"I'm just saying. A baby is going to make it that much harder to finish school. It's already taken her this long. And honestly, having babies out of wedlock these days has become so acceptable."

Isabel glared at her but took another drink of her champagne to keep from lashing out.

"Don't listen to her, Art and Sabrina." Gina's voice was loud and clear. "I for one am very happy for you. You two can always get married later. Finally, a baby in the family. I was getting sick of waiting on Pat and Charles."

Pat's expression turned even more severe. Art and Sabrina exchanged another suspicious glance. "The baby wasn't all we wanted to announce today," Art said.

Pat turned to them, not even attempting to hide her distaste. Sabrina held out her hand showing off a simple wedding band then Art did the same. "We got married last week."

There was more squealing out of the phone. Isabel jumped up again, this time stumbling a little and she giggled. "Oh wow, you guys! This is all so unexpected!" She hugged them again and again everyone else followed suit. The exception of course being Pat whose mouth now pulled tightly to the side. "I agree with Isabel. Wow," was all she said as she reached for the menu.

Everyone ignored her. Gina congratulated them and asked if there were any more announcements. When Art said that was it, she congratulated them again before saying she had to go and hung up.

The second Art and Sabrina walked away to the

buffet table, Pat wasted no time to start in about what a mistake he'd made. "I swear people act like a marriage is something you jump into. She got pregnant so half a thought later they're married. Neither of them have any idea what it takes to make a marriage work."

"Trust?" Isabel said, eyeing Charles.

"That's just one of the elements needed to form a strong union. One that'll withstand not just the ups but the many downs as well. It's not so simple."

What a joke.

"They're both adults, Patricia," her mother warned. "I don't want you lecturing them. That's not why they wanted us here today."

The rest of the brunch was the same, with Pat throwing in jab after jab about how marriage shouldn't be taken lightly. She'd already mentioned the importance of knowing someone well enough to see the signs of future issues. That one was aimed at Isabel, of course.

Isabel was feeling lightheaded and much braver. Her resolve and decision to just ignore her sister and keep changing the subject was beginning to wane. It was when Pat brought up trust again that Isabel couldn't take it anymore. "Because you know without a doubt that you can trust Charles. Right?"

Pat's brows pinched and Charles stared at her. "Of course. We've been married all these years and I've never had reason not to."

Isabel stood up without responding, excusing herself to the ladies' room. She noticed Charles kept his eyes on her. Not wanting to be overheard she texted Romero.

I don't know how much longer I can keep quiet about Charles. Pat is so infuriating! She needs to be told how NOT perfect her marriage is.

It took a few seconds but Romero responded.

She'll know soon enough. You don't have to tell me what a pain she is. Just be cool for now.

When Isabel got back to her seat, her champagne glass had already been filled, as if she needed any more. Her parents and Pat were gone. She could see them over at the buffet table again. Art was busy smooching Sabrina and Charles sat back in his seat. Isabel couldn't help glare at him.

"Something on your mind, Isabel?"

She sat down taking a sip of her champagne again. "No. Just wish Romero was here."

He sat up a little. "You know your family is only looking out for you. They don't trust that—"

"Really is *he* the one that can't be trusted, Charles?"

Charles' brows flew up. Isabel turned away from him when she noticed Art and Sabrina stood up. Art chuckled. "How many of those have you had, Bell?"

She looked down to where he was pointing at the champagne glass in her hand. Too many but she wouldn't admit that out loud. "Are you leaving?"

Just then, Pat and her parents returned to the table, plates in hand. Art explained to them that they had a long drive and were still planning on meeting with Sabrina's family to give them the news.

Once they were gone, Isabel knew Pat would now openly unleash her self-righteous opinions about them. Even though it was rude to text at the table, Charles had done it the entire time so she pulled her phone out and texted Romero again.

I can't take this anymore. But I don't think I'm okay to drive. I had to numb myself with champagne to get through this. You think you can pick me up?

She sipped her water, trying to ignore Pat who was already going off on a tangent when she noticed Charles staring at her. Her phone buzzed and she read the text.

On my way.

Isabel endured, listening to her sister go on and on about what a huge mistake Art had made. Her mother didn't seem to think so, but was a little hurt that they'd gone off and gotten married without having at least the immediate family there. Her father didn't say much as usual except that he agreed with Pat that it would be a lot harder for Sabrina to finish school now. Charles was surprisingly quiet throughout the conversation. He could be just as opinionated as Pat when he wanted to be.

From experience, Isabel knew there was no arguing with her sister so she didn't bother. The waiter had already brought the bill and Pat insisted on paying since she'd picked the restaurant and as usual it was a pricey one on the marina. Of course, she had to throw in a few jabs about not expecting Isabel to pay on her teacher's salary.

Romero's text letting her know he was there hadn't come fast enough. They were all getting ready to leave as well but Isabel didn't wait to walk out with them. If she had to listen to Pat for even another minute, she was going to scream.

She made one last stop at the ladies' room before heading out the front door. The cool ocean breeze felt good against her face. Romero leaned against the side of his car and she smiled at him.

"Isabel."

She turned to see Charles walking toward her. "Is there something you wanna say to me?"

A sudden wave of anger washed over her. There was plenty she wanted to say to him, but she'd wait until Romero gave her the go ahead. "Nope."

She didn't like the way he walked up to her and stood menacingly close. "You made a couple of odd comments in there. I couldn't help but feel they were directed towards me."

She took a step back. "Wow, what a genius. Was that because I was looking right at you when I said them?"

He took a step forward. "So out with it then. Say what you wanna say."

"I'm sure you know perfectly well what it is." She began to turn and walk away.

Charles grabbed her arm before she could turn with an expression she'd never seen on him before. "What do you *think* you know?"

"Big mistake, asshole!"

Both Isabel and Charles turned to see Romero rushing toward them, that unmistakable rage in his eyes again.

Chapter 27
Careful what you ask for

Charles let go of Isabel's arm as soon as he saw Romero. Romero charged at him, but Isabel jumped in front of him. "That's right and don't you ever put your fucking hands on her again."

"Don't please," Isabel pleaded, her hands on Romero's chest.

Romero had managed to stay calm as he'd walked toward them when he saw Charles's body language. He could tell even from where he'd stood Charles was pissed, but seeing him put his hands on her had done it. Only thing keeping him from slamming his fist into Charles's smug face was Isabel's touch.

"You must love getting arrested. But then you're probably used to it, right? Like father, like son?"

Isabel wasn't going to be able to hold him back much longer. Romero was ready to bury his fist in Charles mouth. The door to the restaurant opened and Isabel's family walked out. "What's going on?" Pat hurried toward them. "Is there a problem? Why is he here, Bell?"

"He's taking me home."

Charles shook his head. "Some people never learn." He started to walk toward Pat who had nearly reached them. "Put your dog on a leash, Isabel, before he gets himself into anymore trouble."

Isabel spun around. "You're the dog!" Her parents and Pat stared at her. "You're the one having an affair!"

"Isabel!" Pat looked completely stricken. "Just because you're mad about—"

"It's true." She turned back to Romero. "Tell them."

Charles stared at her. Pat's face went sour and she rolled her eyes. "Oh, I'm gonna believe *him*? Really, Isabel I can't believe you would—"

"He has a girlfriend in Miami, Pat," Isabel insisted.

"No he doesn't." Romero said, feeling a little calmer now.

Isabel turned back with a completely confused expression on her face now. Pat crossed her arms looking a little too self-satisfied, so he laid it on her. "He has another wife and a kid."

No one said anything for a moment then Pat, scoffed. "This is ridiculous."

Charles said nothing, just stared at Romero.

Romero smirked then turned to Isabel's dad who appeared shocked. "He's been taking money donated to the campaign so he can set up his other wife and kid here in San Diego. She gave him an ultimatum. It was either that or she'd come forward and tell Pat." Romero turned back to Charles. "I guess you don't have to move her here now uh? Now that the truth is out, she can stay in Miami."

Pat turned to Charles. "This isn't true right? He's making this up, right... Charles?"

Turns out Romero was off with his theory of Pat knowing about Charles' escapades, because when Charles didn't say anything, Pat dropped her purse and took a swing at him. Her parents rushed to them, Charles managed to grab hold of her arms and told her to calm down. She was hysterical. The scene only got worse as Pat screamed obscenities and her father and

Isabel trying to pull her back. Her mother stood off to the side in near tears pleading with Pat to calm down.

Romero hurried toward them to try and help as people began to gather and restaurant patrons began coming out. Just as he'd reached them he saw Charles grab both of Pat's hands with one of his and the second Romero saw him lift his other hand he knew what was about to happen and he jumped, wrapping his arm around Charles' neck, startling them all but no one more than Charles. Pat probably deserved to be slapped more than a few times through out her life. But not by a fucking man. "Rule number one, you prick—never hit a woman!" Romero's grip around Charles's neck got even tighter, making Charles grunt. "Especially not in front of me."

Romero's plan was to kick Charles' ass, but Pat didn't give him a chance. With Charles in a choke hold, she took advantage and landed a couple of resonating slaps on his face that could be heard clear across the marina, then topped it with a knee to his groin. Romero let go when he felt Charles body go limp. He fell to the pavement with a groan.

Clearly, now wasn't the time to let Pat in on everything his buddy from the mall had managed to uncover in just one day. But she knew the most damning thing already. He'd been having this affair for a few years now but it wasn't until several months ago when his love child was born that his mistress started pressing to be closer to him. That was right around the time he and Pat began pushing for Isabel's dad to run for Mayor.

The idiot had actually gone and married his mistress when she found out she was pregnant to keep her mouth shut.

As expected, Pat filed for divorce and pressed bigamy charges against Charles. Charles was also hit with charges of embezzlement along with a few other counts of fraud. Isabel was furious that weeks later he still hadn't done so much as an hour in jail. His lawyers had him out on bail before he ever went in. Romero warned her that he'd probably get off easy.

Even though her dad knew people in high places, unfortunately so did Charles. As bad as she felt for her sister, she was glad she'd found out about Charles before they had any kids together. Ironically all the time her sister had worried Romero or Sabrina would somehow taint her dad's reputation and harm his campaign, it had been her own husband that ultimately cost her dad the chance to be Mayor. With the scandal that followed about the campaign donations being mishandled her dad decided to resign from running, something Isabel suspected he was secretly relieved about. At least now he could enjoy his retirement in peace.

What Isabel least expected was for Pat to apologize to Romero and even thank him for everything, including jumping in to stop Charles when he was obviously going to slap her. Not only had she apologized, but after witnessing Romero's indignation regarding a man hitting a woman, she told him she was glad someone like him was watching out for Isabel and she admitted she had him all wrong. While she still said his temper was something he needed to work on, she also said she'd never worry about him turning it on Isabel again.

Although Isabel had said many times that she didn't care what Pat thought of Romero, she'd never tell him but a tiny part of her was thrilled that she finally had her big sister's approval, especially about something this important to her.

Weeks after the whole ordeal, Romero had only dropped hints here and there about the ring he'd given her being an engagement ring. A couple of times she'd been asked in front of him if it was an engagement ring. Both times she'd said no, and he hadn't corrected her. Even though each time, she'd she noticed a change in his mood. It obviously bothered him but he hadn't actually asked her to marry him so how could she say it was.

Tonight she'd made a big dinner for him and bought champagne. She told him it was Friday and she'd had an especially good week at work so she felt like celebrating. When they finished eating and moved into the front room with their champagne, she almost lost the nerve, but after one especially long and passionate kiss she did it. "Will you marry me?"

Romero sat up, almost making her spill the champagne she held. "What?"

"Since you won't ask me I'm asking you. Will you marry me?"

"What do you mean since I won't ask you? I thought you weren't ready, the way you acted any time I or anyone else brought it up. You were always so adamant that the ring wasn't an engagement ring. "

"I don't know. Since you never actually asked me, I felt weird saying it was. Anyway never mind all that. Will you?"

He smiled that beautiful smile that had done her in, from the very first moment he called her sexy at the wedding shower. "You bet your sweet ass I will."

Her heart swelled and she felt the tears fill her eyes.

He sat up and kissed her again. "You've never even talked about it. Are you gonna want a big wedding?"

"No not at all." She shook the tears away smiling big. "I'm with Valerie, the smaller the ceremony the better. But I do want my family there. My mom was really hurt about Art and Sabrina eloping the way they did. But after the ceremony I just want an intimate dinner: close family and friends only. I'd rather spend the money on a nice honeymoon."

Romero's eyes had gone from her eyes to her lips the entire time she spoke. "You really want my uncles and Aida at the same dinner table with your family?"

Isabel laughed. "That'll be the best part."

"You ever heard the saying be careful what you ask for?"

"Yes," she giggled. "But I don't care. I'm asking for it. I want them all there. I wouldn't have it any other way."

Romero took the champagne glass out of her hand, setting it on the coffee table then pulled her down onto him, lying back. "Okay, don't say I didn't warn you. You asked for it."

"And what are you asking for?"

"The only thing I can't live without. You."

Isabel felt that familiar lump in her throat she'd felt all too many times since she'd met Romero. But this time it was a good lump. Never in a million years would she have imagined feeling this happy. "Maybe you should be careful what you ask for because you got me, babe. Forever."

Epilogue

The ceremony had gone as smooth as it was going to go. Romero had taken Manny and Max to shop for suits that didn't make them look like pimps but they'd insisted they'd all wear matching fedoras and Romero gave in — only because he knew how much Isabel liked him in it.

They could think of no place more fitting to have their intimate dinner than Moreno's. Since their guests consisted of only her immediate family, his uncles and Aida and of course Alex and his family who were part of Romero's extended family, they didn't need a banquet room. But Alex and Sal still insisted on closing off one of the smaller dining rooms just for them. And they set up small dance floor at Isabel's request so that they could have their first dance as a married couple and she could have her father-daughter dance.

Romero had done enough coaching before the dinner, telling his uncles to watch their mouths, take it easy on the burping and not talk with their mouths open. He planned on having Isabel's family at one table and his uncles at a separate one. He even asked Sal to try and arrange it that way when everyone was seated. But somehow, things got goofed up. Since even Gina had shown up with a date Max and Pat were the only two not paired up so to Romero's horror, they ended up sitting next to each other.

Dinner was going well until Aida's snorting caught Romero's attention. Apparently, his uncle the comedian was at it again. Isabel touched Romero's hand. "Stop worrying. Everyone is having a good time."

Angel and Sarah, who sat across from Manny and Aida, were laughing, as were Alex and Valerie who sat at the same table. It was hard to believe they were all married now. Alex was even expecting a kid. Kids were still a scary thought for Romero, but Alex was totally stoked about it.

Surprisingly, Sal, who was the oldest, had yet to get serious with anyone. Sure he'd brought a date to dinner tonight, but she was a different girl from the one he'd brought bowling with the gang just a week ago. He always said he had too many things going on to settle down any time soon. Personally, Romero thought he was just too damn anal to ever meet a girl who'd be perfect enough for him.

He looked over and cringed when he saw Max talking animatedly to Pat with a mouth full of food. There was clinking of a glass and Manny stood up. "I'd like to make a toast."

Romero leaned over to Isabel. "Isn't there a rule or something for when you do the toast? You don't just get up in the middle of dinner and—"

"Shh… listen."

"I still remember my first words to Moe when he came to me to tell me he was getting married. 'Is she knocked up?'"

Don't laugh at your own joke. Too late. He was already wheezing, his belly jiggling as he laughed. Aida's cackling didn't help either. But they weren't alone, others were laughing, too. Romero could only hope this didn't encourage the comedic act to go on too long.

Romero smiled, trying to be a good sport and

glanced over at the table with her parents. They weren't laughing but they did smile.

"Seriously though, I can't say how glad I am that he's found someone that makes him this happy." Isabel slipped her hand in his and patted it. "I raised this kid. Me and Max did, along with his grandmother, God rest her soul. I've never seen him so happy. You two seem to be made for each other. I've never seen anything like it. It's like you said to me that one time you two broke up for a few days there. You're broken without her."

Isabel leaned into him. "You said that?"

Romero smiled trying not to show his annoyance. Yeah, in *complete confidence*. He didn't think he was going to announce his weaknesses in front of everyone here at his wedding.

"When you asked me and Max to be your best men..." He put his hand on his chest, getting choked up. "I can't tell you what an honor that was. I thought for sure you was gonna ask them pretty boy friends of yours, or that other one. What's his face with their sister?"

Isabel laughed. So did everyone else. "No, really. Huh Max?" He turned to Max. "Isn't that what we were thinking?"

Max nodded. "Anyhow, I just want to say I wish you and your beautiful wife, Izzy, a long and prosperous marriage. I know you're gonna hold off on the babies but don't wait too long. Me and Max need another kid around, now that ours..." He choked up again. "Now that our kid has left the nest." Manny lifted his glass unable to go on. "Salud!"

Feeling a little choked up himself, Romero lifted his glass and took a drink. Everyone clapped and began clinking their glasses. Romero leaned in and kissed his beautiful bride. The memory of the utter despair he'd felt when he thought he'd lost her coming to him. "I really am broken without you. Promise you'll never leave me, Izzy."

"I'm broken without you, too. I promise. I love you."

Romero kissed her softly still unable to believe, she was his forever. "I love you too, baby." Then he stood up taking her hand. Just like Manny, he didn't care if this was the appropriate time or not but it felt like it, so he was going for it. "Get me some music," he said to Sal. "Time for my first dance with my perfect wife." He lifted her hand in his for everyone to see. "Izzy Romero."

About The Author

Elizabeth Reyes is a full time stay home wife, mother of two teens and writer. This is the fourth in the Moreno Brothers Series. As mentioned in the dedication since obviously Romero is not related to the Moreno's he played a side role in the first three and was liked enough to garner enough attention from the readers who requested his story be told. Elizabeth is currently working on the next in the series. The rest in the series are all available on now.

Forever Mine – Angel and Sarah's story.
Always Been Mine – Alex and Valerie's story.
Sweet Sofie – Sofia and Eric's story.
Making You Mine – Sal and Gracie's story.
And most recently released. The first in Elizabeth's new series *5th Street* **Noah**.

For more information on Elizabeth Reyes and her writing including updates excerpts and sneak peaks of her upcoming works visit her website:
www.ElizabethReyes.com

and her FB FanPage:
http://www.facebook.com/TheMorenoBrothers

You can also follow her on Twitter @AuthorElizabeth. She loves hearing feedback from her readers and Romero is proof that she is listening to your requests and suggestions. =)

Acknowledgments

As I write more and more, the stories come to me faster and faster. I already have the plots for the first two in my next series just begging to be written. This means I spend 90% of my time writing. I have to thank my family for their continued support and patience as I spend most my day in front of my computer. Once again thank you Mark since you know that as soon as I upload this one I'll be back to writing Sal's story. It's never ending and I couldn't do it without you! Thank you for supporting my dream, Dr. Doback ← inside joke. =) As for your request I write Manny and Max their own book. Uh not happening. Even I can't romanticize those two. lol

To my critique partner and good friend Tammara Webber. Thank you so much for all your wonderful help. If it wasn't for your complete honesty and telling me to get my "big girl panties on" just as you lay it on me. LOL, I'd miss some of the things that it's amazing how another pair of eyes can read so differently. Also thank you for helping me find my new editor.

Which leads me to my next acknowledgment. My new editor Stephanie Lott (aka Bibliophile). I got to say I owe Tammara big time for this one. I was very impressed with your professionalism and timely turn-around time. I look forward to working with you on my future projects. Sal is just around the corner. ;)

To Ivannia my beta reader and good friend. I know you've been busy getting ready to graduate and all so you didn't contribute as much this time but let me tell you. The little you did was huge. Catching that big "DOH!!" right at the end about the character names. I can't believe everyone else missed it! Thank you for that!

To the rest of my family, parents, brother, sister-in-laws, In-laws and my commadre Inez for believing in me from the very beginning. I love you all and thank you for your continued support.

To my readers, bloggers and everyone who has reached out to me online with your kind words and your loyal following of the series. I've had so many offer to help in one way or another. You have no idea how much it's meant to me through out this journey to read the encouraging emails/pm's/comments from you. I spend so much time and pour so much of my heart and soul into all these stories it's nice to know you are all enjoying them. Trust me I think of you all now when I'm writing, at times cringing. "Oh crrrap they're gonna be mad!" =/

Check my website often for updates on Sal and hints about what the next series will be about!

Made in the USA
Lexington, KY
14 October 2012